THE ALPHA NINA

BOOK 2 OF THE FEMININA SERIES

Author of **Nailbiters** and **Enemies of Peace**

M.K. Williams

Publisher: MK Williams Publishing, LLC
Library of Congress Control Number: 2021919418

ISBN-13:
978-1-7333929-9-0 (eBook)
978-1-952084-14-0 (Paperback)
978-1-952084-15-7 (Hardcover)

1mkwilliamsauthor@gmail.com
1mkwilliams.com

Cover Art: Formatted Books
Interior Design: Formatted Books

All Persons Fictitious Disclaimer:

Works by M.K. Williams

FICTION
The Project Collusion Series
Nailbiters
Architects

The Feminina Series
The Infinite-Infinite
The Alpha-Nina

Other Fiction
The Games You Cannot Win
Escaping Avila Chase
Enemies of Peace

NON-FICTION
Self-Publishing for the First-Time Author
Book Marketing for the First-Time Author
How to Write Your First Novel: A Guide for Aspiring Fiction Authors
Going Wide: Self-Publishing Your Books
Outside The Amazon Ecosystem
The Fiology Workbook

Dedication

To Celeste – My beautiful star-child

Table of Contents

PART 1

"Words have weight, something once said cannot be unsaid. Meaning is like a stone dropped into a pool; the ripples will spread and you cannot know what back they wash against."

– Philippa Gregory

1

The lab was eerily quiet after the roar of the machine cut out. Xander Marks turned to face his lab assistant, who also happened to be his daughter. It was nearly midnight on August 8, 2008. Both exhausted and exhilarated, they finally had a moment to acknowledge all that had just happened.

What they had planned was for Xander to be the first person to walk through the Portal they had invented to a sister device that was located around the world. After his brief stay in Tokyo to take photos and confirm he was healthy after the trip, he would walk back through the Portal. This had been his revolutionary idea to cut down on the carbon emissions from airlines and other forms of transportation. His initial plan had been to travel across the multiverse, but he hadn't perfected the equation to pinpoint the exact location of another portal in time. In space, yes. It helped that he knew the exact location of the sister Portal in Japan. But he couldn't yet find another device in time.

What they didn't realize as they prepared for his initial journey, was that no other functional devices existed in a parallel universe. At least not yet.

So, Dr. Marks strode confidently across the globe by taking one step through the Portal and he returned by exerting the same effort. But that was just his own physical movement. The power required to activate the machines was incredible. He knew that they would have to find a way to reduce the amount of energy required if his invention would ever have commercial applications. But first it had to work.

What he didn't know, what he couldn't know, was that the power being used on that first trip was sending a signal out across space-time, a homing beacon for future travelers of the multiverse.

He may have considered it, but it is hard to think multiversally when you've only ever experienced one reality.

His departure from the lab was a success. He arrived in Tokyo to the cheers of the small team waiting for him. They congratulated Xander and quickly began to execute the plan that had been developed over the past few weeks. Katsumi strapped a blood pressure gauge to his arm and stuck a thermometer in his mouth. Jiro held a Geiger counter up to him and furiously scribbled notes on his clipboard.

Behind the console, Hajime monitored the energy output and recycle. He was making sure that everything would be ready for another trip in just a matter of minutes. Only three assistants had been waiting for him when he arrived. They had agreed to keep a minimal team on hand to record his travel. That way if something went wrong and he didn't go anywhere, there was minimal disappointment. He was supposed to be greeted by his daughter and his boss back in Washington, D.C. But the billionaire mogul who bankrolled his research and all the research at the thinktank, Lionel Rogers, had been called away for a family emergency around 9:30 pm, leaving Xander and his daughter to complete the rest of the preparations on their own. (Not that Rogers was much help, he understood just enough to sign the checks. He was woefully out of his depth when it came to quantum mechanics.)

As he waited for the all-clear to return, Dr. Marks looked out the window on the beautiful mid-day skyline of downtown Tokyo. It was already "tomorrow" here. He wished he could stay longer, explore. But he would be back in Tokyo again soon, he assured himself. Now that this crossing had been successful, he could pop over for fresh sushi any time. Well, any time on August 8, he still had to figure out how to expand the quantum jitters. But that was a problem to solve another day. For now, the world was about to change. He took a deep breath (because Katsumi asked him to as she held a stethoscope to his back) and reminded himself to enjoy this moment. The moment of success before all the additional work began.

With the measurements done, he was good to go. Each of their faces beamed with delight. "Thank you so much for your quick work. I'll have Nina confirm once I am back in our lab and we will be sure to do a real celebration together soon!"

The team in Tokyo sent his daughter back in Washington, D.C. a message when her father arrived and again just before he walked back through. She hadn't acknowledged either message, but it had not been part of the plan for her to respond, so they didn't think much of it at the time. Hajime called out to Dr. Marks that Nina had not responded. But he was so elated at the success of his first trip that he brushed off the warning. Surely, Nina was pacing in front of the machine, anxiously awaiting his return. Perhaps she was so excited that she had begun to celebrate. Both actions would have been incredibly uncharacteristic of his daughter, but he wasn't thinking much about her. He was thinking of the articles that would be written, the prizes to be awarded.

Dr. Marks bowed to his colleagues in Tokyo. The Portal came to life with a pearlescent glow and he stepped through.

He expected to see his daughter behind the console, eager to welcome him back. He expected to have his temperature, blood pressure, and other vital signs checked again by Nina immediately upon his return. He expected a small celebration and then a good night's rest before a big day of alerting the world.

But what he didn't expect was to see that a band of travelers from across the multiverse had already joined his daughter for this auspicious moment.

He didn't expect to learn that the power of the Portal had been corrupted and an evil man named Parker in another universe had used the invention to kidnap and murder.

It appeared that his daughter, Nina, had already been pulled away from their moment of discovery to help these weary travelers find a way back to the correct space and time. It was a lot for Dr. Marks to process. Especially since two of the three travelers were also his daughters, the alter-egos of the one he had just left in Washington, D.C.

As the two other Ninas and their friend, Marie, explained the situation, he knew that he and his daughter needed to act fast to get them back to their place in the multiverse. They had all come from 2018, a decade into the future, and with them brought technological advances that he hadn't dreamed of yet.

First, they had a quantum drive with the saved coordinates for the exact location in space and time that they needed to get to. Apparently, they had solved for this problem, but didn't know how to generate enough power. It was as though the lock and key had finally been placed together. With only minutes until August 8 ended, they had to use the next quantum jitter to walk into the Portal across space-time. There could be more quantum jitters after midnight, but they knew for sure there would be at least one more before the day ended.

The women worked together, the clock wound down, and just as strangely as they had appeared, the three visitors left.

It was a lot of knowledge and emotion to process as Dr. Marks stared at his daughter, his actual daughter from that universe. His salt-and-pepper hair in perfect place, his tweed jacket unrumpled. It was as though nothing of much consequence had just happened. He looked totally normal. But absolutely everything had changed.

He wanted to tell her all about his trip across the Portal, to ask more details about how the travelers came through, to talk about the ramifications of what he had just witnessed. If others used the same logic that those visitors had, there could be more people stepping through the Portal again and again once they dialed into the exact time that the power source was first used.

Nina was the first to make a sound. "Oh my gosh!" She did a small leap in place and lunged forward to hug him. Her smile, the same one she wore since she was an infant, broke out across her face. In that instant he snapped into "Dad" mode. The sentiment, the excitement, the pride all welled up within him, mist drawing to his eyes. He hugged his daughter who quickly pulled away and continued her giddy motions. Nina's arms wiggled as she did her own brand of happy dance. Her black-brown hair shaking and covering her face.

Xander was gob smacked. "We did it!" He finally managed to get out some words through the shock.

Nina paused her celebration and jumped into work mode. She had two clear demeanors with her dad, always trying to remain professional while in the lab. "Okay, we need to take your readings, the team in Tokyo has been sending me lots of messages asking if you got back through in one piece."

It had already been several minutes since he returned, but it felt like a lifetime. His entire world view had shifted. Nina continued to rattle off the list of things that needed to be done. The pale, watery skin beneath her eyes showed every sign of exhaustion, but her voice carried enough energy to get them well into the morning. "Then we need to record everything that happened. I think we should do video testimonials separately so that we don't contaminate each other's accounts." Nina was firing off tasks and follow-up items.

Dr. Marks finally felt his own brain start to fire; his wonder now dissipated. They needed to take action quickly, they were losing precious time. With each moment the details would become more fuzzy, less precise. Xander ran his left hand through his graying hair, slightly greasy and in need of a good shampoo.

"Alright then, you respond to the team and let them know I'm fine. Don't tell them about the rest just yet. You're right, we still need to do my health check and then we need to record our experience."

Nina looked over at him and crossed her arms. "Yeah, I just said that, Dad." As he had often experienced, he went from a hero in her eyes to an annoyance in very little time. He would have never tolerated such insolence from any other lab assistant, but it was clear in that moment that she was not his employee, she was his daughter.

"Well, I was agreeing with you," he said in his usual apologetic tone, so typical of dads who want to keep their cool.

"Great, can you grab the video equipment? I'll get everything else set up," she had already returned to the console and was blasting off one message after another to Hajime.

"Right!" Xander turned on his heel and walked as quickly as he could down the hall to his office. His was the nicest on that floor, a corner office with an expansive open area, enough room for a couch and coffee table, his large desk, and a storage closest for A/V equipment. The plush carpet dampened his footsteps, unlike the hallway he had just come down where his heels clicked the whole way.

He unlocked the A/V closet and looked for the right cameras and their corresponding tripods and cords. Nina had been telling him for years to organize these in distinct bins for easy use. But they were physicists, they never had a video emergency. Until that night. *Oh boy, and Rogers missed all of this*, Xander shook his head. But at second thought, he realized that was probably for the best.

As Xander searched for the right items, he thought he heard the air conditioning kick on. For early August, this wasn't an unexpected sound, but it usually never started on a night when temperatures dipped. He refocused and found the extension cord he was looking for. He placed each item carefully on a dolly so he could roll it down the hall and not risk dropping and breaking the expensive equipment.

Xander tried to roll the cart across the carpet of his office, but the wheels were slow to turn. He spotted the clock on his desk. 11:51 pm. Only a little bit of time left in the day. Just thinking about how late it was made him sleepy, but he knew they had to make their observations now.

As he pushed the cart along the hallway he called out to Nina. "Let's set up your video in the lab and I can record mine in the office."

When he maneuvered the dolly into the lab, he was surprised to see it empty.

"Nina?" he looked around the wide-open room and didn't see her. *Had she run off to the restroom perhaps?* He didn't hear her in the hallway.

Xander decided to start with the tripod so that they would be ready once the quick medical exam was complete. He brought the camera over to the console and noticed a flashing signal on the screen.

"UNKNOWN UNIVERSE CONTACT"

The message flashed repeatedly. He assumed this was a left-over alarm from the travelers who had just left. But his gaze shifted and he noted that Universes Alpha, Beta, and Gamma were clearly marked on the screen. So, what was the Unknown Universe?

His eyes dropped to the message box that was open between Nina and Hajime.

```
    NMarks: Yes, Dad just came back through. Sorry
for the delay. Very excited!
    Hajime504: Great, did you take his readings?
We're all very excited but we need to get the
correct measurements recorded.
    NMarks: Yes, yes. About to take his readings now.
```

    Hajime504: Send them when you are done, please.
    NMarks: Are you sending Jiro or Katsumi through
the Portal?
    Hajime504: No, why?
    Hajime504: Do you have the readings?

The conversation seemed normal. Hajime was always down to business, and in this case Marks admired his tenacity and precision. But what was Nina's question about Jiro and Katsumi about? That wasn't part of their plan.

And where was she? "Nina?!" he called out.

He heard no reply. "Nina!" he bellowed once more before setting down the equipment and heading for the restroom at the end of the hall. He knocked on the women's room door. No answer. He gently pushed the door open and called again for Nina before he saw all three stalls were empty. Without thinking he dashed back down the hall to the break room to see if she was perhaps brewing some fresh coffee. Not there either.

He ran back into the lab and moved the equipment away from the console. Xander plopped down in the office chair and wheeled himself closer to the screens. Dr. Marks dismissed the alert about the Unknown Universe and the screen returned to the standard view of the grid representing space-time. When he and Nina had first designed the console, even without the ability to travel to a different universe, they knew that one day it might be possible. The screen had been a bare grid for as long as he could remember. But now it was lit up with five distinct points. Each labeled: Alpha, Beta, Gamma, Delta, and UNKNOWN.

On the next screen he saw the frequencies for the two Ninas and Marie who had just arrived and taken off. They were all currently in Universe Beta.

And then he saw a third yellow line, a third Nina line. It showed a change in location from Universe Delta to UNKNOWN.

Had she engaged the Portal and taken off to another universe without him? Where was she?

He ran back to his office and unlocked his desktop computer. As quickly as his thick fingers would allow, he navigated to the security footage of the lab. The entire facility had a security team and cameras near the exits.

But he had insisted that his lab have a separate camera feed, a secure line that would only transmit to his computer. The technology was too tempting to competitors. He didn't want to risk someone breaking into the building's system and erasing information or stealing a peek at the design.

Thankfully, he had gotten his way. He was able to pull up the video feed for the lab and watched back as he left the first time. He sped up the recording and saw the trio of travelers spill out of the Portal only seconds later. Then as they left. He saw his daughter hug him and then he left the lab for the A/V equipment.

And then Nina was sitting at the console. *Oh, come on, I wasn't gone that long,* he thought as he watched the playback. Then another figure stepped through the Portal. Dressed in black with a cap on their head, this person pointed a gun at Nina. He couldn't believe it. *Was it this Parker trying to kidnap another person?* He couldn't see the intruder's face. Whatever they said or commanded Nina to do, she followed their orders.

He saw the intruder approach the console and waved at her, gesturing for her to do something on one of the screens. Then they came around and grabbed her by the arm.

The Portal was engaged and the intruder stepped through, pulling Nina along with them. The intruder kept their head down the entire time, no clear sign of who it was. Nina looked up into the corner of the lab where the camera was positioned. Just as she was about to go through, she called out "Help!"

Or at least that is what Xander thought she said from the movements of her mouth. The camera had no sound. Not only was he unable to hear her plea, but he couldn't learn what this person had said or ordered her to do.

He glanced over at his desk clock once more. It was 12:08 am. He had burned the last precious minutes of August 8 scrambling to find Nina. And now, at eight-minutes past midnight, his chance to go after her was closed until the next unpredictable quantum jitter occurred, or until another year passed.

Before he jumped into action and notified the team in Tokyo, before he could process the weight of what had just happened and start searching for his daughter's kidnapper, he sat staring at the clock. He willed it to turn back.

The digital clock updated just as it was intended though, just as it always had.

12:09 am.

2

A decade later, in a universe far, far away, four people spilled through a Portal. But this one was much less polished than Dr. Marks' device. For starters, it looked as though it had been patched together with spare pieces. The lab itself was far less sophisticated as well. Instead of a private facility with well-designed accents that Dr. Marks enjoyed in multiverse reality Delta, this lab was the industrial warehouse type that was commonly found on college campuses. When colleges were still in session in the Washington, D.C. of multiverse reality Gamma, that is. The ceilings were exposed and the concrete floor was in need of sweeping.

It was 11:12 pm on August 8, 2018. After leaving Universe Delta, Marie and Feminina had been on quite a wild ride. They had arrived back into Universe Beta to stop Parker from killing Hank and using the Portal to kidnap someone else. They traveled there with Nina, the alter ego to Feminina from Universe Alpha, and sprang into action. Together, the three of them had subdued Parker and another alter-ego of his with the help of Dr. Thurston.

It seemed that the moment that they finally had the bad-guys under their control with their hands bound, the police burst through the door to the lab. There was no time to act and Nina had run off trying to create a diversion.

Marie had punched in a return trip to their home reality while Feminina positioned both Parkers so she could hoist them through the Portal. They hit the ground first, squirming like worms on the floor since their hands were tied. Marie and Feminina followed, quick to pounce on the two of them and ensure they didn't slither away.

In all the commotion, they had just acted on pure instinct. If the police had made their way into the warehouse section of the lab, they would have seen Hank unconscious, Dr. Thurston on the edge of passing out, and the two of them standing over identical Parkers who were bound and tied on the floor. The scene would have been very difficult to explain even if everyone was happy and getting along. Marie and Feminina knew they had to get out of there and hope that with fewer people, Nina would have less to explain.

Marie also heard Nina call out just before the machine really kicked into gear and it sounded like Dean Winchester was on the other side of the thick plastic partition. *Dean Winchester.* As in her alter-ego in that parallel universe. Marie hadn't believed Nina when she said that she was the Dean of the College of Arts & Sciences in two different universes. She loved her work too much to ever give it up for an administrative role. She would have more time to worry about the implications of that revelation later.

Feminina called out to Marie. "Grab his feet!" She was trying to angle one of the Parkers so that he was propped up against the console by the machine. The two men were potentially shouting obscenities through their gags, but Marie and Feminina couldn't hear them clearly. Nor did they care. One of them was for sure a murderer. He had confessed in the moments before their hasty departure. He had been living with Nina Marks in multiverse reality Beta and killed her when she said it was over. Parker had claimed it was an accident, but Marie and Feminina knew that men could never contain their violence, especially against women.

That was the event that had sparked an entire day of chaos across four different universes. Marie and Feminina were grateful to be back home. But neither of them knew what to do with the two Parkers. They had committed no crimes in this universe and therefore the murderous one couldn't be prosecuted. Marie thought about the consequences of sending him back to Universe Beta. Unless they knew for sure the police were ready to apprehend him, it was a risky move. They didn't have that guarantee so they might send him back only to allow him to escape and potentially murder yet again.

Marie mimicked the same action as she helped Femi move the other Parker. *Oh right, we've got this other nut job to worry about too.*

"What's worse than one woman-hating murderer?" Marie muttered out loud.

"Two," Feminina replied as she wiped sweat from her brow with her forearm. The two women were exhausted. Multiple trips across the Plain would do that to a person. Although they were one of the first to ever travel from one parallel universe to the next, let alone do repeat trips in one day.

"What are we going to do with them?" Marie asked out loud what she had already been trying to riddle out in her mind.

"I don't know, I need to sit down though," Feminina said in an exhausted voice. She shuffled to one of the desk chairs near the console and slumped into it, her weight rolling the chair back slightly on its castors.

Marie began to pace. While she felt just as weary as Feminina looked, her brain was alighted with the adrenaline of the situation. They had just evaded arrest in one Universe, but they couldn't very well hold two men hostage in the building that they were routinely breaking into and not expect legal trouble for themselves. Marie drew her hands to her head, starting to rub at her temples.

One of the Parkers began to move, as though he was trying to flip himself into a standing position. Given how tightly his hands and feet were bound, this was impossible, but his attempt created a loud clang that echoed in the large room.

Feminina was slow to respond so Marie got to him first. She landed a square punch against his jaw and he seemed to wither in her hands. She had likely knocked him out. It was such a harsh action after a night of violence.

First, she had been dragged away from her comfortable apartment on a whim by Feminina and her alter-ego from another Universe. As a scientist who had worked on the Portal for years, the idea of someone traveling the multiverse wasn't necessarily new to her. But she was frustrated that she wasn't the first. And she had to brush Sonali off because of it. Their relationship had one lone sour point and that was how closely Marie worked with Feminina. It didn't matter how many times she reiterated that there was no attraction, for Sonali it wasn't about any physical element. Marie spent more time with her lab partner, shared more of her day, her life with Feminina. She knew that even though she would never cross a line and cheat on Sonali with anyone, it was an emotional affair. Marie relied on Feminina more than Sonali and that was what bothered her.

But she would patch things up in the morning, Marie told herself as she resumed her pacing. She knew what one solution would be, but she was already starting to feel remorse for the last time she took that action. Gus Blanity had attacked them, *what? not even two hours earlier*. He had a vendetta with her and Feminina. So, he had followed them into the lab that night, of all nights, and tried to clobber them with a brick.

Her eyes flashed on the red clay that impacted the floor and broke apart not a few feet away from her. Nina had been slow to respond, she had frozen. Marie and Feminina had taken action and sent him through the Portal.

At the time, it seemed like the best solution. Send him somewhere, anywhere, so he couldn't get back. Except that the three of them, Marie, Feminina, and Nina, had just been looking at Universe Alpha and they had also pulled up the first recorded time that the Portal was ever activated anywhere in the multiverse. Which meant that they had a specific space and a specific time plugged into the machine. Gus didn't go to nowhere. He went back to the evening of August 8, 2008 in Universe Alpha where that Dr. Thurston had a prototype constructed in his office. Not even functional, but a Portal nonetheless. And it turned out that Gus had been the one to kill the love of Nina's life. So, Marie was feeling culpable for his death at the moment. If they threw these Parkers just anywhere in the multiverse, who would they hurt next? The possible consequences were too much to fathom.

"Marie-" Feminina said, trying to grab her attention. But Marie was too lost in her thought-spiral. She moved even faster, power-pacing back and forth and back and forth.

"Marie!" Feminina called out again. This time Marie turned to face her colleague. She noticed that Feminina's face was an eerie pale color, as though she might throw up. Her black-brown hair was matted to her forehead with sweat, the usually loose fringe bangs now smeared across her skin.

"Please. Stop. Pacing," Femi uttered, giving each word its due emphasis. Marie watched as Feminina rubbed her head and started to lean over, bending in half.

"Are you going to be sick?" Marie asked, looking quickly around for a trashcan.

"Well, three jumps across the Plain and a crap load of sugar in my system just might do it," she said as she looked down, addressing her shoes. As Femi spoke the words, Marie started to feel the pain of her multiple headaches compounding. Only by standing still did it start to set in.

Marie knew she should comfort her friend, but there was so much weighing on their next decision. It couldn't wait for a nap and a long debate. They still needed to talk through everything that happened, document as many new learnings as possible so they could replicate the power source they observed in Universe Delta, and agree on a cover story. There was no energy left in her to play the mothering type at that moment. "We can't send them to just anywhere," Marie said.

Feminina looked up. "I know," she sighed. "But they can't stay here."

At this point, the other Parker started to fidget in earnest, trying to wriggle himself loose. Marie didn't have it in her to hit this one too. She had clobbered Gus and sent him to complete his murderous destiny. She had subdued these two guys in front of her and knocked-out the one Parker. After years of training and feeling confident in her role as a powerful woman, as the superior gender, she just didn't have it in her for another fight.

But one was walking right towards her.

"What the hell is going on here?" A husky voice thundered from the other side of the lab.

Feminina's eyes went wide as she caught sight of this new addition to their little group. Marie spun around to see Sonali standing at the partition between the two sides of the lab with her hands on her hips. Her wide and powerful hips. Furious, her large brown eyes burning with rage, her mocha skin flush with anger, her curly hair wild and loose around her face. Marie hadn't expected her girlfriend to interrupt this already hectic moment.

"I can explain everything to you, but first we need to-" Marie started to inch closer to her girlfriend as she spoke, trying to radiate calm with her words even though this was another complication to an already crazy situation.

"Sonali-" Marie heard Feminina start to speak behind her. She turned slightly and saw that she had willed herself to stand.

"No, there can be no *legal* explanation for this! Who the hell are these two men and where exactly are you going to send them?" Sonali snapped back. It seemed that Feminina's attempt to address her had really set off Sonali's rage.

Marie let out a deep sigh. This would take a long time to explain and she just didn't have the energy. Also, they would be due for another quantum jitter any moment. She and Feminina needed to get rid of the Parkers before the day ended and that time was coming in mere minutes. It was a lot to process all at once in terms of the logistics, the science, and the emotional gravity of the situation.

"You told me that she was just stopping by for a visit and then you were going to bed! You promised me that you were done breaking into this building! You swore that this project was done and that you were going to focus on finding a job!" Sonali punctuated each sentence with a jab of her finger. Each indictment was accurate.

Marie had indeed communicated all of those things. Every time Sonali expressed her concern, Marie placated her. She made empty promises because she would never abandon her dream or the project that she started with Femi. But she couldn't say that to Sonali, she was afraid it would push her away forever. Marie wanted to have it all. Have her University lab up and running again, have the glory of success and discovery, have a great life partner in Sonali and a steadfast lab partner in Feminina. *Why was it so wrong to want it all?*

But she couldn't have any of it. The University was shuttered. Any discovery would have to be secretly reported, credit given elsewhere so she could avoid any criminal charges for continuing research on the property. She had lost so much already; she didn't want to have to choose between her best friend and her girlfriend because it felt that at any minute, she really might lose both of them. But she couldn't articulate all of that while Sonali was yelling at her at the worst possible moment.

"I know, and I will explain everything, I promise," Marie softened her tone to one that she didn't even recognize.

"I don't want to hear any more lies," Sonali said as heavy tears spilled onto her cheeks.

In the commotion, Parker had come to and started to squirm again, causing the other Parker to reattempt his escape as well. Feminina clearly had enough of everything going on.

"Stop that!" she thundered at the two men. Marie refocused on her friend, who now had a fire in her eyes, her exhaustion long gone. "Sonali, we have two known killers, two woman-haters here from another universe. They don't belong here and, in my opinion, they don't deserve to exist anywhere. And we have-" she checked the clock on the wall, "-maybe four minutes before this Portal opens up again and we can get them out of here. After everything we've been through tonight, I will hand you the wrench so you can dismantle the Portal yourself and I'll be right beside you taking it apart. But for the moment, we need to work together to clean up this mess."

"I'm sorry, just how do you plan to *clean this up?*" Sonali crossed her arms and Marie knew immediately that Femi had said the wrong thing.

It was only a few hours earlier in real time for Sonali, in Universe Gamma, that she had just confessed that her own brother, Ayush, was about to be subject to the punishment of a Pink Box. Mentioning how to treat woman-haters was not the right thing for Femi to say at all.

"We're sending them back," Femi said.

"Back?" Marie snapped back. *How could she do that?* But then she noticed a subtle change on Femi's face. She didn't mean "back," she meant "out."

"I don't want any part of this," Sonali said as she waved her hands and turned to leave. Without thinking, Marie took off after her. She could hear Femi calling after them. She could hear the men struggling on the ground. But it didn't matter, she couldn't lose Sonali. Not when they both needed each other.

Sonali was long down the hallway, but Marie was just crossing over the threshold out of the lab when she heard the whir of the Portal starting to power up. She glanced back. *Who needed her more in that moment?* Marie continued her jog down the hallway to try and catch Sonali. She would have to ask Femi what happened later.

3

A shiver ran down his spine as the cold water leaked from the ice pack. Hank wasn't even sure what day it was anymore. After he woke up in the hospital around 10:00 pm and was informed that he had a minor concussion, he was escorted into a police car and found himself in a grey room that felt like a small box. He held the melting icepack to his head, but it was doing little to alleviate his headache.

It had been a whirlwind day and although he knew that he would soon be peppered with questions – again – he enjoyed the momentary silence of the room.

Hank had relayed everything exactly as he remembered it to the officers. He had seen his ex-wife a few days earlier and they confirmed that she would move back in with him. They had reconciled and rekindled their relationship. They were going to make it work this time around. She left to go back to the home she shared with Dr. Parker Lovett and then he didn't hear anything from her. He tried calling and texting, nothing worked. She finally answered his call that morning and they met up. He escorted her back to her home to help her pack her things and that was when they both discovered the body in Dr. Parker Lovett's basement. They left and called the police.

This is where they started to scrutinize everything he said. *Why did Ms. Marks delay her move? What reason did she give for her being missing for a few days? What made you think she was missing and not just ignoring your message? Why didn't they call the police right away when they found the body? Why wait until they returned to his apartment? What did they remove from the home? Why did Ms. Marks leave? Why did he go to the University lab?*

He told them the truth, but it made no sense. Even as he explained it over and over, he knew it didn't sound logical. He had seen Nina's dead body in that basement. But he had also been with her, held her, hugged her, that very day. He wasn't imagining this. There would be footage of her on campus that day, surely there was some record of her with him. She had texted him when she needed help and he had called the police, *again*, to say that she was in danger at the University. And she had been. He saw Parker push her.

Hank furrowed his brow at this memory. He swore that he saw Parker lift a barely conscious Nina and then push her down on the ground. Hank had reacted on instincts and lunged after Parker. But Nina didn't hit the ground. At least he didn't remember seeing her hit the ground. And then she was there again. He must have been hallucinating or maybe it was a dream while he was passed out. He could have sworn there were two Ninas working together to fight off Parker. And there were two Parkers. His memory included double-vision, that was how he rationalized it. And then he didn't remember anything until he woke up.

The officers left him to think while they went to "check on a few things." He figured they were giving him time to get anxious. Which he was.

It had been the strangest day he had ever experienced. But he knew he would continue to assert the truth. It was Parker who had hurt Nina, who was now missing, *again*. They needed to find Nina, and more importantly they needed to arrest Parker. He was the one that should be in this room, not Hank.

He finally set the ice pack down on the table. It sloshed and leaked over the metal surface. He tried not to go down the dark hole of emotion that he had been circling for days. He and Nina would be reunited, only she had ghosted him. Then she was back, and while he knew he should have more pride, he wanted Nina more. He wanted everything to be back the way it had been before. But he also longed for their somber ritual. He hadn't gone to Hannah's grave that morning, he wouldn't go until Nina was with him. Just as they had done every year since she passed.

In the whirlwind of finding Nina and going back to collect her things, he assumed their next stop would have been to visit their daughter and pay their respects. But then they found a body, and then Nina was in danger again.

He had let down both of his girls that day. He had betrayed the memory of his daughter, of their daughter. And he hadn't been there in time to save Nina.

The door to the room opened at that moment. It would have been a welcome distraction to the angst Hank was experiencing, if it hadn't been the two officers returning for another round of questions. There was the short guy, whose name he forgot and the normal-height woman who name he was fairly sure began with a W. He looked up and acknowledged their presence.

They took their seat opposite him, the metal chairs scraping against the cement floor. The sound was like nails on a chalkboard to Hank's ears and did nothing to help his pounding headache.

"Mr. Jankowski-"

"Dr. Jankowski," he corrected the female police officer. It was a habit he had formed after years of smart-mouthed college students trying to buddy up to him. His cheeks flushed the moment he saw the police officer's eyebrow shoot up.

"Okay, Dr. Jankowski-" she continued, clearly perturbed by his correction.

"Sorry, you can call me Hank," he interrupted again. He was too nervous to think that he should try to not look nervous.

"Hank," the police officer waited for him to meet her eye. When he did, he noticed that her ponytail was pulled so tight that the veins on her forehead were standing out. "I'm going to need you to focus."

"Sorry," he looked down again. What the officers told him before had to be wrong. They escorted him from the hospital after his doctor signed off on his release. He had asked why and was only told once he was at the police station, inside that windowless room that could have easily been a closet for how tiny and cramped it was. His eyes darted up to the camera in the top corner by the ceiling.

They had said that the woman he found in Dr. Parker Lovett's basement was Feminina Marks, formerly Feminina Jankowski. But Hank knew that was impossible because Nina had been with him when they discovered the body.

W. started again: "Your ex-wife's body was found."

Hank shook his head; in spite of the pain he was feeling. "No!" he cut her off. "No, Nina was with me when we discovered the body."

"Hank, I know this is hard to hear. But your ex-wife has been deceased for three days now. We just received the preliminary report back from the medical examiner." W. slid the file to him. He didn't dare open it.

The male officer cleared his throat.

"That's not possible. I saw Nina today; I was with her. She was the one who told me to get to the lab because she was in danger." He started to explain again, but they weren't listening. "She asked me to come help her, to save her from him," his voice broke. He looked down so they wouldn't see him cry, he could feel the tears starting to gather. He hadn't cried in so long. He told himself to suck it up, showing weakness would make them think he did something.

He heard W. rifling for something and then she pushed a plastic packet of tissues toward him. He was too proud to pick it up.

"You have my phone, right? Check my texts. She messaged me that she was in danger. I ran to the lab as fast as I could!

"Yes, we saw the text message on your phone from earlier this afternoon and we will be following up with Dr. Thurston regarding the identity of the woman who rode to the hospital in his ambulance, but we need you to focus right now," W. responded in on overly calm tone.

"Hank, you've had a very trying day and you've also sustained a head injury-" the male officer started.

"I held her! She was with me!" Hank thundered, he snapped his head up to address the officer directly and pounded his fist on the table.

"Did anyone see the two of you together?" W. asked.

"I called her; we had an entire conversation. And she texted me. You have my phone. You can see the records!" Hank had told them this before as well. He felt like he must be speaking another language or something because they weren't understanding. He folded his arms and looked over at the door, avoiding any eye contact with these morons who were wasting their time asking him something he had already told them.

"How was your relationship with your ex-wife?" W. changed the topic.

"We were getting back together. That's why Parker attacked her. He pushed her, I saw him push her and I just jumped-" Hank repeated these words slowly to make it clear to them.

"You saw Dr. Lovett push Nina in their home?" the male officer clarified.

"No, at the lab! Earlier today. I got her text and ran over as fast as I could. I saw him push her." Hank emphasized his words with his hands, trying to underline his point.

W. let out an exasperated sign. "Hank, Ms. Marks died three days ago, there is no way that you saw her earlier today."

He saw the look that she was giving him. *Pity?* Maybe. *Or did she think he was insane? Perhaps out of it because he hit his head?* No way, he knew what he saw, he knew what he felt. And all this time they hadn't asked one question about Parker. About his jealousy, about his need to control everything and everyone around him.

"You need to find Parker!" Hank had enough. "That's it. That's all I have to say. I'm leaving now." He stood up and headed for the door. He knew he hadn't been charged with anything and was free to go. He also knew that he did nothing wrong and wasn't about to ask for a lawyer and give them any indication that he thought he needed one.

As he reached for the handle, he heard W. from behind him, "Wait, we'll give you a ride home."

"I can walk, thanks," Hank shot back.

"No, we actually need to escort you home. You told us that you removed items from the crime scene earlier today, we need to recover those."

Hank let out a sigh and walked out the door. He rolled his eyes and waited for them to lead the way. This horrible day, this horrible day that he had dreaded on the calendar every year: August 8 had taken on a whole new level of miserable. And it didn't look like that suffering was about to end any time soon.

4

A dark sedan with tinted windows slid silently into the open space in front of the Sciences building. The rest of the street was fairly well illuminated by the streetlights, but this spot was hidden under the shade of a crowning tree. The leaves blocked any light from that specific patch of pavement, the perfect location for them to observe.

Special Agent Nick Noriega turned off the car. His partner, Special Agent Archie Clermont, looked over to him with his stark white eyes, only a slight gray remained where his pupils were. Nick had witnessed the evolution of this change over time as the dark brown color drained from Archie's eyes, but it was still a shock to him sometimes.

Both men had been dispatched as soon as the alarm sounded. The call had only just come in as their evening shift started and Nick had raced to the scene of the anomaly. He was the aggressive driver. Besides Archie's eyesight wasn't what it used to be, but they also had an unspoken agreement to not express the issue out loud. It would mean the end of Archie's days in the field. They both hoped to forestall that as long as possible.

Nick checked his watch. It was 12:28 am 8/8/18. No signs of life around the Sciences building of the University. He and Archie had been tracking the progress of the research that Dr. Norman Thurston and Dr. Parker Lovett had been making. They had been waiting for the day when they would get this call, but they didn't expect it would come so soon after the last alarm.

Two weeks earlier the same alarm had gone off, they had rushed to the scene, and there was nothing. They had staked out the building for hours, but there was no one there. There had been a city-wide power outage at the same time, so the two had reasoned that it had been a false alarm. Although, the cut in power also meant that the security footage their team analyst Mona, would have been able to retrieve, had been lost. It was a dead-end. This time they hoped to catch one of the two scientists in the act.

When the alarm sounded again that morning, Nick sprang into action, but Archie wasn't so sure. "Man, we drove all the way down here again for another false alarm." Archie shook his head as he looked out onto the illuminated green in front of the building. "I've got to get back for Jump Day, I've got more than a few files riding on this."

"Yeah, but look, all the street lights are on. No reported outages anywhere else. This could be the real deal." Nick pointed to the lights around them.

"Well, I'm not going to just sit here. I'll go out and do a check around the perimeter, see if there is any movement, anyone walking about." Archie unbuckled his seat belt and exited the car. Dressed in plainclothes, both of them were meant to blend in, not stand out. Archie used to be able to do that easily. His chestnut brown skin and black hair allowed him to blend in the crowds in D.C. But as his eyes began to lose their color, he started to catch more attention from people. That wasn't a good thing in their line of work.

Nick was anxious about the day that lack of anonymity hurt one or both of them. He watched as Archie set off across the grass towards the Sciences building. He radioed in their position and initial observations to their HQ.

"Hey Mona," Nick spoke into his cell phone, the speaker on.

"Yeah?" he heard a groggy voice answer.

"We're on the scene. Anything showing on your side?" Nick didn't take his eyes off of Archie, his guard up.

"You mean between monitoring everything for Jump Day, trying to hack the local security cameras for the University and city traffic *again*, and monitor any anomalies on the quant, is anything showing?" Her snark was crystal clear.

"Yeah?" Nick retorted, trying to match her attitude.

"I'll let you know when I catch something, but this is a massive amount of information. Clermont running around and setting off new motion alarms isn't helping."

Nick could tell that would be her final response for some time. Mona was excellent at her job, both he and Archie knew it. But he had to ask the question, he had to do *something*.

He saw Archie try to open the side door to the Sciences building, the one they both knew was the closest to Thurston's lab. It must have been locked because Nick didn't see it open. Archie tried to peek in and then started to circle the building. Nick took his eyes off his partner and started to look over the street.

No signs of life, which was odd for a college campus. *Shouldn't some students be out and about?* Nick dismissed this thought; it was Tuesday night after all. *Actually, Wednesday morning*, he corrected himself as he checked his watch again.

This job had not been his first pick. After following the prescribed path that would lead him from local law enforcement to the FBI, he thought he was headed for a field office in a big city like New York or Los Angeles. He expected to be working major cases and climbing the ranks. But somehow or another he had shown an aptitude for *this*... How he could have ever tested for it, he still didn't know. Maybe it was an off-hand comment to an instructor about his preference for reading science fiction, maybe it was a joke about thinking in more than one dimension. Either way, as assignments were handed out at the end of training, he was sent to an address in downtown Washington, D.C. His excitement level went through the roof. FBI headquarters were downtown. Nick Noriega saw visions of himself starting an accelerated career path immediately. Until the GPS directions led him right past the large federal buildings in the heart of downtown. He started to sense that he was heading towards the Virginia border, was he going all the way to CIA headquarters? That didn't make any sense. And then his GPS abruptly announced that he had arrived at his destination. 1863 New Hampshire Avenue.

A run-down building with opaque glass on the windows and door that appeared to have calcified sometime between 1970 and 1980 was not what he had expected at all. But he double-checked the address and punched in the code on his instructions. That was the first time he had ever entered the building that would become a second home to him.

He didn't like it at first. The mission was completely secret, so that was exciting, except that he felt like he would never make a name for himself in an organization that wasn't supposed to even exist. He viewed his job as a punishment. Until the first assignment came in, then he warmed to the agency.

Most days, heck, most years had been calm. But he and Archie had strong evidence that Thurston was about to do something where they might *both* have to intervene. That would be a first in their organization history. Usually, Archie saw all the action on his side of the aisle, Nick was there to make sure nothing got out of hand. But if they *both* had to take action on this case, that would be one for the classified record book.

Archie arrived back at the car and sat down. His brow was sweaty from the humid August air.

"Nothing, not even a squirrel or a pigeon in sight," Archie said as he shook his head.

"Nothing from Mona either," Nick gestured slightly to his agency issued secure cell phone. The black and completely unremarkable sedan belonged to their dual-agencies. They had to be forgettable, and so did their car. Nothing glamorous about that line of work.

"How long do you want to stay?" Archie asked. He had been thoroughly annoyed that the last call hadn't panned out. Technically they were supposed to wait for an all-clear from their headquarters. But there was no field manual for this line of work. And if there was it would have been entirely redacted.

Nick knew that Mona was running an analysis on campus security cameras back in the home office. If whoever caused the anomaly ran, they would get a call to pursue. But no call came in.

Sometime around 3:00 am Archie picked up the phone and asked for confirmation on whether they had a false alarm or not.

"No, this doesn't appear to be a false alarm," a familiar voice issued out from the small device. Mona was very direct, but she knew the pair of them well enough to be able to joke with them when the time was right. This wasn't the time.

"Okay, well the campus is dead. There isn't a single person around. Whoever tripped the alarm is either still inside, or this was a false alarm." Archie could not hide the frustration in his voice. "I've got five files to work today, Mona. I need to get back in."

Nick shot him a look, trying to tell him to cool it. They were all just doing their jobs. But Archie was cranky, it was way too early in the morning for a stakeout where literally nothing was happening.

"Fine, pack it in you two. We'll start to look for camera activity thirty minutes prior to the event and see if we get anything." Mona didn't sound pleased, but Archie sighed with relief at her words.

"Sounds good, let's keep the video feed rolling for the main camera directed at the Sciences building too," Nick spoke through the phone.

"You do know that eventually the University is going to notice this breach, right?" Mona was good, but she wasn't invisible either. Nick didn't want to leave their post and risk that Thurston or Lovett were about to walk out of the lab the second they pulled away.

Little did he know that it was neither of those men who walked out of the building two hours later, after Mona had stopped pulling the University security camera feed. By sheer luck, or perhaps fate, the woman who exited the building did so without any notice. Which was good, she was exhausted and it showed on every inch on her face and how she hobbled home to recover.

5

The standard issue sedan passed under the streetlight directly in front of his apartment.

Hank felt like a common criminal in the back of the car with the two officers. He had no handcuffs on, but he was still in the backseat behind the metal grate. The ride over was tense and silent. He confirmed his address, something he already provided to the officers, and they drove off into the night. The streets were their usual amount of busy for that hour. A few co-eds spilling out of pizza shops, bureaucrats on their way home from a happy hour that extended well into the evening.

Hank had to wait for W. to open the car door for him. He just hoped that none of his neighbors thought anything of his perp walk from the cop car to the apartment.

He fumbled for his keys in the manilla envelope that he had been provided. The hospital removed his wallet, cell phone, and keys and handed them directly over to the police. Hank unlocked the front door and started up the stairs to his apartment. He could hear W. and her counterpart trudging up the stairs behind him, their feet clomping like horses. *They're probably going to wake up every person in the building.*

They reached the door to his apartment, which he unlocked. As he opened the door, the officers pushed him aside so they could enter first.

"Sorry, it's protocol to make sure you don't tamper with anything," W. said with a shrug.

Hank didn't even pretend that he wasn't offended. He was ready to be rid of these two. He could have refused to let them in, but he wanted to prove he had nothing to hide. The sooner they got to work finding Nina – and Parker – the better.

Everything was just as he had left it when he ran out of the apartment earlier that afternoon, or maybe it was yesterday already. He had left Nina to start to unpack her things and he dialed the police to report what they discovered in Parker's basement. After repeating the address multiple times for the dispatcher, he was able to get off the phone. He called out for Nina, but she didn't answer. Then he saw the open window leading out to the fire exit.

She had run. From him? It was too painful to think about what would have made her do that, but then she texted him and he took off towards the University. W. quickly located the two bags that Hank carried over and dropped in the living room. The male officer made his way down the hallway. "There are two more bags in the bedroom!" Hank called out after him.

W. stood silently waiting for her partner to return.

Hank leaned up against the breakfast bar separating the kitchen from the small dining area in the apartment. He rubbed his eyes, the exhaustion from the day, his weariness inevitable at that point. "Will you return her items once this investigation is over?" Hank asked.

W. stood there silently for a moment. Perhaps waiting for Hank to elaborate on his request. He just looked at her and waited for a response.

"Yes, be sure to contact our office with your request," she pulled out a business card from her back pocket. Detective Patricia Wells. *At least he got the "W." part correct.*

"And don't forget this," Hank said as he nodded to the note on his kitchen counter. It was the scrap of paper he had discovered on the nightstand after Nina left. He had climbed out onto the fire escape, hoping to catch a glimpse of her, which direction she had set off. The scrap of paper nearly flew onto the floor after he shut the window. But it was Nina's handwriting, he would recognize it anywhere.

Detective Wells stepped closer to identify the paper. She put on a plastic glove and carefully dropped the note into a plastic bag that she had pulled out of her pocket. "You touched this?"

Hank wanted to roll his eyes at the ridiculously obvious question. *No. I looked at it from afar with my hands tied behind my back because I knew this would become critical evidence.* "Yes, Nina left it on the nightstand before she left out the fire escape." Wells didn't respond, instead she jotted something down in her little pocket notebook. "That's Nina's handwriting." Hank asserted.

"We'll test for her fingerprints and run a handwriting sample, Dr. Jankowski," Wells muttered without so much as a second glance.

Her counterpart finally lumbered down the hallway, one large bag on each shoulder. The bags had been perfectly balanced between Hank and Nina earlier, but this detective was short and stocky so he walked off-kilter with the bulk of them. He set down one of the large bags and handed Hank his card as well. Detective Thomas Holcrum. *Yeah, never would have remembered that name.*

Hank pocketed both cards. He would be sure to call and ask for updates as to their search for Parker. He wouldn't stop bugging them until Nina was found, or avenged. He still hadn't accepted that she was gone, he couldn't do that. But he knew Parker had hurt her, and he needed to pay for that.

"Well Hank, if you think of anything else give us a call," Wells said as she headed for the door. But apparently her partner felt the need to add in the final word.

"We'll be in touch with more questions as we continue to investigate. So, don't leave town," Holcrum said as he hoisted one of the bags back on his shoulder, both arms weighed down by the bulky luggage. *How cliché*, Hank thought. Wells grabbed the other bag and they set off.

Hank watched as Wells opened the door, struggling to maneuver with the heft of the bags. Just before they were out of the apartment, he stopped them.

"Wait, I did just realize something," he said, causing both officers to take a half-step back. They both looked over at him expectantly. He was pleased to see them waiting while still holding the heavy bags of Nina's things.

"It looks like it takes two people to carry all that," Hank nodded at the bags. They couldn't reasonably think he had carried all of that by himself. Nina was with him, they had to believe that now. The officers exchanged a look that told him that he had made his point. "Guess I didn't walk all that over here by myself after all."

"Have a good evening, Dr. Jankowski," Wells said, her tone completely changed, harsher and more frustrated.

The officers left and Hank locked the door behind them. He could hear them clomping all the way down the stairs. As much as he wanted to stay up and continue to sort through everything that happened in the past twenty-four hours and find another clue, another piece of the puzzle, he needed sleep. Hank sauntered down the hall and crashed headfirst onto his bed, his head ringing, his shoes still on.

He fell into a deep sleep. But instead of closing his eyes into a dream, he found that a completely dark sleep allowed him to escape the nightmare for a few brief hours.

6

Nick Noriega stirred the powdered creamer into his bland coffee. He was less than enthused at the prospect of another cup of the break room blend, but he was on a government salary, so this was his go-to. To anyone who stumbled across their building, and somehow managed to get past the front door, they would see a long white-walled hallway with abysmal recess lighting and opaque glass doors locked with thumbprint and retinal scans. The only room any pedestrian could hope to enter was their lackluster break room and kitchenette.

As he made his way back to his desk, Nick faced the impersonal hallway, just as he had every day for the past several years. They had their administrative teams towards the front. Payroll, Help Desk, and the really secret stuff was towards the end of the hall. That was where the teams were divided: left or right. Chronos or Kairos.

Those were the names for their joint departments. Founded in the late 1940s, the U.S. government knew that advances in physics would soon bring about massive safety concerns. Other departments were also created, but Nick wasn't read in on those. The joint-team at 1863 New Hampshire focused on time. Nick was a member of the Kairos team and Archie was his counterpart on Chronos. With theoretical physics starting to articulate multiverse theory over half a century earlier, there was a need to police any movement between realities. Because any movement to or from a parallel universe would require a time-machine, by definition, there were two distinct security concerns. The first was that people would come to this Universe and bring technologies we couldn't handle, disease, or dangerous ideas. In general, Nick's mission was to ensure that everything stayed in the correct universe or at least nothing that wasn't supposed to be in our universe ended up here. The overall function of Kairos was to keep everyone in their place in spacetime. The second concern was the movement of people through time to alter major events in history in their reality. That was the focus on Chronos, Archie's division. Because there had been so little activity beyond theorizing, the agents always worked in teams, one member from each department, until they knew for sure where or when someone came from. Then a team would be assigned based on the type of incident they were facing.

Nick hoped that Thurston and Lovett hadn't done anything to disrupt the balance of the universes. Nick liked his job and perhaps would have enjoyed more in-field opportunities, but he had so much anxiety over the responsibility. If someone from another universe showed up with a deadly weapon and started killing people, that would be on Nick. If they brought a plague, or if they were just comprised of anti-matter, there would be mass devastation. The more he thought about traveling to another reality, another version of this world at the same exact moment in time, the more unstable he felt. As though the ground beneath his feet could shift at any moment.

He paused and scanned in at the door on the right, erasing his worries from his mind for a moment. He entered the darkened office space, illuminated only by strip lighting on the floors, the monitors at each work station, and the large screens on the front wall with global updates. There was a small video feed at the lower right corner of the main wall showing a grainy figure approach the entrance to a building on a repeating loop.

After the call on August 8, there hadn't been many developments on the power surge detected in Thurston's lab. When he and Archie returned to the office, they had met in the joint conference room with Mona. She had given them enough sass over the radio, but her job was very difficult. There were five camera feeds that she was monitoring while trying to keep the firewall for the University from locking her out. She had been keeping an eye on the live feeds so she hadn't yet discovered the recorded video of the lab before the alarm went off.

The following day on August 9 she had finally been able to pinpoint a clear view of a figure approaching the building late on the evening of August 7. From the view, it appeared to be a person carrying a large bag over their shoulders and entering the lab at about 11:30 pm. The lighting was poor, but based on the surveillance they had been doing, Nick and Archie agreed that it was Parker Lovett who was entering the building. Height, build, and gate analysis confirmed it. Although they had no idea what was in the large bag he was carrying, it looked like a body bag, but they reasoned that it would be too bold for a man to walk around downtown Washington, D.C. at night with a body bag without being stopped.

The two continued to monitor the situation, but without more to go on, they were at a bit of a standstill. When Nick returned to his desk with his subpar coffee, he saw an alert from the metro police. A missing person's report had been filed for Parker Lovett the previous evening. Nick picked up his desk phone before he even opened the document and dialed Archie's extension.

"Get over here, now," he said and then hung up. A minute later, Archie appeared behind the console that Nick was working from. The open office plan allowed each team member to use any console they desired, all having access to look up at a bank of common screens that reported on relevant metrics. As was the office pattern, Nick had a favorite console and often left his files there instead of locking them in the central filing cabinet system.

"What took you so long?" Nick asked. He knew that Archie's side of the building had the same exact layout, a mirror image. Their two departments were separated by just that bland hallway. Both teams worked together so much, Nick didn't quite get why the teams were kept apart to begin with.

Archie didn't respond to Nick's question, instead he pulled up a chair and sat down. "What's up?"

"Parker Lovett was reported missing yesterday," Nick said as he opened the file. The benefits of working for a clandestine government agency was their ability to access this information without jumping through hoops.

Archie muttered as he read through the document. "Missing since August 8. Last seen evening of August 7 with girlfriend. Didn't report to work."

"Yeah, the girlfriend filed the report. It says here they met for dinner and then parted ways for the evening," Nick scrolled through the document.

"Well, that doesn't sound like it was a very good date," Archie commented. Nick nodded in agreement. "Who filed the report?" Archie asked. Nick rolled his eyes, especially since he had just given this information.

"The girlfriend did, but it looks like Thurston was there because he is heavily quoted on the document too."

Archie grabbed a piece of paper from the desk and started to jot down some notes.

"What is the girlfriend's name?" he asked, squinting to see if it was on Nick's screen.

"Feminina Marks." Nick read the name out loud.

"That name sounds familiar," Archie commented as he wrote it down.

"Well, it says here they've been together for three years. Maybe we've crossed her before during our surveillance." Nick offered the rational explanation.

"Hmm, I don't know. I'm thinking of it from somewhere else, someplace else." Archie shook his head.

Nick shook his as well, but for a different reason. This happened a lot with Archie, he experienced déjà vu more than the average person. Occupational hazard perhaps, but it bothered Nick. This "sense" of familiarity would cloud Archie's judgement sometimes. He would focus in on details that didn't help them move forward.

"Well, whether you already know her or not, we should make a point to question her this week," Nick added her home address and workplace to his own notes.

"Let's make sure we read anything else the local police post on this," Archie added. "I don't want us to go in too soon and have the local police asking questions about why we were also there." Nick knew exactly what Archie was referring to with this. There had been another incident three years earlier that involved a case on Archie's side of the hall that went horribly wrong. Not only were people killed, but the investigation had been bungled with local police trying to chase down the 'shadow agency' that had interviewed witnesses before they had a chance to.

"Alright," Nick added and with that Archie headed out of the open office and back across the hall. Nick stared at the name on the screen for another moment. *Feminina Marks. Who are you?*

7

Universe Alpha

Archie crossed back over to his side of the hallway. For as much as he enjoyed working with Nick and knew that both of their agencies had an important mission, he often felt that his was just ever so slightly more important. He had never voiced this, but Nick just had to make sure people stayed put in their place in time. Archie had to ensure that the chronology of their universe remained unperturbed. He was constantly working to make sure that the present didn't change because of damage that could be done in the past.

His concern about waiting so that they didn't interfere with the local police investigation stayed top of mind as he made his way to his preferred work console. Archie pulled out his case file on the unsolved murders from three years earlier. Usually, their agency wasn't called in for murders in the District. It's a big city, there are a lot of people, there are bound to be homicides. But, when there is a temporal displacement alert, he usually got the call. Just like the alarm that had gone off the other evening, the agencies had sensitive equipment that monitored the energy output and quantum readings of their assigned territory.

The agencies had field offices operating in the cities where known quantum research regarding the multiverse was taking place. Archie had been asked to assist on a case in Tokyo once, which was ultimately fruitless, but a thrilling trip nonetheless.

As Archie flipped through the file in his hands, he recalled the details of the murders, brutal attacks on three women. All Caucasian, so the press covered it much more than any of the other murders that summer. They had each been stabbed fatally, no weapon recovered from any of the crime scenes. But there was a clear pattern. Each woman was attacked at night in the Dupont Circle area. The crimes all happened between 1:00 am and 3:00 am, the bodies discovered later that morning. There were no witnesses to any of the crimes.

The alert of a temporal displacement, meaning someone with too much or too little time on their body, meant that Archie was called out to investigate as well. As is well known, each and every person is dying. It is the only guarantee in life, plus taxes. When someone travels back in time, it means that they will relive the same years over, compounding their decay exponentially. When someone jumps in time, they are lagging on their decay. Archie had traveled back and forth so much that his decay clock was completely out of whack. Chronos calibrated their measurements to exclude any of their officers from inadvertently tripping the alarm.

Sure, messing with his own biological clock was a clear occupational hazard, but Archie enjoyed his job. Looking at the files with fresh eyes, he read through the details again. The women murdered in this case had trace amounts of radiation on them, indicating that their killer had a severe temporal lag.

He finished flipping through the file, light as it was. There hadn't been much evidence to glean, but Archie and his commanding officer agreed that the killer had been from another time, and potentially another universe as well. There had only been one joint alarm with the Kairos agency that summer, when the unknown criminal arrived. There was no alarm signaling their departure. Which meant the murderer died or they were still living in this universe. That was the curious part that always tripped Archie up about this case. If they had died, then surely their body would have been discovered. Traveling through time and across The Plain of the multiverse left physical signs on a person. Archie's own milky eyes were proof enough of that. Any time-traveling body examined by a hospital or county morgue would have been brought to the attention of the authorities. But no such claim ever came into the agency.

He flipped to the last page and read over his final notes. As he went to close the file and set it back in his drawer, he noticed that there was indeed another item in the file behind his sheet of handwritten comments. Archie didn't remember adding anything else to the file, but then he looked at the picture. And then, yes, he did recall this information now. That unsettling feeling that often accompanied his work came over him. As though he was standing on unsolid ground, that the soil beneath him had been shifting all along. That the case was unfolding presently, three years in the past.

Archie removed the photo and scrutinized it. Something he had done several times before, although it still felt as though this was the first time he had seen it. A grainy color photo showed a dark figure exiting a convenience store. Archie closed his eyes and the memories, the brand-new memories, flooded his mind. This had come from a shop not twenty feet from the location of the final murder. Just before Audrey St. Claire had been cut down, this shadow figure had exited the nearby corner market. The cashier had reported that this person seemed shiftless, just roaming the aisles as though they were killing time and then left without buying anything. They had on a loose black sweatshirt with the hood pulled up over their head. Given the height of the person, 5'3", and their thin legs, barely visible beneath the tent of black cotton, Archie had surmised that this person was female, which didn't fit the psychological profile for a potential murderer. Still, he filed it away.

As Archie replaced the photo in the file, he remembered his initial suspicion that maybe this action had been intentional. Almost everyone who has ever been in a quickie-mart, or gas station store, or any kind of stop-and-go establishment knows that they can easily access a vast array of energy drinks, slushies, and poor-quality food. But they're also aware of multiple mirrored cameras around the building and a height marker on the doors. These stores are the unfortunate common prey for everyday criminals and such security measures often lead to the quick arrest of whoever decided to steal a couple hundred dollars from the register. It was almost comically dumb for anyone to rob one of these stores. Which is why most of the time the local police caught teenagers doing this. Some more experienced criminals at least knew to keep their faces down, hidden from camera, and stoop low to throw off the height marker.

But this brazen individual stared back up at Archie from the photo. They appeared to have paused as they exited the store, turned, and looked directly at the back camera. As though they wanted to be found. It was a clear shot of their face and height. The camera quality was poor so it wasn't exactly the best photograph. And no results popped up when they ran it through facial recognition software. Their eyes appeared black; the irises too small to see any color. But their skin was stark white, almost blindingly so. A thick lock of bright white hair fell out from under the black hood.

The face was eerie, ghoulish. There was something off that Archie just couldn't place. Not able to find the source of his unease on this review of the photo, he put it away and shoved the file back in his cabinet.

Taking a deep breath, Archie leaned back in his desk chair and glanced over at the clock on the wall. His stomach growled; he would text Nick to see where he wanted to go for lunch soon.

Archie cast his eyes to the right just slightly. Next to the clock was the picture of the current Commander in Chief, an image that always elicited a heavy eye-roll from him and several of the other agents. Immediately next to that image was one of the founders of the joint agencies. A black and white photo that seemed to never fade with age, she looked confidently into the camera lens, her eyes sparkled with the glow of the light the photographer was using, or perhaps it was a touch of destiny. Archie often wondered if she had known how important these agencies would be. And then he stopped himself, of course she did. She was the first person to ever travel through time.

PART 2

"The two most powerful warriors are patience and time."

– Leo Tolstoy, War & Peace

8

The hot liquid squirted into the carafe. Dr. Xander Marks watched as the coffee sputtered into the container. He was both alert and exhausted, focused and confused. His panic had fueled him for so long. But his mind, his graceful, intelligent, incredible mind, needed sleep. And when he refused to relent, to stop looking for Nina, he knew he would need a stimulant. He had lost count of how many batches of coffee that he had brewed since Nina went missing seven hours earlier. His hands were shaking, jittery.

Since Xander first played that security footage, he had been busy. He recalibrated the Portal. He called her cell phone. He pinged the team in Tokyo, asking if they had any odd readings on their end. He ignored their questions about why he was up so late; couldn't this wait until the morning. Didn't he deserve to sleep? He knew that he would need to ask them if Nina had stepped through to their end, but he wanted to wait just a bit longer. He knew that if she appeared through the Portal, they would have said something by now, but he still held out a small bit of hope. Maybe, just maybe.

His time was running out, though. Soon the dedicated weekend crew that filled the other offices on their floor would filter in. They would be eager to hear about how the test went. They would ask where Nina was. He would have to admit that he didn't know or he would have to lie.

Xander grabbed his mug as soon as the coffee stopped dribbling. The first sip was too hot, but he was almost too numb to care. Ever since he realized that Nina was missing it seemed that he was living in a fish tank, immersed in water, his movements and thoughts dulled.

He headed back to his office and reviewed the notes he had started to write down. As always, his method for sorting out his thoughts was to put them on paper. Even though these were memories he didn't want to commit to something as permanent as a notebook. He was struggling to separate his emotion from the situation. He needed every last bit of his mind focused on the facts of the situation and a possible solution. He couldn't afford to have any brain cells not focused on finding Nina, but at the same time he couldn't stop himself from panicking. *What if he never found her? What if he could never get her back?*

Perhaps the coffee was making it worse, his agitated mind really didn't need more juice. But he needed to stay awake. He vowed to not sleep, not rest, until he found Nina and brought her back.

From his desk he could hear a few voices out in the hallway, the standard crew of early arrivers was making their way to their offices, exchanging the usual pleasantries. *How could he tell them what happened?* While other careers afforded a comfortable five-day workweek and relaxing weekends, many of the experiments run in this building required daily monitoring. The Saturday morning crew was just as dedicated as the Monday morning team.

It seemed like another lifetime ago when he had stepped back through the Portal and seen the first travelers of the multiverse in his lab. Since he had sent them on their way and hugged his daughter, it was as though his life ended the moment she vanished. But how could he tell anyone that his machine had worked so splendidly without then telling them how it had gone so wrong?

He ran through the checklist on his notepaper. He had backed up the data of all the Portal jumps. He added a note next to it that he would need to develop a quantum drive similar to the one he had seen Feminina and Marie, the travelers from what they called Universe Gamma, using to help with their device. Next, he ran through the order of events again. He had a list of potential ways to calculate the location of "UNIVERSE UNKOWN," but he would need time in order to walk through each of those options. In spite of the fact that he knew he would be able to rescue Nina the second she arrived in that foreign reality, he still worried about each moment that passed.

The first forty-eight hours in any disappearance are critical. *But what if she had been taken years into the future*, he wondered. *Or into the past?*

A knock at his office door pulled him back into the present moment. Denise, one of the lead scientists working on their floor whose area of study focused on renewable energies, was leaning against the doorframe.

"So, how did it go?" Her question was tentative. Perhaps Xander's exhaustion was written all over his face, something that could easily be misread as failure.

"Well, I didn't have time for sushi, but it was great to see the team in person," Xander managed to compose himself and offered his response with a sly smile. He surprised even himself in his ability to share the success of one part of the evening without revealing the complete disaster that followed.

"What! No way!" Denise responded, her eyes bulging with delight.

"Oh, ye of little faith," Xander pretended to rebuke her.

"No, I just assumed that if you were here today that would mean back to the drawing board. Otherwise, I would have expected you to call in sick with a champagne hangover." Denise took a few steps into the office. She and Xander had a good rapport, their research teams often worked together to help power his device. At times, he wondered if he was perhaps too familiar with her, his own attractions starting to show through. But he never dared to cross a line, to suggest drinks after work or a shared meal. Besides, he wasn't sure how Nina might handle the idea of him dating again, even though Elle, her mother, had passed when she was so young. Denise was tall, taller than Xander, and she was what some people might call "big-boned," but Xander didn't mind looking at her figure no matter the terms applied. She didn't look a thing like Elle, so much for having "a type," but there was the same ambitious fire in her spirit that Xander found compelling.

For the hemming and hawing he had done, the worrying about their professional relationship and how neither of them would ever sacrifice their research for anything as simple as love, he was relieved in that moment that he had maintained his distance. If they had grown closer, into good friends or even lovers, he would have had to recount the entire evening to her. He would have felt compelled to share his worries and fears, to ask for help. But he couldn't do that, and he was glad that he didn't have some kind of obligation to do so. He needed to solve this situation before he alerted others to it, he needed to be able to concentrate and get it done.

"Perhaps I'll do just that, but I wanted to take down all the notes and recollections, make a list of next steps for our team," Xander responded to Denise, his tone still polite but markedly less inviting.

"Of course. Well, a celebration is in order. I can order in lunch for both of our teams today and you can regale us with the story. I'm sure Nina is thrilled," Denise offered a warm smile.

"Yes, she is delighted, lots of hard work on her end too," Xander moved some of the papers on his desk as he spoke. He couldn't look at Denise as he said this. Perhaps his deception was extremely obvious, but he hoped that she wouldn't read too much into it.

"Great," Denise cooed. "Did she stay through the night with you? I didn't see her in the lab when I passed by."

"Oh, no. She is following the advice that I should have. At home resting. Weeks and weeks of long nights, I thought a bit of recuperation was in order," Xander rushed these words together, his lie too difficult to stomach. He marveled at how he hadn't thought of what he would say when people asked. Had he really believed that he would be able to find her and bring her back already? He didn't even know when the next quantum jitter would be.

"Well, I'll look forward to congratulating her when she is back tomorrow then," Denise smiled and dismissed herself, picking up on his tone.

He offered a weak half-smile, although she wasn't there to see it. He rubbed his forehead and tried to refocus on his plan, or lack thereof. Rogers would be asking questions soon, Xander was surprised that he hadn't been peppered with questions yet. As much as he didn't want to, he knew he needed the help of his team in Tokyo. He could trust them, and they were the only ones who could do the necessary analysis, all while keeping this under wraps.

Xander pulled up the inter-office chat system and pinged Hajime, he always worked later than his counterparts. It was well into the evening on his side of the world, and a weekend day to boot, but Hajime seemed to revel in his position as the one who always arrived early and stayed late. Always online, always working.

Unsure of how to begin the conversation, Xander wrote out the question that he desperately hoped would reveal the answer that he needed.

"Hajime, I trust you had a good workday. By any chance, did Nina happen to walk through the Portal after me? It would save me a lot of time and energy looking for her if you could assure me that she was safe in Tokyo with you and the team."

He knew it was a foolish hope. He replayed the footage over and over; he saw that she had been taken. And if she had been in Tokyo, she would have pinged him by now, he would have received pictures of the team out for drinks or karaoke. But, ever the scientist, he had to rule out all of the simplest explanations first before moving on to the more complex ones.

An icon popped up at the bottom of the screen indicating that Hajime was writing a response. The three dots recycled into infinity as Xander waited to see what would come through.

Dot. Dot. Dot.

9

Knock. Knock. Knock.

Hank didn't even realize he had fallen asleep until he heard the pounding. It was a rhythmic hammering on his front door, someone really putting their muscle into it. Hank sat up on his bed. He had fallen asleep still wearing his clothes from the previous day. They were beyond wrinkled. He shook his head and moved his hands through his hair as the sound continued.

He had a wretched headache, one of the worst he had ever experienced. But getting beat to a pulp by Parker Lovett, slamming his head on the concrete floor, and then being interrogated by the police didn't really set him up for a pain-free morning. And then there was the other pain, the one that couldn't be eased by over the counter or even prescription pain killers.

Where was Nina? Where was the love of his life? The only cure for that pain was to find her.

The knocking on the door didn't help the other pain though. Hank slowly stood up, letting each of his joints take their time stretching out. It was only as he stood that he caught some of Nina's shoes peeking out from the closet.

That's right, because she was here with him yesterday, starting to move a few things in. The thought filled him with hope, and a stolid certainty that he could prove that she had been there and that she therefore couldn't be dead and that the police needed to stop jerking him around and start searching for her in earnest.

As this passed through his mind, Hank realized that it could be Nina on the other side of his door. Suddenly very awake, he darted for the front door. He hastily unlocked the deadbolt and swung the door open.

But it wasn't Nina who greeted him. Instead, he saw a petite woman with short-cropped hair, shiny in spite of summer humidity.

"Carol?" Hank asked, bewildered. He hadn't seen her in years. Not since he and Nina had originally separated. He was surprised that he remembered her name.

"Hank!" Carol let out a deep sigh. She brushed past him, inviting herself in. She began to pace immediately. "I didn't know where else to go! I just heard it on the news." Her face was warped as her mouth remained open, caught between being shocked and gulping for oxygen.

Hank closed the door and ushered her over to the couch. Thick and brown, it was the perfect relaxing oasis for a young college professor and the best hiding place for years of crumbs that were surely gathering between the cushions. "Here sit down," he could tell that she was worked up.

"But we have to go to the police!" Carol pleaded with him.

Hank let out a grunt. "I'll get you some water." He didn't really have a very high estimation of the local police at the moment, but he did indeed need to visit them again. *How could Nina be gone since last week if she was with him yesterday moving her shoes into the closet?*

"Hank! They're saying on the news that Nina was murdered last week! And now Parker is missing!" Her voice was shrill, reaching its peak volume.

"I know," Hank said as he set some water down in front of her. He looked at her, but she didn't take the water. Instead, Carol peered up at him. And as if she was finally seeing him, she startled.

"Goodness, Hank! What happened to your face?" Carol's face was aghast once again. Her demure khaki and blush pink outfit was too prim and proper for the situation she found herself in. She almost seemed comically polished in spite of the situation, but Hank couldn't find the energy to laugh.

"That bad, huh? I haven't looked in the mirror yet this morning," Hank touched his fingertips to his left cheek gingerly. It was sore and the pain flared at his touch.

"You look like you've been in a fist-fight!" Carol declared. *Poor demure Carol,* Hank thought. He began to recall all of her mannerisms that he and Nina had remarked on back in the glory days of their relationship.

"That's because I have been," Hank answered as he sauntered back to the kitchen and grabbed an ice pack from his freezer. The frost on the outer part of the package was painful as it touched his skin, but started to numb it within a few seconds.

"What? Who did that to you? What is going on?" Carol demanded more answers than Hank had time to process.

"Parker," was all Hank could grunt out as he plopped back down in the arm chair across from his couch.

"Parker did this to you? Well, you have to go to the police-" Carol started in, her words spilling into each other.

"Carol," Hank interrupted her and only continued once he had her attention. "I spent most of yesterday evening with the police. I answered all of their questions, but they still don't believe me."

"Well, maybe they'll believe me. Nina told me all about how she was planning to leave Parker and how she was nervous about telling him. I can provide context around their relationship and how they need to be looking into the idea that he kidnapped her." Carol said it all in one breath.

"They told me they are going to look into where Parker went, especially since I do intend to press charges of assault," he said as he gestured with his right hand to the ice pack still held up to the left side of his face.

"Okay, well they're looking for Parker, but what about Nina? On the news this morning they said she was found dead!"

Hank didn't have an immediate answer. His mind flashed on the body he had found yesterday, the woman in the plastic tarp that he had cradled in his arms. But he hadn't been alone when that had happened. He had been *with* Nina. But his mind still told him that the woman in the tarp was Nina as well.

"I know, they found a woman's body in Parker's basement. But-" Hank let his thoughts die on his lips. He needed physical proof that it was Nina who had been with him. Nina who he had seen struggling with Parker when he arrived in that lab.

"Well, it simply can't have been Nina! Especially if they're saying this woman died last week. I mean I feel horrible. A woman is dead, but they aren't investigating what happened to *her*. If they think it's Nina then this other family will never get their closure. No, Nina is alive Hank!" Her bobbed hair shook with the vehemence of her words, her tight hands clenching and releasing as she spoke.

Hank nodded his head, this he knew. Perhaps it was the residual exhaustion or just the cold pack pressed against the side of his head, but he had a slightly delayed response. "Carol, how do you know for sure it wasn't Nina?" He couldn't hide the note of suspicion in his voice.

"She was at work yesterday morning. Came in late complaining of a headache and then made a scene on her way out. Knocked into one of the media buyers, scattered papers everywhere. It was a big mess. I was worried about her, but I figured she has so much going on with moving back in with you and all. And the family issue she had last week."

What family issue? He hadn't heard of this. But then his mind switched back to the matter at hand. Hank stared unblinking at Carol for a moment. "Carol, will you attest to this under oath? Who did she knock into? We need to get the both of you down to the police station now. Do you think your office security videos are backed up? We need to prove she was there."

Carol sat up, at first shocked by the complete one-eighty in his temperament but he saw that her worry had quickly transitioned into steely resolve. Carol gave him a resolute nod and pulled her cell phone out of her purse; she began typing into it with determination.

For the first time in days, since Nina went M.I.A., Hank felt like he wasn't losing his mind. He had a witness now, he had multiple witnesses perhaps, something to prove that Nina was alive and now potentially a kidnapping victim. He let out the smallest of sighs, the tiniest bit of relief at knowing he had a next step in the plan to find Nina.

Now he just had to wrangle witnesses, convince the police to collect the security tapes before they were recorded over, and prove that he was indeed innocent so that they could start their investigation in earnest. It wasn't much, but it was a start.

10

Sunday morning, bright and early. Feminina arrived at the lab at 4:00 am sharp, just as she had for the past three years. There was work to be done. She waited outside for Marie until 4:10, the balmy summer air starting to turn her pin-straight hair into frizzled kinked ends. Frustrated, she let herself in, no longer worried about who might follow her.

Gus Blanity, the man who had been stalking her and Marie for months would no longer be a concern. Only days earlier, *gosh was it only four days ago?*, they had sent him through the Portal and into another universe and another time. Feminina did have concerns about the damage he would cause, had already caused in Universe Alpha. She saw the devastation on her own face, the face of her alter-ego, as she realized that it wasn't Gus' alter-ego who had attacked and killed her boyfriend ten years earlier, it was that exact Gus.

Messing with the multiverse had severe consequences. Feminina knew that now, had experienced it now. But that didn't deter her, it only spurred her to make improvements. To do better.

She let the chain and padlock lay on the floor, hoping that Marie would be along any minute now. Feminina had a long list of items to tackle. She entered the lab using her palm print and began to restore the items that had been moved about the other day. She righted a chair that had been left in the middle of the lab, pushed back from a computer console. Right, Nina had been browsing the Mesh. Feminina took out a folded piece of paper from her back pocket and added an item at the bottom of the list. *Wipe Nina's Search Records.*

She had tried to recall as much as she could from their brief trip to Universe Delta. While that trip had also taken them ten years into the past, the machine there was more advanced. She had several items on her list from this experience.

Automated Portal Positioning. Feminina already knew where to find the castors and mechanized parts to add that element to the Portal. She would need Marie's help in programming the quantum computer to issue that command.

Supercybin enhanced with a pain killer. That was a stroke of genius as well. Unfortunately, their chemist had also been Blanity, so getting a new formula created would be tricky, but it would go on the list. They had three vials of their existing stash of supercybin left. They had a much larger store of it, but apparently Gus had been supplying Parker with their vials. *To what end?* She still didn't know. He would have only needed a few extra in order to go to Universe Alpha and bring Nina back with him to Beta. Another one or two extra for his additional trips and when he sent Nina to their reality. But they had dozens and dozens of vials missing.

Feminina had that on her list to riddle out as well. When she, Marie, and Nina had left for Universe Delta on Wednesday they had seven vials. It wasn't actually enough to get everyone back in their place in the multiverse, so it had been a blessing that their father had given them three of his vials to help in their journey.

Dad. That was the final item on the list. She knew it was reckless, but she wanted to go back. She wanted to spend more time with him. She knew that the man she saw in Universe Delta was not *her* actual father. He was the alter-ego of her dad, another version of him from another dimension. Her actual father was gone. The long-buried memory of his painful death had been resurrected the instant she saw him alive again, or saw his alter-ego alive and well in Universe Delta.

This had been the main focus of her mind over the past few days. Not the ramifications of the events set in motion on August 8 and their impact across multiple realities. Not any guilt over sending two Parkers into an unknown region of the multiverse. Not even the potential ways in which the machine could continue to be misused. No. Feminina was focused on how she could get her father back. Not just another day-trip to Universe Delta, although she would certainly enjoy that as well. But how could she use the Portal as a true time-machine and go back in time in her own reality and prevent his cancer from spreading.

She looked at the chalk board and white board and debated which one would need to be erased so that she could make room for a whole new string of equations that would allow her to do just that. It didn't feel right to erase anything until Marie arrived though. She checked her wrist watch and glanced back at the door to the lab.

Still no sign of her lab partner.

She decided to continue cleaning up until Marie arrived. Feminina took the brick that Gus had tried to attack them with and moved it towards the back exit of the lab, it would make a good door stopper. She cleaned up the papers that had scattered to the ground and put them back in lopsided piles on the console. Carefully, she placed the remaining vials back in the locked cabinet and then started collecting the half-empty coffee cups and cola cans from their late-night caffeine crash.

As she moved about the lab, her eyes carefully avoided the frame of the Portal. While she had daydreams of traveling back in time to save her father, she couldn't actually face the device. Every time she skirted too close, her memory flashed on the keystrokes that she input the other night. The actions that she took, alone, to condemn two men to the vacuum of spacetime. Something in her soul just couldn't handle looking at it again, standing there, reminding her of her worst crimes.

Feminina had most of the lab cleaned up when she remembered something else. Something that would need to go on a list for Marie. They needed a new quantum drive, having left theirs in Universe Beta. They would need to re-create it and then go back and save the past coordinates to it again. It would be cumbersome rework, but it was doable.

They had a year, perhaps less, until the next quantum jitters would allow the Portal to open again. They had time on their side.

Or that is what Feminina thought. But given that an hour had passed and there was no sign of her lab partner, she began to worry that time had lost all meaning. She could feel herself becoming more and more annoyed with each passing minute. *Was Marie just going to flake on her?*

Impatient, she began to look through the cabinets on the far side of the lab for the items she would need to mechanize the Portal. They had been forced to move it manually, a very delicate and imprecise process. Getting the device to automate that function would make their machine more efficient and accurate. Plus, it had been a super cool feature from the device in Universe Delta.

Feminina heard the distant sounds of the front door slamming shut and footsteps heading towards her. She sat calmly, leaned back in the desk chair as she sipped on her energy drink. She was still reeling from the events of the previous week, but she and Marie had more work to do.

After Marie had run out in the middle of a crisis, Femi had to handle the *two* Parkers all by herself and close up the lab. She wanted to be mad at Marie, she wanted to rant at her. But instead, she had decided to just move past it. Or rather, she had decided to silently hold a grudge and let it fester, but it seemed to be the better option over confronting her research partner.

That lab had been the only bright spot left for Femi. After they closed the University, she went a little stir crazy and she needed to see the project through to the end. She welcomed the opportunity to spend more time with Marie, to learn together, to complete their mission.

Marie strolled through the first section of the lab and into the large open area where Feminina was waiting next to the Portal.

"Hey," Marie said, looking down at her shoes.

The two of them had only exchanged brief text messages to arrange that meeting. Nothing else had been said in the past few days. It was clear that Marie was unhappy with Femi as well, although Femi didn't see how she could be.

"Hey," Femi said back, matching Marie's tone.

"I'm sorry about-," Marie started.

"Whatever, it's fine," Feminina cut her off as she stood up from the chair. "We need to document our findings. We've probably already lost some of the fine details, but we can't let that stop us." Femi focused on adjusting the stray papers on the console that they had used to scratch out calculations that fateful night.

Marie approached Feminina and handed over a notebook and thumb drive. "I already recorded my observations in writing and in video." She placed them on the desk.

"Oh," Feminina blinked, looking down at the items. "Good. Then I'll just need to do the same-," she carried on before Marie cut her off this time.

"What did you do with them?" Marie asked. Feminina knew what she meant. What had Feminina done with the two evil Parkers who she had left her with in the lab? What happened after Marie abandoned her?

Feminina looked over at Marie, making eye contact. "Do you care?"

Marie raised an eyebrow and crossed her arms. Her pursed lips were locked shut, as though she was seriously considering letting her first thoughts out.

Femi raised her eyebrows as well, daring Marie to correct her assumption.

"Look, Sonali was dealing with a crisis. She needed me," Marie started.

"*We* were dealing with a crisis, and then I was left to clean up the mess. That's not how this partnership works," Feminina started in. She had told herself she wouldn't air such grievances, but here they were having this argument anyways.

"You think I liked having to run out? But I also needed to be there for Sonali! It's not fair that you expect me to stay 100% focused on only this just because you are!" Marie shook her head. This was an argument that they had been skirting around for months. Feminina was hurt when Marie cut back her commitment to the project, Marie assumed she was jealous of the attention she was giving to Sonali, but it was deeper than that. Feminina had lost everyone, her mom and then her dad, she had lost the University, and was about to lose the project that meant the most to her. She didn't want to lose Marie too.

But, of course, she never verbalized it that way. Femi never enunciated that to Marie to help her understand why her friend was being so needy. She was needy because she needed her friend.

"Well, then, I guess I just need you to recreate the quantum drive and update the system and we'll be all set." Feminina said in a cold tone, dismissing her lab partner. She wasn't about to beg Marie to be her friend or make time for her. Femi could tell that with Sonali in the picture that she would be seeing less and less of Marie. *Why drag this out?* Why make Marie suffer, feeling like she had to pick one or the other. She knew Sonali would win anyways, love always does.

"Yeah, losing my prototype was a tough blow," Marie said with sarcasm, not catching that Femi had just dismissed her from the project.

"Cool, let me know how long you think it will take." Femi rolled her eyes as she picked up her list. "Also, I'll need your help taking the Portal off the track. One, so we can set up an automatic repositioning element, like we saw in Delta. And for security until we are ready to use it again."

Marie scrunched her forehead. "Ready to use it again? We need to dismantle this thing."

Feminina reacted, repulsed by this notion. "What do you mean dismantle it? Absolutely not! We have more work to do now than ever before."

"You do remember everything that happened this week, right? People were murdered because of the power of this machine. We have to take it down!" Marie was passionate about this point. But Feminina crossed her arms, resolved to keep it operational.

The two women stared at each other for a moment before Marie turned on her heel and stalked out of the lab. Neither were known for their ability to compromise or handle conflict well. They had some arguments over the Portal in the past. Feminina hoped it would blow over like it had every time before. But in her gut, she could feel already, this was different than before. Everything had changed since Wednesday.

She sat with her arms folded, her eyes burning into the spot where Marie had stood for another moment or so. It was only after the sounds of her exiting the building had faded, after the sounds of the clock on the wall had seemed to grow louder and louder, that Feminina moved back to the console.

She had a list to complete, she had work to do. She just started to do it on her own, hoping that Marie would come back next week. They would figure it out, they just needed some time to cool down.

After another hour or so of work, Feminina grabbed her energy drink and headed for the door, only remembering one final item on her list as she reached the exit.

Right, wipe Nina's search logs.

She quickly unlocked the computer and navigated to the browser history. Nothing too dangerous, some basic history searches. A look-up for Parker Lovett. Now that was damning. That had to go. She hovered over the "erase" button before she spotted one search item that caught her eye. "Dr. Henry Jankowski."

Maybe it was curiosity, maybe it was the omnipresent influence of the Portal even when it was powered down, maybe it was the remaining particles of quantum foam that lingered in the air. Whatever it was, Feminina felt a pull to look. She clicked on the link and reviewed the page. A biography for a professor of English Literature at the Ghent University in Belgium. His headshot was handsome. Feminina pulled out her list once more and scribbled his name and the University on the backside. She didn't know what she would do with this information, probably nothing. But she had it now.

She cleared the logs, locked the computer, shut off the lights, and left the lab.

Feminina planned to be back in one week, making more progress on her list. Working towards her larger goal. Marie would be back next week with a box of donuts as an apology and they would carry on like nothing happened. *Right?* At least that is what she hoped would happen.

But none of it came to be. Marie never showed up. Not the next week or the week after or the week after. The two exchanged terse emails until Femi agreed to dismantle the device and put it in storage before she left town.

Feminina was on her own, trying to piece together what to do next in her plan to see her father again.

11

Nick waited for Archie to catch up to him. He noticed that his partner was moving a little bit slower now. It had been a gradual change. At first, he thought it was just Archie slacking off with his physical training requirements. As federal agents, they were required to meet a basic fitness level. Nick took advantage of the gym more often than he needed to, but he didn't have much of a social life, so he didn't mind the extra reps. Archie had always joked that he was employed for his mental aptitude, not his running speed.

When Nick first noticed that Archie was slowing down, he chalked it up to long hours, exhaustion. But now it seemed as though he was moving like an old man, wheezing slightly as he finished the last half-flight of stairs of the walk-up apartment building. Archie smiled up at Nick as he finished the final two steps to the landing.

"You okay?" Nick offered.

"Yeah man," Archie shrugged off his partner's concern. Nick eyed him, looking for any sign of pain. Some visual cue that he should follow up, but this wasn't the time or place. He could see sweat beads across Archie's hairline, but the stuffy stairwell wasn't air conditioned so that wasn't exactly a sign of physical strain, just another hot day in the District.

"Let's see if she's home," Nick muttered as he knocked on the door. Their previous stop, to visit Dr. Norman Thurston at the University, had been… interesting. The professor was clearly concerned for his colleague, but provided little to no detail on their current work. He kept insisting that Parker's disappearance couldn't have anything to do with their research and grew increasingly hostile towards the agents. Nick made his notes, all of which would be cross referenced with his source at the University.

But Nina Marks was an unknown variable. How much did she know, how much had Parker alluded to or shared with her? And, what if she had something to do with his disappearance and this was just a standard case of domestic murder? Nick knew that this interview would be critical to determining if they needed to stay involved in the investigation or not.

After a respectable amount of time, Nick tried the door again, this time calling out, "Ms. Marks?"

"Yes?" he heard a response. But it didn't come from the other side of the door, instead the small female voice was to his right, the answer carrying up the stairs ahead of her.

Both agents turned to face the woman as she continued toward them. A light sweater draped over her hip-length leather bag, she looked tired and confused. Her dark hair, so brown it appeared black, was pulled back, the edges matted to her face with sweat. It was early August in the swamp of D.C., of course she was flush and hot after a walk outside.

Nick checked his wrist-watch. Wow, the day had gotten away from him. It was nearing 5:45 pm. They must have caught her as she was arriving back from work.

"Hello," Archie broke the silence. Nick was still gathering his thoughts, so thoroughly jarred to see her approaching from behind them.

"Can I help you?" She seemed hesitant, but only stopped when she reached the top stair before the landing that the two men were occupying.

"Yes," Nick snapped to attention. "I'm agent Noriega, this is Agent Clermont. We're here to ask you a few questions about Parker Lovett."

Nina nodded quietly and the men parted so she could gain access to her apartment. "Come on in," she mumbled as she unlocked the door.

"Great, thank you," Archie said with a very distinct tone of relief.

"We could always chat somewhere else if you would be more comfortable, perhaps at a coffee shop. Your order on us, of course," Nick said, his words lost in the sound of Archie's reply.

"Isn't it a little late for coffee?" Nina Marks glanced back at the agents as she held the door open for them. Her blazing blue eyes were pinched beneath her quizzical brow.

Nick and Archie entered the apartment, Archie immediately headed to the couch in the center of the living area. Covered in a thick blanket and lumpy pillows, it looked inviting. Nick observed Nina as she set down her bag and moved into the galley kitchen. "Can I get either of you something to drink?" she called out as she opened the refrigerator. There was a gap between the cabinets and counter where Nick could see her moving about.

"Nothing for me," Nick said.

"Water, please," Archie called out. Distracted from their task for just a moment, Nick looked over at his partner. Winded, exhausted, thirsty. Archie had never been one to let any weakness show, even when he was dog-tired. *What was happening now?* Whatever was going on with him was definitely getting worse since Jump Day.

Nina walked back towards the living area and handed Archie a water bottle, the outside already covered in condensation. She uncapped her own and guzzled half of it in one swallow.

"Gotta love August in D.C.," she muttered before setting the water bottle down on an end table and sitting in an arm chair facing the couch. "How can I help you? Have you found anything about Parker?" Her eyes darted between the two men. Nick joined Archie on the couch, responding to her as he moved.

"No, nothing yet. His case has been assigned to us. We just need to ask you some questions. Do you mind if I record this?" Nick pulled out his smart phone and pressed a few buttons before Nina even responded.

"Of course, I gave a recorded statement to the police last week as well." Nina seemed nervous to Nick, but it could just be the situation. Her boyfriend was missing, she was being questioned. He tried not to read too much into her demeanor. He had other ways of determining if she was lying.

"Yes, well we like to be thorough and do our own investigation," Archie added between sips of water.

"Can you tell us the last time you saw Parker Lovett?" Nick started right in.

"Last Tuesday, August 7. We had a date at the tapas bar down the block. After dinner we each went home, Parker said he had a big work day on Wednesday."

"Okay, and you didn't hear from him after that?" Nick confirmed.

"No," Nina shook her head.

"Did you reach out to him at all?" Nick asked. But this was a question he had already verified the answer to. He had been able to see the call and text log from both of their cell phones.

"Yes, I think some of the food we ate was bad. I spent most of the night and early morning hurling into the toilet. I texted him in the morning to ask if he got sick too. I didn't hear anything, so I assumed he was in just as much trouble as I was." Nina's arms wrapped around her stomach as she recounted this detail. Nick noticed that she broke off her eye contact as she relayed this story. *Could be a lie*, he thought.

"And he never called or texted back to see how you were doing?" Archie asked.

"No, but he's never been a very affectionate person. And I just assumed he was sick too." Nina looked down at the smart phone that Nick had laid on the coffee table.

"And when did you reach out to Dr. Thurston?"

"Thursday morning. Whatever had made me sick was out of my system by mid-morning on Wednesday, but then I slept most of the rest of the day. When I got up on Thursday, I felt fine. I wanted to see if Parker was okay too. He didn't answer his phone at all. So, I tried him at work. That was when Dr. Thurston answered Parker's office phone. He said there had been a break-in at the lab, some equipment was missing or damaged. That's when he asked me if *I* had seen Parker. I knew something had to be wrong. Parker isn't always the best at responding to my texts or calls, but he is committed to his job. There is no way he wouldn't respond to Thurston's messages." Nina recounted.

"And you're okay with that? That his work takes priority over you?" Nick prodded. This was certainly an unusual sentiment, or at least one that he couldn't relate to.

"Look, when I met Parker, he was already in a relationship – with his research. I knew from the outset that I was second fiddle to his dreams," she paused for a moment. "I'm not one of those girls who is just so desperate for a boyfriend that she accepts being treated as less than. It's not like that. I knew going in that research was his priority, it was actually very sweet and telling just how much time he did devote to us, when I knew he would prefer to be in the lab. But I have my own share of quirks too. Our relationship works," Nina concluded.

That's hardly a statement of enduring love, Nick thought. But it would certainly rule out any passionate lover's quarrel.

"Where do you think Parker could be right now?" Archie asked the million-dollar question.

"I have no idea," Nina shook her head and sank back into her chair. "He's never once mentioned a desire to run off to Aruba, he's never hinted at wanting to leave his job. I have no clue where he might be right now." Her forehead wrinkled, the worry on her face was genuine. She was telling the truth.

"Aruba?" Nick confirmed.

"I mean, any tropical island really. He's wasn't one to take vacations, planned or sporadic." Nina smiled briefly and then it faded.

Archie surveyed the room as Nick continued to ask questions. He confirmed more known details. Parker's only family were a few scattered cousins in Idaho. No real connection there. No group of friends outside the other research fellows at the University. A few had moved on to postings at other labs around the country, but he hadn't kept in touch once they left. Nina began to fidget with her necklace, moving the ring on the chain back and forth as she spoke.

"That's a very pretty ring," Nick commented. He instantly regretted saying this, because of course that meant he was looking at the ring, which was in her hand, which was right in front of her chest. But a witness with a nervous tick during questioning was something he had to make note of.

"It's an heirloom," Nina responded as she dropped her hands to her sides.

"So, do you know if Parker had any enemies? Any chance there was another woman in the picture?" Nick resumed his questioning.

Nina laughed a little at the question when Archie interrupted. He grabbed at his phone in his pocket. "Sorry, I need to answer this, Nick you got this?" He stood and unlocked his phone before Nick could respond.

Archie moved over to the small dining area off the kitchen and focused on his phone.

Nick looked back to Nina who was now appraising him. "Uh no. Parker didn't make enemies with people. Some students may have not liked their grades, but no one stood out as troublesome. And Parker didn't have the *time* or the *energy* for me, let alone another woman. Besides, he wouldn't do something like that. He would just think that was wrong."

"Hmm," Nick nodded at that response. Archie walked back over to them, but didn't sit down.

"Everything okay?" Nick asked Archie. In the middle of questioning someone about a very active case, he really didn't want to have to worry about his partner. But he could tell by Archie's expression that something was off. Was it a call in from the office, was there another energy surge? Was it something he had seen in Nina's apartment? Given the completely unsubtle shift in Archie's attitude, Nick knew they needed to wrap things up and get going.

"Yeah, man," Archie shrugged as he grabbed his water bottle and took another long swig, gulping down the contents in one long sip.

"If you need more water, I can get you some," Nina offered. It was obvious that Archie's odd behavior was starting to catch her attention. Nick was sure that she was probably thinking that these are the two weirdest officers she had ever met. And they were, but they were usually much better at hiding how unusual they were.

"No, don't worry about it. We're going to head out now anyways. Thank you for answering our questions, Ms. Marks. We appreciate it. We'll be in touch if we find anything or need more information." Nick grabbed his phone and pocketed it. The pair were almost to the door before Nina had a chance to react.

"Okay, yes, please let me know if you find anything. Is there a number I can reach either of you at if I want an update?" Nina rose to see them out.

"Ah, I forgot my cards in the car, I'll drop one off later," Nick said as he mimed checking his pockets before he opened the door. He was flustered, he hadn't anticipated that question. Most people didn't want anything to do with law enforcement or any type of official if they could avoid it. Also, their secret agency had no business cards.

Archie was already down on the landing before Nina reached Nick at the doorway. "Oh, okay then. Well, thank you for taking the time to find Parker."

Nick paused, realizing that their behavior was going to throw some alarm bells in her mind, the last thing he needed was for her to call to local police and inquire about the agents who just visited her. "Of course, we'll do everything we can. Don't worry Ms. Marks, no matter where Parker is, we'll find him."

With that he headed down the stairs, Archie was already long out of sight. He heard the door to the apartment click closed and he glanced back up for a moment. *Had he really gotten enough information? Did he have a feeling, one way or another, about how much she knew?*

When he finally got out of the building, Archie was already sitting in the passenger seat of the car. Nick pulled out his own phone, making sure the recording was off and saved.

Nick climbed into the driver seat and turned on the car, mainly to get the A/C cranking. "Okay Archie, you've got to tell me what's going on, man." He looked over at his partner.

"Aside from the aches and pains, the constant fatigue, and the calcification on my irises?" Archie didn't look up from the screen of his phone as he offered his sarcastic retort.

Nick let out a sigh. He knew Archie was a proud man, and his physical declines had to be taking a toll of his psyche. But he needed to be able to rely on him too. "Yeah, other than that? What was going on in there?" Nick waited for his partner to respond. Because their relationship went deeper than just two coworkers, a paired team. Archie was Nick's closest friend. They understood the demands of the job, the secrecy required. The thought of losing Archie for whatever reason, job related or otherwise, troubled Nick.

"I was just hot and exhausted. The water was great," Archie commented as he held up the empty water bottle. Nick eyed it, *well at least he remembered to take it with him.* As a rule, they weren't supposed to leave any trace when they worked in the field.

"Yeah, it's hot as all get out," Nick agreed. He decided to drop the topic, when Archie was ready, he would talk to him. Nick glanced at the phone screen as he plugged it into his car charger.

"She seems nice enough, and perhaps a little naïve, but I think there is more that she isn't telling us," Nick said as he looked out the windshield at the hustle and bustle on the city street.

"Absolutely," Archie agreed. "What tipped you off?"

Nick picked up his phone and tapped the screen, making the display visible for Archie. "Well, for starters she has a twenty-seven-hour time lag reading." The device had been recording her words, but had also been aimed straight at her the entire interview. It picked up on her vital signals and most importantly, her metabolism. It was the most reliable system for detecting temporal lag.

"No way!" Archie leaned into the phone. "I thought she sounded pretty convincing at first, until one of the photos on her bookshelf caught my eye."

Nick and Archie had a good routine down. Nick asked the questions and ran the temporal lag scan. (If Archie had run the scan, it would have been all out of whack because of his own lag. Nick had never crossed the Plain so he was the one who always ran that test.) Archie would stay silent and take in the surroundings. Even with the calcification on his irises, his eye sight was still razor sharp.

Archie placed Nick's phone back in the cup holder to charge and held his own up. His urgent message had been a decoy after all. Nick glanced at the row of photos from Nina's bookshelf on the image. One of her with an older man, likely her father, at a graduation. Nick already knew it had to be a high school graduation since their background research revealed that Nina hadn't finished her college degree. The next was a framed postcard of the Grand Canyon. And the last picture looked like a candid family photo at a summer bar-b-que. There were two women in the image, one was older, one was maybe in her twenties, and the younger one was holding a baby. The photo was aged, yellowed over time, but the faces were distinct.

"She look familiar to you?" Archie asked as he pointed at the older of the two women in the photo.

Nick squinted, as though that would help his memory place the face before him. She did indeed look familiar, *but where did he recognize her from?* Archie must have sensed his thoughts because he jumped right in with an answer. "You see her photo every day at work, right above the door."

And then it snapped into place. The old woman in this photo was indeed the same person, only several decades later. The woman who founded the joint Chronos-Kairos agencies was featured in this photo, that happened to be on Nina Marks' bookshelf.

"How is that possible?" Nick asked.

"I think maybe that's her grandmother?" Archie offered as he pulled up a photo of Elle Marks, Nina's mother on his phone. No doubt that was also the woman holding the baby in the photo. But how had a familial connection to the agency not come up in their background research on Nina? Surely, Mona would not have missed that critical detail.

Nick looked up from the phone and glanced at Archie.

"Well, this just became a very interesting case," he stated as he buckled his seat belt.

"Oh yes, indeed," Archie replied as he did the same and tucked his phone back into his pocket.

"Any chance this is a coincidence?" Nick asked as he adjusted the gears of the vehicle, throwing it into drive while his foot rested on the break.

Archie shook his head. "Man, you know better than that. No such thing as coincidence in an infinite multiverse. Each action happens, it is inevitable. It was bound to occur, somewhere, sometime. Or, more elegantly put," Archie paused and waited for Nick to meet his eye. "It is destiny," he finished his thought with dramatic flair, offering a smile that Nick matched. He shook his head, *oh Archie.*

Nick checked both ways before he pulled out of the spot on the street, then he glanced upward. He could have sworn he saw Nina Marks looking down at him from her apartment window, but he couldn't be sure.

12

Hank did his best to steady his right leg, it had been pumping uncontrollably as he waited. The motion was not a result of the late afternoon coffee in his hands, no it was a result of his anxiety and his impatience.

The city bench beneath him was uncomfortable. He leaned forward, his elbows on his thighs. He hoped that might quell the jumping in his leg, but it didn't help. Instead, this posture only exacerbated the dull ache in his lower back. Hank adjusted again, reflexively taking a sip of his coffee, it was starting to cool, the flavor starting to dull.

Here he was again, waiting on someone who may very well not show up. Although, he had no evidence that Carol would blow him off. She seemed just as concerned about Nina's disappearance as he was. He did remember that Nina mentioned their relationship had been a little strained ever since she had been promoted to Director. Maybe Carol felt guilty for that. Maybe they had been making amends. Carol knew about him and Nina getting back together after all. He tried to focus on what Nina might have shared with Carol. It was easier than focusing on the raw panic that he felt when he thought about where Nina was.

The woman in the basement couldn't have been Nina. He knew that and he felt more certain of it by the moment. When the police told him that Nina was dead, he felt something inside of him break, something that he thought had already been broken long ago.

But with each memento of her that he found in his apartment, with each review of the messages they exchanged last week, and now with Carol's assertion that she had seen her as well, he knew that the woman in Parker's basement couldn't have possibly been Nina. That woman had died on August 6 based on the estimate from the medical examiner. But he and Carol had seen Nina on August 8. So, it simply couldn't be her. An identical stranger, a doppelganger, but not his Nina. *But then why did his heart ache as though she was gone forever?*

Hank pushed the thought from his mind. No, he had proof that she was alive, and he needed the police to take their investigation more seriously. Parker disappeared before he could be apprehended. Hank didn't remember a thing after he hit the ground, some images danced in his mind but they weren't reliable. The only thing he knew was a true memory was waking up in the hospital to lots of questions and a killer headache.

If Carol hadn't visited him in her own state of worry, he might have eventually convinced himself that those detectives were right. But Carol's account matched his own, that couldn't be a coincidence. Nina was scared and now she was likely kidnapped by Parker. Hank looked to his left and right, he checked his watch. Again.

Some passerby glanced at Hank. Mostly their eyes passed over him without any notice, the way that strangers in a city cross paths with each other, generally ignoring the people around them. A few gave him curious looks, perhaps his haggard appearance had them concerned. Or confused. His hair unkempt, his demeanor off-kilter, but his clothes were nice. He was an anomaly to these few curious people who bothered to look, to notice.

To avoid making eye contact, he checked his watch again. A tick to alleviate the tension, if only for a second. Carol had scheduled time to go in and meet with Detectives Wells and Holcrum that afternoon. He was anxious to hear what their reaction had been to her updates as well. The weekend had flown by and he had heard nothing. Each day that passed without an update only fueled his neuroticism.

He had classes to prepare for, his own worries to handle. But nothing seemed to matter while Nina was in danger. Even though a part of him felt like she was gone forever, her soul gone from this Earth, he also felt that she was still reaching out to him and that he could save her. Somehow. Perhaps it was his years of reading the classics that had given him this complex as the man who needed to do the rescuing.

As he began to think back on the early days of his and Nina's romance, he spotted Carol crossing the street towards him. She was walking quickly down the diagonal path, her shoulders tight, pinning her handbag to her side. He gave her a brief wave as he tried to not read too much into her expression.

Hank didn't realize it, but he had been holding his breath as he watched Carol approach him. He exhaled as she got close and finally said "Hi," as she took a seat next to him on the bench.

People continued on their way, passing close to them, but Hank didn't notice them now. He focused on Carol's face, waiting for her to start telling him about her experience with the detectives. He felt himself growing impatient as she fidgeted.

"So, how did it go?" he finally asked.

"Ugh," she grunted as she pulled her arms tighter around her body. It was a hot day so Hank knew it wasn't because she was cold. "I was there for hours and they kept asking me the same questions over and over. I told them that Nina couldn't have been the person they discovered in Parker's basement because I had seen her at work. And I showed them the texts she had sent me last Monday as well saying that she would be out of work for a family emergency." Carol swiped her hair behind her ears.

"But they didn't believe you?" Hank prompted.

"I can't tell. They didn't seem to care. The one detective, the female-" Carol began.

"Wells," Hank clarified for her.

"Yes, Wells. She was in a real mood. She said that based on the testimony from another potential witness, I'm guessing you," Carol nodded his way as she said this, "they went to the building manager for our office and requested the security tapes but said that they had already been wiped."

"Dammit!" Hank pounded his fist into his knee.

"It's just like they have already made up their mind that she is dead, even though we saw her!" Carol's voice hit a peak before it began to break. Hank looked over to see the woman's face was bright red, her eyes pooling with tears.

Unsure of how to comfort her, Hank tried his best to say something helpful. "Hey, we'll keep on them about any leads. They still have to find Parker. My guess is that Nina is with him. We just have to keep-" Hank fumbled for the right word here. "Going," he added a second too late. He didn't want to use the word "hoping." That implied a defeat was on the horizon. But it was starting to feel like hope was all he had left.

"It's just, I'm sure she is so scared wherever she is and those detectives aren't even looking for her!" Carol spat out; her own words unaffected by Hank's comment. "She's already lost so much and now this!" Carol grabbed for a tissue in her purse. She was wiping her nose before she realized her error. "And you've lost so much too, Hank, it's just not fair."

Hank nodded, accepting her additional statement as a sort of apology. Yes, Nina had lost a lot. But so, had he. Losing their daughter all those years ago had changed everything. They lost their joy. But he and Nina had also lost each other. Their grief just took up too much room, it crowded them out. And he had been so close to getting Nina back. Hank turned his face to look away from Carol, he could feel his own emotions starting to get the better of him. He couldn't cry. If he did, then this moment would feel too real. Too grounded in reality, that Nina was gone, this time for good. And he had to stay strong so he could fight to find her.

"We'll just keep trying. Look, she was at work, she walked with me to her place so she could grab things to move, she went to the University. There has to be footage of her somewhere. Someone else saw her, once we can prove she is still alive, then they can start treating this like a missing person's case." Hank said this aloud, his words firm and resolute. Carol nodded along, agreeing that this was a logical next step, even if it would be incredibly difficult. She didn't realize that Hank was saying this for his own benefit, to galvanize his own strength.

Carol watched him as he stared blankly ahead. Clearly, he wasn't gazing at the cars and pedestrians passing by, but seeing through them. Looking for something, or someone, who wasn't there.

PART 3

"There are only two ways to live your life. One is as though nothing is a miracle. The other is as though everything is a miracle."

–Albert Einstein

13

A blast of harsh audio feedback pierced the ears of everyone within range of the ceremony. The auditorium had been transformed with flowers and banners. Usually, graduations took place on the quad in the spring. But for those who graduated after the fall semester, they could elect to walk in the winter, inside, or wait until the spring to walk outside.

The small group of students who completed their degree that term only filled the first three rows of seats. Their associated friends and family filled in the rest. With the winter graduation, the office in charge of ceremonies could be a bit more generous with the family ticket allotment, even if the budget for flowers and decorations was significantly cut.

Nina had given her tickets to Carol and Sonali. The two had been so supportive of her sudden drive to go back and finish her degree. After the incident the previous summer, she had been on the precipice of another tailspin into darkness. But, in spite of the fear of letting her own emotions best her again, she instead focused on limiting any further damage that could be done by the Portal.

She had deconstructed it with her bare hands, but she still had to be sure. After she had filed a missing person's report for Parker, she had been subjected to questioning. That she expected. She stopped by the University weekly to ask Dr. Thurston and Dean Winchester if they had heard anything from Parker. She knew they wouldn't, but she needed to play the role of the concerned girlfriend. And she wanted to make sure the Portal remained dismantled. Thurston was annoyed at her inquiries, he seemed to have been grilled pretty hard by the investigators. In one of her early interviews two local police officers had asked her about a disagreement Parker and Thurston recently had. Nina genuinely knew nothing about it. But it seemed to be the lead they were following.

When Nina stopped in to chat with Dean Winchester, she had been kind and compassionate, if not mildly irritated by her ad hoc interruptions. On one of Nina's visits in early September, the Dean changed topics quickly. She had pulled out Nina's old file from a decade earlier. She pointed out that when Nina had left, she was on track to graduate with honors. Nina shrugged it off. But the Dean continued.

"Nina, with your work experience you could apply for 'life experience' credit for most of the remaining coursework. You would just need to finish out one more elective and you could earn your degree."

Nina was so surprised by what the Dean had offered. It was a generous comment, to give her this information. The idea had never crossed her mind, never occurred to her that she could finish her degree. Winchester handed over the file with her sticky notes on the front. And the pieces started to fall into place.

"I know you are focused on finding Parker," Winchester continued. *If only you knew*, thought Nina. "But, do this for you. It will take your mind off of Parker and you'll finally get your degree. He mentioned to me once or twice that you were thinking about it."

Winchester had her hooked until that final statement. Of course, he did, because her Parker, while not a murderous kidnapping psychopath, had still been very controlling. He had been pushing her and pushing her. Or likely, he felt that he needed to explain away his girlfriend's lack of degree with a plan on the horizon that he had never actually mentioned to her.

Her frustrations with the real Parker aside, especially since the evil Parker did murder him and she felt bad about that, Nina decided to take Winchester up on her offer. The Dean allowed her to enroll right away, even though the term had already started a few weeks earlier. She pushed the paper and cut the red tape, paving the way for Nina to have a legitimate reason to hang around campus. Nina took an art history elective, the final liberal arts credit she needed to graduate. Winchester handled the paperwork for her to apply for 'life experience' credit towards her applied mathematics degree. She was, after all, using big data and statistics every day in her role at the ad agency.

The biggest benefit at the time, was that Nina had a valid excuse to be on campus. To drop by Dean Winchester's office before her evening classes to follow up on the necessary forms and to say thank you. Nina had a way to check in to make sure no one was fiddling with the Portal. She maneuvered a specific path so that she could pass by the lab on her weekly checks. This has been her way in. Knowing that each week she could check that Thurston wasn't rebuilding the device gave her peace of mind.

Carol and Sonali were surprised and incredibly supportive when Nina broke the news. Nina expected that they both worried that she would 'go dark.' Carol especially so. Once Parker was reported missing, Nina noticed that Carol was extra cheery around her. She told them one day at lunch about her class. The news seemed to be a relief to her coworkers. Both helped her study important dates and artwork at lunch breaks. Carol even stopped by her apartment a few nights in a row as Nina crammed for a mid-term.

It seemed perfectly natural for Nina to invite the two to her graduation. But Nina also felt so very sad. The people that she really wanted to be there would never make it. They would never help her celebrate any moment, big or small. Hank and her dad would never witness her cross the stage, move her tassel, hold the empty prop diploma.

The morning of the ceremony, Nina debated if she should even go. She had started the final term to keep an eye on the Portal, but she had finished because deep down, she wanted her degree. She wanted to do something for herself. But she was so alone in this moment. Yes, Carol and Sonali were her friends, but they didn't love her the way her father did, or Hank did. They wouldn't cheer for her the way she imagined that Femi and Marie might.

But Nina knew that wallowing in her isolation would only make it worse. She had nothing else to celebrate, she had nothing else that she could share with her friends. So maybe, she could let herself have this one nice day.

As Nina sat crammed between her fellow graduates, almost all of whom were a decade younger than her, she craned her neck to see if she could spot Carol and Sonali in the crowd. Before Nina could really take in the moment, the ceremony had begun. Unlike the spring event with a marquee speaker, this ceremony had a small speech by an accomplished recent graduate and then remarks from Dean Winchester.

Nina wondered if she ever sensed what her alter-egos were doing in the multiverse. Did Winchester feel destined to this position, one that she had in Universe Beta as well? Did she feel a twinge of regret in moving away from research, away from the chance to make a big discovery, like she did in Universe Gamma?

Nina's view was suddenly blocked by the solid mass of blue polyester. The row in front of her stood and began to march towards the stage. Nina had missed all of the sage advice that was dispensed while she was too busy thinking about her connections in parallel universes.

Nina shifted her concentration to not stumbling as she stood. Not stepping on the heels of the young man in front of her. She reminded herself to take slow, deliberate steps up the stairs and across the stage.

"Feminina Marks," the emcee called her name into the microphone and Nina crossed the stage to Dean Winchester who already had her hand outstretched, ready to hand Nina the faux placard and shake her hand. For a moment, she pretended it was Marie from Universe Gamma, and hoped she would whisper a sassy comment in her ear like, "it's about time girl." But instead, Dean Winchester, the one from that universe, leaned in and said, "I'm so proud of you, Nina!"

And that was probably better. Maybe Nina did have another friend. Maybe they were also destined to be a pair, close friends in this universe as well.

As Nina moved her tassel, she looked out in the crowd. With foolish hope, she looked for salty white hair and deep blue eyes. She looked for gentle curls and a smile that could knock the breath out of her lungs. She looked for her own face. But her father, Hank, and Feminina were nowhere to be seen. She did catch Carol and Sonali waving and clapping for her. Nina beamed back at them and waved before returning her focus to her feet so she didn't drop off the stage.

After the ceremony, Nina returned the fake degree and rented robes and headed out to a bottomless mimosa brunch with her friends. They nestled inside a café with stacks of waffles and toasted over and over. First to Nina and her degree. Then to Carol and her new boyfriend. Then to

Sonali, for finishing a project at work on time. The toasts became sillier after that. Nina was congratulated for not falling on the stage. Carol was toasted again for doing her laundry. Sonali was given a shout-out for doing her taxes already, even though it was only mid-January.

When they were thoroughly full and sloshed, the three women parted ways with lots of hugs. They each stumbled towards their own homes, ready to hydrate and sleep off their buzz. Nina walked aimlessly, not ready to call it a day. She wanted to let her high from that morning last a bit longer before she resigned herself to her apartment and another Saturday in with her cat.

In her silent wanderings, she realized the weight of what she had just done. The course had been just one, a means to an end. But it was so much more. Finishing her degree was the landmark in her life, the flagstone that said "here you shall come, but no further." It was the penance, the empty spot on her wall to remind her of just how much she had lost. Hank, her father, her ambition, her promising future. But today she had completed the degree. In the whirlwind of studying for class, spying on Thurston, keeping up appearances for Dean Winchester, and her long nights replaying her reunion with Hank over and over again, it hadn't occurred to her that she would be finishing her degree. It was the first mark that she had moved on from those decade old tragedies. But in so many ways she was reliving those losses anew. She had only just seen Hank, held him in her arms, even though he was from another universe. And her father had just told her how proud he was of her, but she didn't feel much pride in herself... Not until that very afternoon when she crossed the stage.

As the magnitude of this moment hit her, she worried that it was some kind of signal that she was moving on. But how could she ever do that when everything was still happening, replaying on an infinite cosmic loop, destined to repeat over and over. It was a cycle she both did and did not want to escape.

Soon, Nina found herself crossing the Mall, her heels numb from the cold and oblivious to the harsh concrete below. Finally, she passed by an empty memorial. Odd for a Saturday in Washington, D.C., even if it was freezing. An oversized Albert Einstein was reclined on a set of massive stairs. Nina, feeling playful stuck her tongue out at him, but he didn't return his iconic pose. He stayed there, in his same relaxed position.

Nina looked down at the plaque on the memorial and read it. Then she read it over again. Perhaps she was meant to walk here at just this moment. She was allowed to get one of her wishes that day.

So, Nina looked for the marker on the ground and moved to stand directly on top of it. The design of the memorial was more than just the lackadaisical Einstein sitting back as if ready to hear your theories. The structure was set so that if you stood in a certain spot, the exact spot that Nina happened to be standing on, that you could say something, anything, and you would hear your own voice echoed back to you. You could hear your own voice as others hear it. Pretty cool for the average person. But Nina wasn't thinking about it being her echo, she just wanted to hear from her alter-ego. She wanted to know how she was doing, what happened after she ran through the partition in the lab to act as a diversion.

She couldn't will the wind to carry that back to her. But she could pretend for a moment that she had been there all day, been there in the crowd to celebrate her moment.

"You did it, Nina!" she whispered. And just like magic, just like the quantum mechanics that had delivered her to Universe Gamma, she heard the voice of Feminina in her ear. Nina smiled and wiped a single tear from her cheek.

14

Universe Beta
October 15, 2018

Dr. Norman Thurston leaned against the lab table, embracing the silence that surrounded him. He rubbed the bridge of his nose with his eyes squeezed shut. Holding his glasses in his other hand, he tried to let the world just melt away for a moment.

Usually, this was his tell that he had a headache, but there wasn't any actual pain this time. Stress? Frustration? Disappointment? Yes, to all. But no actual pain.

He had hoped to spend his afternoon grading term papers before attending a faculty meeting that evening. When he heard a knock on the door after he dismissed his freshman Physics seminar, he expected that it would be a student returning to retrieve a forgotten book or some other item, or perhaps someone hoping to ask him some additional questions on their assignment.

Instead, it was Detectives Wells and Holcrum who were at the entrance to the lab. Immediately, Thurston felt his shoulders tense. He hoped they hadn't noticed.

After that crazy, crazy day two months earlier he expected to hear from them again, but he was still shocked by their surprise visit. Thurston had last seen them in the early evening hours of August 8. He finally succumbed to sleep after speaking to Nina, the one from Universe Alpha, as she held his hand. When he woke up Nina was gone. In her place was a pair of local police detectives.

Thurston had been able to tell a clear story in spite of his fatigue and concussion. And any areas where he wasn't sure, he simply said he didn't know, didn't remember. A plausible enough explanation given the head trauma he sustained.

Now the two detectives had returned to ask him more questions. He confirmed what he said before. Parker had been on edge and visibly stressed. Thurston was concerned about his mental health after he learned that Nina had been planning to move out, but Parker was committed to his work so he wasn't terribly surprised about the change in their relationship. On the day of August 8, he had been called to meet with his boss, Dean Winchester, about excessive energy uses coming from the lab. Parker was with him for the beginning of that conversation, but Nina arrived in the lab and appeared flustered. Parker mentioned that there had been some kind of family emergency earlier in the week. Thurston didn't think to interfere with personal matters. It was after business hours when he was in the lab working on a computer and he heard a noise from behind him. He didn't have time to defend himself when he saw Parker lifting a fire extinguisher over his head. The rest was blank; his recollection erased. He attested that he had no idea why Parker attacked him or when Nina and Hank had arrived on scene. But Thurston was told that he helped to stop Parker's attack.

Or that was the story he told the detectives. Really, he knew exactly what Parker's motives were. He knew the true depth of his power madness and violence. Thurston knew that the power of a door to the multiverse had warped Parker's mind. But he couldn't exactly say that to the detectives. He left out the bits where he overheard Parker explain to Nina that he had brought her from another Universe, that their Portal across the multiverse worked, and that he suspected that Parker had harmed the Nina from this reality and tried to replace her with her alter-ego from another universe. They would think he was crazy if he said that.

And he certainly couldn't tell them his recollection of protecting Nina and her alter-ego, and his boss's alter-ego from two versions of Parker. No, he couldn't say a word about that.

The detectives appeared disappointed with his inability to remember the pivotal moment of the attack in question. They were keen to confirm that he saw Ms. Marks earlier in the day, hours prior to his concussion.

Thurston was adamant on this point. Which meant he couldn't really recant it.

He heard the news when he was still in the hospital that a woman's body was found in Parker's basement. Initially, the report said that it was Nina, but apparently his statement and that of other witnesses caused the police to change their story. Now they considered this victim an unknown body and they had listed Nina Marks as a missing person, along with Parker Lovett.

Thurston relayed his story again with calm precision. He patiently waited as the detectives made their notes and follow-up inquiries.

Detective Wells, the woman, seemed skeptical of his answers. The furrows between her eyebrows were deep, her doubts writ large on her face. She kept asking for confirmation on the exact times that he saw Nina Marks present on campus. Thurston gave his best estimations.

"Didn't you pull the security videos?" Thurston asked her, his voice filled with certainty. Surely, if they would just check the tapes then they could stop asking him.

"The hallway cameras show Ms. Marks entering on the morning of August 8 and then leaving shortly thereafter with Lovett. We see them both enter the lab again several hours later and then Lovett heads to your office with you. We never see Ms. Marks leave but we do see her enter the lab again around the end of the business day." Detective Holcrum rattled off these details from his list of notes as though he were reciting the items on his grocery list. "We see her exit one last time, accompanying the stretcher that is taking you out to the ambulance after the alleged altercation with Lovett."

"So, Dr. Thurston you were the last person she was seen with." Detective Wells jumped in here, a heavy layer of suspicion in her voice.

"I- I- I- don't recall a thing after I was attacked. I didn't even know I had been in an ambulance, although it makes logical sense since I did wake up in a hospital." Thurston shrugged his shoulders and waved his hands. He tried his best to appear bewildered. Wells and Holcrum looked at him silently. Thurston broke first. "And what do you mean by alleged altercation? Do you need to see the scans they did at the hospital of my swollen brain? Do you need to see your own case photographs that you took of the lump on my head and the blood on my face?" Thurston felt an anthropomorphic rage bubble up in him. *They were accusing him of something? Him?*

"Well, as you pointed out, we have the security videos from the hallway. But we can't see anything that happened inside the lab. And if Lovett fled the scene here, how did he kidnap Nina from the hospital where we haven't seen him on any of the footage and where we can clearly see Ms. Marks exiting the building by herself?" Detective Wells asked this question, but Thurston expected that she didn't anticipate an actual answer.

Thurston hadn't thought about any footage outside of the University. He had taken care to wipe the video logs within the lab. Of course, he had security cameras on the machine, it was an expensive device and their competitors would love to know what they were working on. But he wiped that footage back through the middle of June so it looked like the camera had malfunctioned separate from the events of that day. He also made sure to amend the video feed in the hallway for later in the evening of August 8 when Nina returned one final time to activate the machine and head back to Universe Alpha.

Detective Wells sighed and raised her eyebrows. Perhaps she did want Thurston to provide an answer.

"I don't know. I'm a smart man, Detective. I have been reliving as much of that day as I can remember for months now trying to think of something *I* missed, something I could relay to you to help in your investigation. But I know it was Parker Lovett who was standing over me with a fire extinguisher before my memory went blank. I know he had been exhibiting violent behavior and had been upset at Nina's decision to move out of their home. I don't know how it works on your end, but that sounds like motive to me."

It seemed the three were at an impasse. Holcrum let out a sigh and said, "Well, if you do think of anything, please don't hesitate to give us a call."

Thurston could only offer a frustrated grunt in response. They thanked him for his time and left the classroom. The moment they were out of the room he felt his chest release, as though he had been holding in his breath the entire interview.

Perhaps the oxygen deprivation had caused a phantom headache. Thurston strolled over to the warehouse side of the lab, past the ordered line of lab tables and the cleared computer desks and through the opaque plastic tarps. He had once reveled in the hours spent there, but now he avoided it when he could. The posters removed from the wall, the large console and track dismantled and put into boxes in University storage, it was a grim reminder of what had once been. The wide-open space where the massive machine once stood was now a desert of empty concrete.

Thurston looked at the space on the ground where the track had been bolted, the holes from the thick screws the only evidence that the device had once been there.

It was worse than any physical scar, of which he had none. His bruises healed just fine after the attack. But having to put away the machine, that hurt him much deeper than any punch or kick. He knew that he achieved his life's goal, he found a way to travel the multiverse. The device worked; all of the pieces put together. But he couldn't tell anyone. Because then he would have to explain why it was put away and the body count that the machine left in its wake. Or worse, someone might dismiss the concerns over the power that clearly went to Parker's head, the ethics of meddling with spacetime, and they might seek to reactivate it. He couldn't stand the thought of either, so he was left with this equally painful third option.

To stand guard at the place where the Portal once stood, to ensure that no one else could come through or leave. It was his pain to bear, the burden to rest on his shoulders. He helped to create it, and now he would protect the multiverse from it.

He mourned the adventures that would never happen, the papers and journals he would never publish, the accolades and applause he would never receive. But such is the life of a sentinel at the edge of the multiverse.

He just hoped whoever stood on the other side was guarding it just as thoroughly as he was. He wondered who they could be, what they were doing at that very moment to ensure that this never happened again.

15

Nick scanned the room, a force of habit that had been instilled in him after years of training. He picked a table in the back corner of the café, no chance of someone coming up behind them. Archie was waiting at the counter for their orders. Even though it was the lunch-time rush, the two enjoyed their weekly routine of grabbing food and talking shop. Strictly speaking all of their work was confidential, but there was an anonymity as their voices got lost in the din of the café. Something about discussing their cases in broad daylight, surrounded by strangers too self-absorbed to bother listening in made them feel normal.

Finally, Archie walked over with their sandwiches, chips, and soft drinks.

"Thanks, man," Nick said as he scooped his hoagie off the tray and started to unroll it.

"Good find," Archie commented. Nick managed to grab the table he preferred. It didn't wobble and it was close enough to the side exit that they could easily leave if they had to. They were hard pressed to find temporal emergencies, after all Archie could go back and forth on their timeline on Jump Day, but that was still months away.

The two men began to eat, taking a bite of sandwich before they had even finished chewing their chips. Their hunger would not be inhibited by table manners. The two had become good friends and carried on with each other as most men do, they weren't going to judge the other for their eating habits or a wanton lack of decorum while lunching.

Once Nick pushed the last bite into his mouth, he managed to mumble. "So, what is your case for this week?" This was their routine. While they worked together on initial reports to determine which agency would handle the matter, they each worked separately on a case once it was assigned. They both had a firm deadline to either conclude their investigation and take action to rectify the situation by Jump Day, or the case rolled over to the following year. The pair found that they could bounce ideas off of each other, get new insights that they hadn't considered before. Nick was able to help Archie connect dots in the past. Archie did his best to help Nick, but it wasn't until that previous summer that he had even landed an actual case to work.

Archie started in on his triple homicide. He had already gone over the details of each gruesome crime scene with Nick. The weapon was a knife, efficient and messy. Based on the medical examiner report it was a serrated blade, six inches. As Archie ran through the high-level details again, Nick nodded along, his memory refreshed.

"Have you gotten anywhere with enhancements on that convenience store image?" Nick asked.

"No, that's the best the digital team can do without distorting the picture." Archie shook his head. He described the image to Nick on one of their previous outings. "She may be alabaster white with bleached hair and no identifying marks, or at least none that I can see on this grainy photo, but her soul is dark. I can see it in her eyes."

"So, you're sure the person in that photo is our perp?" Nick prompted Archie.

"That's what I believed when I put the image in the folder, which is something I now remember doing a couple of years ago, but it must have been on one of my jumps. It's not as clear as my original memories." Archie explained. This was an occupational hazard for both men, although Archie ran into this issue more often. Nick didn't catch many cases that were strictly people out of place in the multiverse. More often than not, the cases they were called in on fell under Archie's purview, people out of place in time. Each year when Archie would make his jumps, as they called them, to go backwards or forwards and correct the problems, he would be able to gather additional information on open cases as well. It appeared that was the case with this mysteriously appearing photo. Lately, Archie began to wonder if this mystery murderer wasn't from their reality and if Nick would be able to help the investigation.

Archie took a deep breath as he recounted the physical description once again. "Yeah, with that sweatshirt there could be a scar or tattoo hidden that we just can't see," he rationalized.

"Alright, so we have a 5' 3" female who three years ago had bleached hair. She could have changed that by now. She could also be anywhere in our universe at this time." Nick knew that Archie would have to look outside of just Washington, D.C. for this murderer. He would also have to look for them in every year and every city.

"Right, no signs that this individual has left yet." Archie confirmed that all signs pointed to their still being in the present, no chance that they 'skipped town' to head to another time yet.

"But the murders stopped over three years ago, in 2015?" Nick verified.

"Based on what I have in the folder," Archie nodded. The two were stumped. Nick tried to think of something he could provide to Archie to help him over the course of the next week. But he was coming up empty handed. It seemed that they would need another clue, or worse, another victim, before they made any headway.

"Alright, enough about my phantom," Archie announced. "What have *you* got for me?" He seemed almost delighted to be on the opposite end of the review, for the chance to provide help to Nick.

"Still no sign of Parker. The energy traces from last August were hot, but unless I can get in to see the logs on *their* quantum computer, I'm going to be flying blind. Mona did some digging and she did see some distortions around the time the call came in," Nick remembered that early morning rush call down to the University very well. "But she said that if someone left that they likely also returned at the same instant given the energy readings."

"So, if Parker left and came back, then where is he?" Archie raised an eyebrow.

"Exactly, it doesn't make any sense."

"Unless *two* people left and only one came back. The energy signature would just show us that a jump was made, not how many people went through."

"But it's not safe to jump with more than one person," Nick corrected Archie.

"Well, I know that, and you know that, but do you think our little crew of scientists knows that?" Archie rationalized as he took a final pull of cola from the cup in front of him, the air in the straw creating a slurping sound.

"Hmm," Nick muttered, the wheels in his brain starting to spin. "I'll see if my contact can get me access to the logs, although last time I asked they said they were wiped clean." He took his cell phone out of his pocket and began typing a message.

"You trust this source? Maybe they were the one to wipe the logs?" Archie speculated.

"Nah, I saw the security footage too, they weren't anywhere near the building when the energy surges happened and it is likely whoever was there to handle the jumps was the one who did the erasing." Nick had already walked down the mental path Archie suggested. In his mind, there was one person who was likely able to operate the machine, clear the logs, and dismantle the Portal. All of these pieces of evidence had been tampered with prior to his initial meeting with his source, and he had reached out to them within hours of the call to the University that early, early August morning. Nick had Dr. Norman Thurston down as his prime suspect. If not in the disappearance of Parker Lovett, then at the very least destroying evidence.

It seemed that Archie was reading his mind. "Do you think the two aren't related at all?"

Nick sent the text message to his contact and put his phone face down on the table. "I've thought about it, but," he stopped himself to make sure he worded his next thought correctly.

"But what? Maybe Parker was there with Thurston for the jump. Then Lovett left and his girlfriend killed him and hid the body."

Nick sat up straight, his train of thought completely derailed. "I don't know. Nina Marks doesn't seem to have the physical strength to pull it off. Parker looked kind of lean, but she doesn't seem the type to me."

"Oh, she doesn't seem the type, huh?" Archie questioned Nick with a knowing lilt to his voice.

"What?" Nick barked back.

"Seems to me that Miss Nina Marks is more *your* type then?" Archie said with a laugh.

Nick wanted to deny it and tell Archie to shut up. But he also had to admit that he was partially right. Nick knew he should have followed up on her as a potential suspect months earlier, but he couldn't bring himself to do it. As much as he would have liked to see her again, he certainly didn't want it to be under such grim circumstances.

"Yeah, whatever man," Nick finally said, trying to change the subject.

"You can't let a pretty face cloud your judgement here. Maybe she is some femme fatale and you can't see past those pretty blue eyes." Archie batted his eyelashes in an exaggerated manner.

Nick balled up one of his unused napkins and chucked it at Archie.

"What?!" Archie asked, his laugh continuing.

"Alright, I'll investigate your angle," Nick finally conceded. He felt a trill of excitement as he thought about the opportunity to see Nina again. Although if he was interrogating her, he knew he couldn't let his little crush get in the way. Discovering she was a murderer would certainly put an end to any affection.

Archie nodded. "Thank you," he said with a smile.

"But," Nick continued with his index finger pointed in the air. "I do think there are too many coincidences. That somehow all the pieces we are finding have to be connected. We're talking about a time machine. There are paradoxes at play that we have only just started to understand. No way there is something loose rattling around here. All these strings will surely come together," Nick concluded.

"That's the theory, man," Archie said as he stood, grabbing his tray so he could clear it. Nick followed him and they bundled their coats tightly as they walked back to the office. Nick had a next step to help on his first big case. He didn't have much hope that he would find Parker Lovett alive, but he would at least uncover the truth about what happened on August 8, 2018. Of that, he felt certain.

16

Marie promised herself that she would quickly type out the responses to the emails she couldn't get to on the train. But five minutes had turned to ten, had turned to thirty. Her day had started at 4:00 am in New York. She was in hair and makeup to prepare for her interviews on the morning shows talking about her "latest" discovery. Then she was off to a round of radio interviews and somehow the day had flown by in time for her to make a dinner with a potential distribution partner. She caught the last train from New York back to Washington. Marie shuffled into the apartment as silently as she could somewhere near midnight.

She glanced at the lower right corner of her desktop computer screen. It was almost one in the morning. There was always more to be done, but she loved the energy of it all. She was exhausted and overworked. Messages were surely getting missed, she hadn't done one lick of research in months, but she was thrilled to finally be at the pinnacle of her career.

It had been later in 2018 that she had turned all of this on. No pun intended.

She released her findings and announced the quantum drive in The Journal of Modern Computer Science. No one reads that but other nerds like her. But it's the nerds who have the power. Within weeks she had calls from multiple companies all vying to license the technology and build their own version.

Marie was not just a scientist anymore. She was a scientist who was actually earning a living, and getting noticed.

It had been a tough decision. She had decided to move forward with the announcement of the quantum drive after extensive internal debate. It was her brainchild after all. The release of the technology would fund years of additional research. And it wouldn't necessarily compromise the truth. That she and Femi had actually been able to travel the multiverse. She could explain that in their theorizing they realized this technology would be a necessary component, so she developed it.

She had naysayers who asked if this drive posed a threat to modern society. With it, hackers could store information on prime numbers up to fifty digits and potentially unlock secure bank accounts. This could be the first step to a self-aware AI that could overthink its human creators. But she pointed out that they could also map the human brain, download a human consciousness, and *hypothetically* travel the multiverse. As though the first two were somehow more likely. As if she herself hadn't already experienced the third first hand.

Marie was wrapping up an email politely declining an invitation to speak at a university commencement because she already agreed to speak at a different ceremony the same day. She heard a noise behind her. Marie turned quickly, the last bit of caffeine leaving her system made her jumpy.

She turned to see Sonali shuffling down the hallway from the bedroom, half asleep. She was wearing her loose oversized nightshirt and bright pink sweatpants. "I thought you would come to bed right away; you must be exhausted." She rubbed her eyes as she spoke, even the dim light of Marie's desk lamp was too much. Looking at her, Marie realized just how lucky she was to have such a beautiful woman waiting at home for her. Even half asleep and wearing her pajamas, Sonali still took Marie's breath away.

"Had one cola too many on the train, I figured I'd get through some emails now and save some time in the morning." Marie responded before turning back to the computer screen.

Sonali knew well enough that time savings wasn't her only motivation. "Nothing from Femi still?" she asked as she wrapped her arms around Marie's shoulders before moving to give her a brief shoulder massage.

"No," Marie exhaled. She paused and let her hands drop from the keyboard and into her lap as she sank into the rolling motion of Sonali's hands on her shoulders.

It wasn't just the stress of travel that needed to be relieved. It was the other big looming elephant in every room Marie had been invited into that day. The conspicuous absence of her lab partner. To say that Marie's relationship with her closest friend was strained was putting it lightly. The two women disagreed on what should happen with the machine. Marie knew deep down that Femi wanted to use it again to see her father. Marie wanted to shout their success from the rooftops, but she felt the burden of her own actions weighing on her conscience. The machine was too dangerous, the power too uncontrollable. Marie wanted to take the machine apart and never put it back together. They were at an impasse, but decided for security's sake to dismantle the device and store it to prevent Gus Blanity or some other malcontent from stumbling through. *Just until they could come to an agreement,* they promised one another. They never discussed when they would reassemble it, but Marie assumed it would happen eventually.

Then Femi left for Belgium to give a lecture on quantum theory and apparently 'fell in love.' Marie rolled her eyes at the thought. Femi was not the kind to just abandon her life's work. Their emails were short and concise, but still cordial. They both had so many questions they still wanted to explore. And then when Marie decided to publish her first paper, all communication stopped. Marie sent Femi a long message, pages and pages of her explanation for her decision, how it would be good for them, how they could still help the world with what they had discovered. Marie said she would be happy to keep the supercybin secret. That served both of them well so that they didn't have to answer any sticky questions about Gus Blanity. Marie promised Femi that she would say nothing about the power source until she had her okay on it. Femi never responded.

It had been months of silence.

Every time Marie checked her inbox or her phone, she secretly hoped to see Femi's name pop up. Even at this late hour, she knew it was almost dawn for Femi. There was no way she would be writing a coherent email response right now. But still, Marie hoped.

Sonali yawned and moved back from Marie's desk. "Come on, those emails will still be there in the morning. No one expects you to be sending responses at 1:00 am."

Marie looked up at her and gave a half smile. She knew Sonali was right. She turned off the monitor and followed her down the hall. She could unpack her bags in the morning too. It seemed as soon as she stood up that the exhaustion of the day finally caught up with her. She had been going for almost twenty-one hours straight.

If only there were more hours in the day, Marie thought as her head hit the pillow. A smile breeched her mouth, she would have laughed out loud at her own private little joke if she had any more energy. The lavender that Sonali always put in her essential oil diffuser had permeated the smooth cotton of Marie's pillow case. A deep inhale and she felt instantly calmer. She drifted off to sleep quickly, thinking about all the ways she could get more done by just creating more hours with her time machine. *Their* time machine.

Even though she slept soundly, Marie still awoke before 7:00 am. She hoped her body would give her more time to rest, but she was wide awake. Lying as still as she could to avoid waking Sonali up, Marie stared at the ceiling and the way the light coming in through the crack in the curtains moved with the sun. In the silence of the morning, she had nothing to distract her from her own mind. All those thoughts and feelings she had been avoiding.

The most basic, the most prevalent was pain. She was hurt by the loss of her friend. Marie felt a genuine sadness that she didn't have Femi to share this success with. Sonali, still soundly asleep, understood on the surface level of what Marie created with Femi, but so few people actual got the magnitude of it, how difficult it was.

Marie felt abandoned, but she also felt guilty. *Shouldn't Sonali's love be enough?* Friends grew apart all the time. And Femi was acting childish, ignoring her emails. She could at least let her know she was okay.

Annoying, that's what this was. Annoying. Marie ruminated on this jumble of feelings. She was a woman of science; this emotional part wasn't her forte. And in that mess of sorting out how she felt about it all, she decided to reassemble the Portal as she had initially planned. She could run diagnostics and pull out more data. She didn't want to ever power it up again, she just wanted to make use of the quantum computer and write a paper (or more likely a book) on the mechanics of actual cross-dimensional travel.

Clearly, Femi is done with this project so it is mine now to do with it as I see fit. Once she made a decision that was it, her stubborn brain wouldn't let her give it up.

Marie felt better now that she had a path to run down, even if she was running this whole thing alone.

17

Time travel can really take it out of you. The exhaustion, the nausea, the headache. Nina thought she would have been used to it after her secret adventure the year before. Although it wasn't a fun trip, more like her sojourn back home. But she did find a kind of poetic irony as she studied her itinerary before departing on her two-week venture.

As a gift to herself for completing her degree, Nina booked a trip to Tokyo. She was looking for a way to commemorate this milestone in her life. She really wanted to be able to go with Carol and Sonali and make it a girl's trip, but all three of them couldn't be out of the office for that long. Besides, her two closest friends had already tapped into their paid time off for the year and didn't have nearly as many days banked as Nina did.

So, it was a solo trip. Nina was excited by the prospect of discovering such a vibrant city all on her own. She tried to convince herself that the pull was for the history and beauty and food. But deep down she knew the real reason. Her dad, at least the version of her father she had seen in Universe Delta, traveled from Washington, D.C. to Tokyo by crossing through his Portal. She was hoping for some sign while she was there that would lead her back into the magical world of multiverse travel. Even though she kept telling herself to let it go, she just couldn't. She promised herself that she would help to protect her universe from further incidents, but she couldn't help but think about the possibilities, the positive ones.

Her trip was chock full of fun day trips with other American tourists and two weeks later her phone was now overfull with high resolution photos of water lilies in urban parks, bustling street vendors, sacred temples, and the shadow of Mount Fuji. But no signs of cosmic gateways. No inklings of research being conducted nearby that would lead her back to the version of reality where her dad was still alive. Or where she could be with Hank.

On the long flight home, she chided herself for being so silly. Surely, if quantum research was being conducted in a lab, the facility would have been locked and those who worked there wouldn't have been spending their day at tourist traps.

But the trip hadn't been entirely fruitless. She felt a new sense of confidence. Nina was nervous when she departed, unsure of what to expect. She'd never traveled anywhere on vacation by herself. Let alone another country where English wasn't the predominant language. She was exhilarated by how much fun she had on her solo trip, she made tour bus friends with other travelers, and she felt more in control of her life than ever before.

Jet engines and recycled air vents provided a loud hum that drowned into white noise throughout the flight. The sound was soothing, nothing like the roar of the other machine, the real time travel device that amplified noise as it opened the Portal to other realities. As the plane touched down at Reagan International Airport, Nina resolved to do this again. Maybe not the same exact trip, but to venture out on her own more often. And she came to another important decision. It was one that had been weighing on her ever since she completed her degree. Without any good reason to continue to pop by campus, she felt inept. How could she possibly ensure that Dr. Thurston, the one from this reality, didn't reconstruct the Portal? How would she be able to casually just pop in to chat with him or Dean Winchester? She wasn't personally close with either of them. The only weak tether she could pull from was the ongoing search for Parker. But she knew she couldn't continue to ask for updates. For starters, she wasn't a very good liar and she already knew where he was, he was gone. And second, she didn't want to play the role of the weak girlfriend. She felt that was dishonest to the person she was now, the person she was becoming.

So, she decided that she would strike out on her own again, only this time for work. She had a bachelor's degree now and could apply to work at the University teaching math for business and marketing majors. She knew all the latest trends in digital marketing analytics that would help college students when they got to the real world. She could even stay on long enough to get a master's degree at the University too. Then she would be able to keep a better eye on Thurston to make sure the Portal was never reconstructed.

And she would make herself proud. Nina didn't want to admit it, but she was still stinging from the idea that her lackluster life and career had been such a disappointment to her alter-ego. A job at a university would be impressive to all. Not that she would ever see her fierce alter-ego from Universe Gamma again. But she saw a version of herself the previous summer, one that was brave and capable. Nina couldn't unsee that possibility, couldn't unknow her true potential.

This idea re-energized Nina in spite of her ridiculously long flight home. Her mind was flitting between one thought and then another as she contemplated about how she would approach this topic with Dean Winchester and what she would tell Carol and Sonali at work. *How could she ensure she could be near enough to the Sciences building to be able to monitor Thurston without seeming too obvious? What kind of pay cut would this mean?* Each new question revealed another and another. She jotted them down quickly as the plane began to descend. After picking up her luggage and heading for the Metro she tried to quiet her mind just a bit so that none of these thoughts would get lost.

This mental energy kept her wide awake until she rolled her bag down the sidewalk leading to her apartment. As she dug for her keys in her purse, Nina felt all thirteen hours of her direct flight weigh on her shoulders and eyelids. Her flight took off from Tokyo at 10:55 pm Saturday evening and she arrived back in Washington, D.C. at 10:35 pm Saturday. She smiled at her ability to time travel without the Portal as she hefted her bag up the stairs to her apartment.

Nina let herself in and saw that her apartment was exactly as she left it. After two weeks away she thought something would be different, but her inanimate belongings were all patiently waiting for her to return. The only difference was how Nina felt, full of gumption. But completely wiped out. She debated crashing onto her bed fully clothed, but decided against that since she had been stuck in that outfit all day. She tucked her bag just inside the door to her bedroom, she would unpack that tomorrow. She began to unbutton her jeans so she could change into her pajamas when she heard a knock at the front door.

Startled, Nina stood still for a moment. *Who could that be? Had she been followed? What if it was evil Parker, back to enact his vengeance? Or Gus?* Surely nothing good could come from a knock on her door at eleven o'clock at night.

Another knock broke her train of thought. She quickly readjusted her clothes and tip toed to the peep hole in the front door. She hoped whoever was on the other side wouldn't hear her approach. But the light was on, so they would clearly see that someone was home. And Nina realized, in disbelief, that she had forgotten to lock the deadbolt behind her when she had walked in. Her fuzzy exhausted brain was failing her.

As she peered through the hole, she spotted a tall man in a suit who looked vaguely familiar. *Where did she know him from?* As he moved his head, she could see his profile a bit better. And then it clicked in her mind. He was one of the investigators who stopped by to question her after Parker was reported missing.

For a second, she debated opening the door. *At this hour he would only stop by with important news to share.* News as in Parker had been found, which she knew was impossible since evil Parker had sent the real Parker out into the nothing of the multiverse. *Unless, evil Parker was back.*

Suddenly panicked, she swung open the door. "Yes?" she asked, looking directly at the man before her.

"Ms. Marks? I'm Agent Nick Noriega, we met last August," he started. *Noriega*, Nina thought, the name finally clicking into place in her mind.

"Yes, do you have any updates on Parker?" Her question released with incredible speed. No time for introductions, she needed to know if the man who had kidnapped her the previous summer was back, not that this Nick Noriega would know anything about the existence of the multiverse and evil alter-egos.

"Uh, no. But I did have some additional questions for you. Do you mind if I come in?" He seemed shocked at her response. *Had he thought she wouldn't answer?*

"Sure," Nina agreed and stepped aside, her mind trying to jump back into overdrive and desperately fighting the exhaustion that was trying to slow her down.

The agent strode confidently over to the couch and sat down. Nina sat across from him on an armchair, waiting silently for his first question. He seemed to be looking around the apartment, perhaps searching for clues.

"Oh, I'm so sorry, would you like some water?" She finally asked, ever the polite hostess, just as she had been raised.

"No, I'm fine," the man in front of her responded, his attention now back on the woman across from him. "Have you heard anything from Dr. Lovett since we last spoke?"

"No," Nina shook her head vehemently. "I-" she didn't know what to ask next. If the real Parker Lovett from Universe Alpha was "back" he would have reached out right away. If this had been a case of a man who just wanted to get away from it all, maybe not. But Nina knew the truth. How could she respond without giving away what she knew?

"We haven't found him, Ms. Marks," Agent Noriega clarified in a soothing tone. "But, always good to ask, just in case." He pulled out his cell phone and set it on the coffee table. "You don't mind if I record this again?"

"Uh, sure," Nina agreed. "Have you found any new information about where he might be?"

"Well, we are hoping to find out more about what was going on leading up to his disappearance. Do you recall any changes in his personality?" The question itself was innocuous, a logical thing to ask. But to Nina, it struck terror into her heart. The two weeks that she spent with evil Parker, thinking that her boyfriend just turned over a new leaf, popped into her mind. She came home one evening to find sweet romantic gestures were going to be the new normal after years of perfunctory interactions. She regretted how naïve that Nina was, the Nina who didn't stop to think how abrupt the changes in Parker's personality were.

But she couldn't say that to this agent. Or, at least not all of it. "Well, he was really busy with work, more than usual. Maybe he sensed that he had been spending too much time there, he had started acting sweeter, more romantic. Like in the beginning of our relationship. Roses and candlelight dinners. That sort of thing." Nina looked down, perhaps this agent would think that it was out of sadness. But really it was out of disgust. The reason this other version of Parker had been so affectionate and loving was his own perverse sense of guilt for murdering her alter-ego in his own reality.

"Hmm, and did he say anything about his work relationship with Dr. Thurston?" He continued on with his next question, seemingly unphased by her revelation.

"They were very close. We had dinner with Dr. Thurston and his wife several times. I think Parker really looked up to him. Why?" Nina told the real truth here. But a kernel began to pop in her mind. If Thurston was somehow implicated in Parker's disappearance, she might feel more comfortable that he might lose his job or get arrested. Then he would never be able to rebuild the Portal. Although, her conscience was quick to snap back that even though the man had been a bit of a jerk, he was innocent of any wrong-doing in this regard. She shouldn't wish incarcerations on an innocent man.

"We're following up on every possible lead, Ms. Marks. I have to ask." Nick Noriega nodded as he said this. Nina wasn't sure if he was waiting for her to add something else. Did she miss another question? Had she fallen asleep for a second and dozed through his next inquiry?

"I'm so sorry, it's really late and I am exhausted," Nina apologized, not knowing what for, as all women in her reality were socially conditioned to do. "I just got back from a long trip, could we schedule a better time to talk? I'd like to get some rest."

"Of course, my apologies," Agent Noriega said as he stood from the couch and scooped up his phone. "You know Ms. Marks, when we said to not leave town, we also meant international trips to Tokyo." She held the door open for him, trying to will herself to stay awake and cordial until he was out of the apartment, but his latest statement chaffed her.

"You never said to not leave town…" she replied reflexively.

"Ah, sorry." But it didn't sound like he meant it.

"Am I a suspect?" She couldn't think of any other reason why she shouldn't leave town. At least that was what she had learned from hokey detective shows on TV.

"Have a good evening, Ms. Marks," was his only response. Polite, but not an actual response to her question.

It took her a few moments after he left and she dead-bolted the door to realize that she had never said *where* she had been. Somehow this agent knew she had been out of the country. Nina got an uneasy feeling that he wasn't actually there to question her about Parker's relationship with

Thurston. *Maybe she was a suspect in his disappearance.* This only added to her irrational worry that evil Parker was somehow back in her reality. She suddenly didn't feel much like sleeping at all. She wanted to sit on her couch and stare at the door, ready to defend herself if anyone tried to come through.

18

Universe Delta
August 10, 2008

"**J**iro, I think the feed cut out again," Xander declared as the image before him froze. One of the downsides of working with a team that lived halfway across the world was the inevitable communication issues. Though Xander spoke passable Japanese and his counterparts were fluent in English, it was the video calls that tripped them up. It was always very early or very late for either him or the team. The feed would cut in and out on a whim, slowing their conversation.

We developed a quantum power source, but we can't get this dang call to work. Xander was about to type, 'okay smack, the monitor,' to see if that would help when Katsumi's voice popped through.

"I think it is just the video feed for now, we can still hear you," she assured him. He could see each of their faces individually, they dialed in from their respective offices. Hajime had his camera faced so that his background was the blank white wall of his office. Very professional, clean, precise. Just like Hajime.

Jiro was the complete opposite; his wall was covered with posters and pictures. Xander had spent years on calls with Jiro and witnessed the evolution of memorabilia from different movies, video games, and trips. He got a sense of Jiro's adventurous side with the changing patterns on his wall.

And then there was Katsumi. At first her background had been plain and white like Hajime's. But she added a bonsai tree and an assortment of 3D printed figurines to the shelf above her. There was an elegant simplicity to the design of her office space. Still professional, but not devoid of color. She was the balance between her two comrades, in more than just aesthetic.

"Okay, good," Xander was quick to respond. He was much older than the rest of his team and he felt that any small glitch with technology could quickly be chalked up to user-error where he was concerned. He worried at what frame his video screen had frozen on. Hopefully he wasn't mid-sentence with his mouth hanging wide open, adding to the overall chaotic look of his space. His bookshelves were overflowing with manuals and his collection of post-it notes on his side cabinet were always visible in the frame as well. He didn't usually worry about how his office looked, but this was the small purview that the team had into his world, his life. "So, we feel confident that we can get all of this done by next August. How long should we estimate for the quantum drive development?"

"I'm good with computers, but Nina was our lead engineer. With her gone, we don't have much of a hope of completing this on time." Jiro sounded as disappointed as Xander felt.

Ever since he messaged Hajime on the morning of August 9, the group had been working nonstop to find Nina and bring her back. The team in Tokyo initially suggested that Xander get on the first flight to Japan so that they could work together in person. After all, they had a machine set up in their lab as well. Despite their very generous invitation to stay with the team, he declined. He wanted to stay in his lab, just in case Nina showed up. *Just in case.*

So, the team worked remotely as they had for the past several years. Each team member focused on their area of expertise. But they had reached such a pinnacle on their August 8, 2008 trial run. They had poured their collective lifetime of knowledge into the Portal. They had a shared vision for how the machine would function and what would be needed. But now they needed to solve for this pressing issue and they didn't exactly know what the solution would be.

They had their power source. They had supercybin and confirmed through additional blood tests that it had no negative health effects on Xander after his trial runs. They had a console that operated the machine. They had two functional Portals. And they had the coordinates for an unknown universe. That was it.

"Well, we'll just keep working at it. I know we can create it, it's been done before," Xander encouraged the team.

"Technically, it hasn't been developed yet, not for another nine and a half years at least," Katsumi corrected him. Dr. Marks nodded silently. She was right. At first, Xander was worried that the team wouldn't believe him. But they all understood the metaphysical and ethical quandaries of building this machine. They caught up quickly and were able to work through the potential scenarios where Nina had been taken to the past, future, or an alternative present without skipping a beat. After a lifetime of study on the topic, he was amazed by how quickly the team had been able to think multi-dimensionally. He felt all the more inept at his own failures. He hadn't considered the possibility that this would happen. He hadn't prepared for any safe guards against this kind of a situation. He recognized his own hubris and it revolted him.

"Well, we can try to calculate the exact date, time, and celestial location on the current quantum computer, but then that is all it would be able to do. Rogers will notice. With the drive we could save our work and return to it the following day without pulling the energy all day and night." Xander reminded the team of the realities of the situation.

Lionel Rogers, the CEO of the thinktank they all worked for, was tolerant of the eccentric scientists that he employed. He had a business background and was interested in capitalizing on the discoveries made by his team. Because each scientist was delighted to get an exclusive invitation to work for him and receive full funding, many were just fine with signing over the intellectual property they developed in the lab.

Fortunately, the development of the power source had been a great win for Xander, Nina, and the team in Tokyo. Rogers was working with his business development teams to license the technology to cities around the world. But, Xander could feel that his long leash was about to get cut.

First, Rogers had asked where Nina was when he popped in Saturday morning to inquire about the test. Xander lied and said that she went home to rest and Rogers didn't seem too interested in asking about her whereabouts again. What he wanted was a minute-by-minute account of what he missed after leaving the night before.

Rogers wanted detailed reports on how the trans-global walk went. Xander had been building up the excitement for the test run for months.

He had received permission to run the quantum power source in order to do the test. The infrastructure for their city hadn't yet been upgraded to handle that power load, so it was a big ask. But Rogers saw even bigger dollar signs, so he pulled the necessary strings.

Rogers kept on him all day Saturday, while Xander was trying to lead his team in Tokyo. It had been a dizzying game of chess. "I understand that not all tests are successful Dr. Marks, but I need to see some evidence that it at least took place. Your counterparts in other labs are all able to comply with my requests for these updates. Please have your full detailed report to me by Monday morning."

That email had hit Xander's inbox Sunday morning. He was stuck in a jam. He hadn't left the lab since Nina disappeared; the hours flew by as he tried to riddle out what was needed to bring her home. He couldn't hide this from Rogers forever.

He could lie, falsify the records and say that the test was a complete bust. But there were perhaps too many documents to destroy and hide. Security cameras in two different countries to try and corrupt. And then there was the problem of erasing the very data that he needed in order to find Nina. While he had been delaying and obfuscating, he hadn't explicitly been untruthful about the test. He was just avoiding the topic as much as possible.

But if he revealed that not only did the test walk between two cities occur, but that it was a rousing success, then he faced another ethical dilemma. Xander knew Rogers would be on cloud nine. He had already been spinning up daydreams of travel stations set up around the globe allowing for the largest disruption in travel since the invention of the hyperloop train. The technology would be licensed and used as frequently as they could manipulate it. Which meant more Portals. More doorways open to visitors from other dimensions, more exposure to dangerous actors and viruses and all manner of things that couldn't be controlled. The ramifications of the truth seemed far more dire than this one omission.

But, without telling some version of the truth, Xander knew that Rogers wouldn't clear another use of the quantum power source to keep the calculations running, let alone for a trip out across the multiverse to go and find Nina.

The team in Tokyo had been silent for a moment while Xander's thoughts spiraled out into the multitude of bad scenarios that were likely to play out as his report deadline loomed on the horizon.

"Did we lose the feed again?" He asked the air around him, sure that he would feel foolish for talking to himself if the line had disconnected.

"No, we're still here," Hajime replied, a timid reluctance in his voice. "Maybe it is time that we tell Rogers the full truth. He has unlimited resources; he would put the full weight of his money and lab behind finding Nina." It sounded like this had been a rehearsed statement, the logical step that was so apparent to his team that Xander hadn't been able to see.

Xander rubbed his hands over his face, trying without success to rub the exhaustion off his skin. "Yes, he would do that." Dr. Marks knew that Rogers was a good man, but he also knew that he was a business tycoon for a reason. "But imagine how quickly he would move to market and sell a Portal to another Universe? What would he use it for? There are an infinite number of ways that could go wrong."

And it all came down to the worst decision Xander would ever have to make. Which was more important, the fate of the entire multiverse and everyone in it or the safety of his daughter?

There was no question in his mind, he just had to reconcile with the guilt he would feel.

His team on the other end of the line didn't answer. Either because they didn't have an answer to the questions he had asked aloud, or because they knew the answers and still felt that Nina's return was more important.

"Alright, I'll tell him." Xander finally said and he could hear the sighs of relief from halfway around the world. "I'll let you know what he says and if we get any help."

"You're a good man, Dr. Marks," he heard Hajime say before their line disconnected.

Was he? Would history remember him that way? He didn't need a time machine to reason out how this would all unfold.

19

Nina sat bolt upright, her hands shaking and her lungs gasping for air. She fumbled for the light by her bedside and switched it on, certain that she would see that the shadow in the corner of her room was Parker. *Evil Parker.* Somehow back in this reality and ready to attack her again.

She turned as soon as the light flashed on and saw that there was nothing, no one there at all. Just the towel she had hung from the top corner of her open closet door. Nina let out a sigh, not of relief, but frustration. She hadn't been able to get a solid night sleep in months. So much haunted her each evening. Refreshed memories of the attack on Hank all those years ago. The knife that had been meant for her, but had killed her soulmate instead. And now adding to her regularly revolving carousel of night terrors was a replay of the attacks by Evil Parker when she was fighting him in Universe Beta.

In her mind, she always referred to him as Evil Parker. She did have three years of memories with her Parker. Not all great, but the beginning had been sweet. But even if he wasn't a great boyfriend, at least he never tried to kidnap or murder her. I guess when you use that criteria it is easy to sound like an amazing partner.

But Nina needed to compartmentalize for other reasons. After she reported Parker missing the police had stopped by. Then federal agents. Then the local police again. When a person goes missing the assumption is that they are dead. And when a person is dead the first suspect is their significant other. The surprise visit from Nick Noriega on the evening she returned from Tokyo had rattled her.

Nina was confident that she wouldn't be arrested for Parker's death. Because she had nothing to do with it. Also, because there was no body or sign of foul play. He had simply disappeared. Vanished. No trace of him to be found. She sometimes worried that she might be implicated in his disappearance. She did know what happened to him, after all. But no one would believe her. And she had been earnest in her interviews with law enforcement. This was why she had to keep her Parker and Evil Parker straight. She couldn't let her anger at Evil Parker show through.

It also helped that Parker and Thurston had a mild tiff the day before he disappeared. The federal agents that visited her seemed to be very interested in asking her about Parker's boss and their work in the lab. She tried to remember what it was like back before she truly understood what Parker was researching, before she had experienced traveling across the multiverse herself. It was hard to un-understand what she had learned last summer.

Her most recent rash of anxiety was not brought about by her worry about incarceration. No, a secure cell might make her feel better, safer. Locked away where Evil Parker could never reach her. It hadn't occurred to her that the man responsible for kidnapping her could come back, but now this shadow of a thought loomed over all others.

Fully awake, she got up and headed into the kitchen for a glass of water. This had become a new habit of hers. She would crawl out of bed, too spooked to go back to sleep. After a drink of water, she would sit up on her couch reading books on multiverse theory. They might have put her to sleep a year earlier, but now she was enthralled by the text. She was searching for answers, for a way to make sense of everything in her mind.

As she shuffled about for her cup and poured filtered water from the jug, her new cat danced between her ankles, daring her not to trip. Her eyes passed over the little phrases and notes she had carefully taped up on the cabinets and refrigerator. These affirmations and positive action quotes had buoyed her, but she was in no mood for them now. Her mood was sour as she knew it would be another long night without the sleep she so desperately needed and wanted.

It struck her as odd that she should have so much trouble now. She had expected this type of reaction upon her return from the multiverse. But it seemed that her psyche was operating on a long delay, just now processing the trauma. Forcing her to relive it each night. These nightmares, the violence of them was so real. She was jumpy. Nina made a note in her daily planner to call up her old psychiatrist, Dr. Syvilak. She had found the old business card and even dialed the number, but the line was disconnected. Her information wasn't online anymore either. *Oh well, guess she retired. Not that she would believe the truth anyways.*

The crisis had passed, but it didn't feel over to her. Knowing that someone could pop up at any point in time while the Portal had been set-up and alter her present made her anxious. Unfortunately, the Thurston she knew wasn't much like the one she had encountered in Universe Beta. The curious and kind scientist in the other reality was nothing like his alter ego here. This Thurston, Universe Alpha Thurston, was cold and rude. He had an air of entitlement and superiority about him. Nina's gut told her that he couldn't be trusted and that she should especially not give him any details about the events that had unfolded the previous summer. He did ask a few pointed questions after Dean Winchester had assigned him to a new position and removed him from any of the practical research he had been doing in the lab. But Nina played dumb, how could she know anything about why his boss moved him to a new role? She asked him if he thought that the Dean suspected him of being involved in Parker's disappearance. He stammered and didn't ask any more questions after that.

Nina knew that she had everything to do with his reassignment. She had left a detailed anonymous note under Dean Winchester's door after she dismantled the Portal. Nina had been glad to hear that her advice had been followed, but she still worried that someone might piece it back together.

She finished her water and poured another glass before heading over to the couch. Her kitten Bonnie, who was quickly growing into a full-sized cat, mewed softly as she strutted off to her post in the corner. After Nina curled up with a blanket and opened her latest book at the spot she left off, Bonnie sauntered over and made a ball at her feet.

Nina had found a way to secure the Portal and ensure that no one would ever rebuild it. She had developed a careful plan and was about to make good on it. Tomorrow, or rather, later that morning, she would shower, dress, and head off to interview for a new job. An adjunct professor in applied business statistics working at the University, specifically the Sciences building as math was considered a science. She would be one floor above the lab and her classroom would be down the hall from Dean Winchester's office. She had appealed to Dean Winchester's practical as well as emotional nature. Not only did Nina have years of experience working in digital marketing attribution and mining data for her clients, she also said that she wanted to feel closer to Parker. It was a one-two punch. Surprisingly, the Dean acquiesced even though Nina didn't have the advanced degree required. Nina did not feel one bit guilty for using the "missing boyfriend" card to aid in her application. She needed to protect the universe from whatever else could come out of that Portal.

She had found her "something more" that she had been yearning for, that unnamed need to feel like she was contributing. She would stand guard to ensure that no one else came or went from the Portal, ensuring the safety of others while keeping herself within arm's reach of the one thing she truly wanted. More time with Hank.

She wiped that thought away as she attempted to re-read the page that she just glossed over. No, she couldn't have him back again. That she got any more time with him at all was a miracle, she couldn't push for more. She couldn't use the machine for her own personal gain.

"We have to be better than those who would manipulate the science, don't we, Bonnie?" Nina asked her sleeping cat, giving it a soft scratch on the back. The kitten didn't stir. But she didn't need her pet to validate her. She knew her alter-ego would agree. Nina thought that she might make her proud.

20

Universe Beta
February 15, 2019

There was no *thud*, no impact to signal that he had reached his limit. It had been a rough few months, and this was rock bottom. The students shuffled in and out of classes without much energy. Hank couldn't blame them. He was only giving his minimal effort to get through the semesters. How could he focus on teaching college kids about dead authors when he the love of his life was missing? *Still*.

He was grateful to receive the news back in November that Nina's case had been reclassified as a "missing person," which meant that the detectives would start to look for her. That was three months after she disappeared. If the first forty-eight hours were the most critical, where did this leave them? Hank tried not to go down that mental path.

There was a ray of light on the horizon. Not only did he have a sense that Nina was out there and that he would see her again soon, but he had a lead to follow up on. Hank had been exchanging messages with Carol regularly. Carol usually reached out once every other week to ask for updates and to send support. He appreciated that she never forgot about Nina, never pushed her memory aside. It had been a few months earlier that he finally had something to report back to her regarding the case.

Detectives Wells and Holcrum were to thank for this lead. Though indirectly. Back in October, Hank was crossing campus to get to his car in the faculty lot when he spotted the detectives heading for the Sciences building. Hank probably wouldn't have noticed otherwise, but he just happened to look up at the right time.

Curious, he followed them. Not in a creepy way. He just found himself walking behind them towards a building he rarely visited. He had once proctored an exam on the second-floor years earlier, but it was rare that he had to ever go to this side of campus. The University was pretty good about keeping courses in the same building as the offices for each of the associated departments, but sometimes scheduling was tricky.

Hank recognized several of his own students as he entered the building, backpacks slung lazily on their shoulders, faces lost in the glow of their phones. He saw the detectives turning into a room at the far end of the hallway. Hank casually followed, but soon saw that the hall ended shortly after the classroom they had entered. He didn't want to risk passing by and being spotted. When he returned the next morning, he stopped in front of the door. It was closed and locked with no sign on the outside. He was heading out, thinking that he should just check again later when he passed by something that caught his attention.

"Dr. Parker Lovett" The nameplate on the office door to his left caught him off guard. It was like graffiti on a church door, it was a hate-message spray-painted on a car. His blood began to boil. For all anyone knew this man was a criminal who had kidnapped Nina and the University still had the audacity to leave his name up? Hank felt a rage build up in him that he hadn't felt before. A powerful anger that rumbled through his hands and joints.

Hank turned quickly, and was about to punch the wall to his right. He needed to release this tension, this hatred that he felt at the sight of Parker's name. Before his fist could make contact with the cement wall, he noticed the name on the door across the hall from Lovett's abandoned office.

"Dr. Norman Thurston."

Hank stopped in his tracks; his right arm raised mid-air. As the wheels in his mind started to turn, he realized a few things at once.

First, that Wells and Holcrum had been here yesterday. The door that he had seen them go into, the one that was now closed, was probably a classroom or lab that Thurston worked in. Second, he reasoned that the detectives had been there to see Thurston. Perhaps with updates, or to ask questions. And third, that Dr. Thurston might have seen Nina that day as well. In fact, he realized that the name wasn't all that unfamiliar. *Wasn't he the guy who stopped Parker from attacking us?*

Energized by these revelations, and the adrenaline still pumping through him after seeing Parker's name, Hank shot a quick text over to Carol. They met for lunch later in the week to discuss the implications. When Nina's case was reclassified a few weeks later the two of them agreed that it must have been related to the detectives visiting Thurston. Carol pointed out that they didn't know who else the detectives may have spoken to, but Hank was convinced it couldn't be a coincidence.

The weeks continued to pass without further development. The holidays came and went and Hank hadn't heard anything new. He had visions of celebrating these special days with Nina, of starting 2019 with her back in his life, back in his arms. But instead, he rang in the new year with a bottle of whiskey as he flipped through their old photographs from before they lost Anna.

He let himself wallow for the days that he had off during the term break. The boxes of takeout stacked high in the sink; the empty snack bags decorated the coffee table. Hank existed, but he certainly wasn't living.

And then he decided that he needed a plan to find Nina, not just passively waiting for updates that weren't materializing. He couldn't take the one development in the past months as a sign that the detectives were seriously looking for her. Hank made up his mind to talk with Dr. Thurston himself. They both worked at the University, surely, he could find a way to run into him at some faculty function. When Hank told Carol, he expected that she would be eager to join him for a planning session. He was caught off guard when she responded with, "are you sure that's the best idea?"

There it was, the first signs that her faith was wavering. Her devotion to their shared cause was flagging. He spent his life teaching students how to read between the lines of text in a story. How to squeeze the meaning out of each word, wring out the truth from the narrative. While the face value of Carol's response may have appeared to be one of concern, Hank knew better. Her loyalty to their cause was fading. He was alone on this journey now, searching for Nina by himself.

So, Hank pushed on with his plan. As the new term began, he took steps to put himself in Thurston's path. He attended every faculty meeting and seminar. He went to more events hosted by the Sciences department. Hank informed Carol after each event, letting her know if Thurston had been present or not. She usually responded, but sometimes he had a sense of unease if her message didn't come through right away.

By February, Hank was planning to just cut to the chase. He told Carol that he would drop by during Thurston's office hours and ask for his help. Instead of replying to his text, Carol stopped by his apartment thirty minutes later.

Hank was caught off guard, he wasn't expecting company. He could tell from Carol's expression when she walked in that her concerns were confirmed by the scene in front of her. His living room was in disarray. Stacks of bills on the counter, glasses and plates left lying about on different tables, jackets strewn about. Hank felt embarrassed, he fumbled to make excuses. "Sorry, I didn't know you were coming over."

"Hank," Carol began, unbuttoning her prim mauve peacoat. Her voice was calm and metered.

"I just haven't had a chance to clean up lately," he insisted cutting her off before she could try to talk down to him.

"I know, I should have called first," Carol agreed as she took off her coat. She sat herself down on his couch, smoothing her hair with the open palms of her hands, waiting for him to join her around the coffee table. Once he sat down across from her, she began.

"I'm starting to get a little worried. I want to find Nina just as much as you do-"

He knew what this was. An intervention!?! That set him over the top. "No! You don't! You don't think about her non-stop! You don't picture her lost and scared and hurt! Don't start in with that, Carol." Hank snapped. He was frustrated at a lack of progress and Carol took the brunt of it.

"Hank, you're right. I miss my friend, but I didn't love her as deeply as you did," Carol continued in her clinical voice, as though she had perhaps rehearsed her words to be calming and soothing, even if the actual message was upsetting.

"I do love her, still!" Hank corrected her.

"Yes, of course. But you can't lose who you are while you search for her." Even though she never raised her voice, her tone made him take notice. At this, Hank's retort stopped in his throat. His confused expression was enough of a pause that Carol continued. "You're right, maybe this Dr. Thurston saw something. Or maybe he didn't. Maybe there is no progress on the case going on. But when Nina is found, you still need to be Hank for her. Imagine how she will feel if she comes back, and you've lost everything that makes you Hank. She'll feel like she isn't home at all. Do you know what I mean?"

Hank let her words sink in. He hadn't considered this before. Had he really been losing himself? He certainly took no joy in his work, something he used to love. He hadn't done anything outside of work since Nina went missing. He had been locked up in his apartment for months. His life had been consumed by the search, or lack thereof. He wondered at what he would do once Nina was back. When she asked him what he had been up to, he would only have one response, "looking for you." He mulled these thoughts silently, feeling shame start to creep up from his toes all the way up his back.

"Look, I'll help you make a plan to talk to this professor," Carol continued. "You can't just go up to him and start asking questions. It will put him on the defensive, and it will make you look suspicious too."

Hank took in her words. Carol was right, he couldn't scare this Thurston off. Especially if he had been close with Parker, maybe he hadn't helped the detectives at all. Maybe he had tried to cover for Parker, or insisted that he keep the missing scientist's name up on the vacant office all this time.

"You're right, I can't just rush in too fast," Hank nodded, considering the best angle to take.

"And, you need to talk to someone," Carol continued.

"Yeah, I need to talk to Dr. Thurston," Hank quipped back without letting the implication in Carol's words hit him.

"No," she clarified. "I mean you need to talk to a therapist." Before Hank could cut in, she continued right on with her reasoning, holding up her hand to stop him. "You were attacked last year too. You woke up in the hospital to learn that Nina was missing, possibly dead. You went right from that to trying to find her without processing what happened to you."

The full force of what Carol had been trying to relay to him sank in. She would help him, but only if he "got help." Hank nodded, silently agreeing to her terms. He didn't want to talk to Carol about it, or to anyone about it. But he knew he couldn't find Nina without any help.

"Okay, we'll meet later this week to talk about a plan to get you in front of Thurston in a natural way," Carol dictated the terms as she pulled a small card from her purse. She reached out to hand it directly to Hank, but redirected herself and laid it on the coffee table instead. Hank offered her some water or coffee, trying to make a pass at normal conversation after this… intervention of sorts. Carol shook her head softly and declined. "No, let's connect later this week. We'll both have fresh eyes and clear minds."

Carol offered a sheepish, "goodbye," before she slipped out of the apartment. Hank sat silently for a while, letting his thoughts run in a dozen different directions. His concentration finally broke when a dog outside began to bark, snapping his attention back into the present moment. Leaning forward, Hank grabbed the business card that Carol left. He felt the stiff edges between his fingers, a fresh business card that she must have just picked up for this conversation.

Hank looked over the details. The address was close by, but he didn't recognize the name. "Dr. Andrea Syvilak."

Hank headed into the kitchen and pinned it up on the refrigerator with a magnet. He would call, he promised himself. He would do it. Just not right now. In a bit. Maybe tomorrow.

PART 4

"*If you are silent about your pain, they'll kill you and say you enjoyed it.*"

– Zora Neale Hurston

21

Universe Alpha
June 3, 2019

"**D**ammit!' she swore as the makeup liner skirted her lashes and made contact with her eye ball. Reflexively she rubbed at the eye, getting it to water and alleviate the sting.

Nina did everything she could to mask the bags under her eyes, but her coverup was no match for this level of exhaustion. She wanted to look good for the first day at her new job. She was starting with a summer session class. Fewer students, easier schedule, a good way to ease into the life of an adjunct professor. Her sunken eyes were the result of another poor night sleep, this time instead of finding her life in mortal peril from Parker, she found herself lunging after Gus as Feminina and Marie sent him back to Alpha, back to commit the crime that would ruin her life. It was at least something different this time. For the past few weeks, she had the recurring nightmare that she was trapped in thick opaque plastic, suffocating, unable to breathe. The new nightmare was still scary, but at least it was a different kind of terror. Her mind must be processing through something.

She hadn't been able to get back to sleep afterwards, reviewing the contents of her secret shoebox once more. Turning over the quantum drive that was effectively useless to her since the Portal had been dismantled. Re-reading the list of historic events from Gamma, one that Nina had already memorized. It had been almost a year since her adventure across the multiverse. This little treasure trove had all her reminders of her trip, the only way she could be sure that it had all been real. That ripped page from the history textbook in Universe Gamma was too outlandish to be anything but proof of her time there. The quantum drive was too weighty to be anything but operational. And then there was the wedding ring that Hank handed her in Universe Beta, now a charm around her neck, a daily reminder of what could have been.

When the sun began to rise, Nina put the box away and set about the routine of getting ready. Her clothes were laid out, the first day of school routine ingrained in her from childhood. Her excitement peaked and waned as her body fought against the exhaustion from months of poor sleep.

The makeup helped, but it didn't magically give her extra energy. She was in need of some serious caffeine before arriving on campus. Nina didn't even bother to brew her own mug of coffee at home. No, she needed the full sugar-added, syrup pumped, coffee from the shop she would pass on her walk over to the University.

As she breezed down the sidewalk, she could already spot a line forming outside the café. Dozens of University students and staff, as well as local residents of the area, crammed into the shop to order their morning drinks. Nina stood at the back of the line, wondering if the heat outside was worse than the cramped interior of the café.

Nina looked over at the store window to her left. An abandoned building, tattered signs covered the window. They advertised jobs, concerts from months earlier, a reminder to keep vigil for three homicide victims whose murders remained unsolved four years later. Nina frowned at that sign. She had missed the news of the murders when they originally happened. But four years earlier she was in a decent relationship with Parker and had her blinders up to the rest of the world. She was still wandering, pretending to have her life together, even though she had yet to process the loss of Hank. Or that is what she told herself. Every so often a piece of news would pop up or some headline from the recent past would come up in conversation and Nina would nod along. She was never one for current affairs, but every so often she felt a chill run up and down her spine. Had she returned to the correct Universe Alpha? Or had more damage been done to the timeline in this reality for the ten years that the Portal stood in Thurston's lab, time enough for all manner of multiverse crimes to be committed.

The line advanced and she found herself standing in front of the café window, able to see the pandemonium inside. Nina knew this could not become a regular routine, waiting this long for any treat, even one that would give her the needed jolt to stay awake through her morning class, was not worth it.

Within fifteen minutes she had her iced coffee in hand and could already start to feel the sugar lifting her mood and energy levels. Her first class started at 9:30 am. She might have enjoyed the later start to her morning if she had been able to get a good night sleep. Her phone buzzed just as she was walking into the Sciences building at the University.

A text from Carol, "We miss you already :(Come back!" The message included a photo of Carol and Sonali standing over Nina's emptied out cubicle with sad faces.

Nina smiled and shot back a response, "Miss you too! Happy hour Fri?"

It was tough leaving them behind, but they both supported her decision to make a career change. Carol bemoaned the absence of Nina's much deserved promotion and Sonali joined in, although the passed-up opportunity had predated her. Nina didn't even recognize the person who had tried to go above and beyond to get that promotion, the woman who had been pressured by Parker to "reach for more." When Carol brought up the missed promotion as a rationalization for Nina leaving, she just went along with it. The real reason was one that Nina couldn't share.

But she would still miss her two good friends. Carol and Sonali were an amazing support system as Nina quietly recovered from some of the trauma of the previous summer. Although they didn't know exactly what Nina was coping with. To them, Nina was dealing with the disappearance of her long-time boyfriend. But in reality, Nina had lost so much more. She had lost her sense of reality, her feeling of safety, and once again, she had lost Hank.

A student brushed past Nina on their way out of the Sciences building, bringing her attention away from her phone. She looked up and faced down the hallway, the one she used to travel down to visit Parker, the one she had run down almost a year earlier in two different universes. The same bright white walls, the same dark spot where the lights never worked. Nina stared at the doors further down the hallway, the entrance to the lab, for a moment before turning left and heading up the single flight of stairs to the second floor.

The hallways here were also white-washed, but had no lights out. Just that one difference changed the ambiance significantly. Nina continued down the corridor with purpose and paused for a moment outside her classroom. Just as she had seen in Universe Gamma, her name was on the door. Feminina Marks. But this time it was really *her* name. It was as though she had brought some of that other reality back with her. Once she saw what was possible, she could make it happen for herself.

Nina started to set up the desk at the front and removed her lesson plans from her shoulder bag. She set her coffee on the far corner of the desk, the condensation pouring off the sides of the plastic container. Even though it had been a short walk from the café to campus, she had already slurped down half of the coffee. Nina found a stray napkin in her purse and set it under the plastic cup, trying to keep the moisture from spreading out across the desk, warping the words on her carefully typed papers.

As she started to write out the course title on the whiteboard, "Statistics for Marketing and Business," she heard a noise behind her. She assumed it was the first student, abnormally early.

But she was greeted instead by a handsome man in a suit. His thick black hair was perfectly gelled, his stubble appeared to be tattooed on. Her eyes narrowed. Any woman might be flattered to see such a man standing before her, given his powerful shoulders and attractive features. But not Nina.

"This is harassment," she said and then tightened her lips. She had seen him far too often, answered the same questions too many times. And after his last visit, she had been thoroughly unnerved. He was one of the federal agents who had stopped by on multiple occasions with no warning to grill her about Parker's disappearance. The last time the local cops did the same she told them that she didn't see why the two groups couldn't coordinate. She was getting questioned every other week. She had no new information. The local detectives seemed puzzled by her reference to the federal agents who had stopped by. She had her guard up, something wasn't right.

"Hey," Agent Nick Noriega drew his hands up in defense. "I was passing by on my way to ask the Dean a few questions." She could tell he was waiting for her to react to that statement. She kept her face still as stone. "I saw your name on the door," he pointed with a nervous smile on his face.

"Yeah, I start teaching today," Nina said as she crossed her arms. She noticed that she was eager to share this, even with someone who decidedly didn't like. *Did that make her pathetic?*

Nick nodded at the whiteboard. "I can see," he said and crossed his arms. Was he waiting for her to say something else? She didn't necessarily want to start her first class ever with a federal agent asking her questions in front of her new students. It wouldn't necessarily lend any credibility to her as their instructor.

"Well, good luck with the Dean. Hopefully you haven't badgered her nearly as many times as you've bothered me and maybe she'll be willing to answer your questions," Nina gave him a fake smile and returned to the papers on her desk.

"Well, I have new evidence that I need to discuss with the Dean," Nick retorted and started to turn from the classroom.

Nina popped her head up. "New evidence? About Parker?" The fear in her voice that he might have discovered the Portal and their ability to travel the multiverse must have shown as the genuine care and concern of the grieving girlfriend.

Nick turned around; he had clearly wanted to see how Nina would react to this news.

"Not directly, but it could be a lead," he said as he walked closer. "We got a message from an inmate at the Institute for the Criminally Insane."

Nina made sure to look confused, puzzled. But she instantly knew who the note would have come from. The only person it could have come from, the man she had just tried to stop in her nightmare not a few hours earlier: Gus Blanity.

"Well, what does this note say?" Nine tried not to sound too interested.

"Oh, that you and the Dean pushed this inmate through a time machine," Nick paused here, trying to judge Nina's response. "And that she likely planned to do the same to Parker. Oh, and that all this happened a decade ago." Nick smirked. For a moment she wondered how much he did know about the Portal. But there was no way, no one else knew about what happened the previous year. At least no one in that universe did.

"Wow, this is crazy," Nina said with a shake of her head.

"Especially since the Dean was in Pasadena ten years ago, nowhere near Washington, D.C." Nick rolled his eyes and started back out of the classroom. Nina wanted to correct him that location had nothing to do with time travel, that he was only thinking in one dimension. But she didn't want to give away her own expertise in the topic. She didn't want to continue the conversation. She needed to focus on her plan for an inspiring first lesson to get the students excited about big data and how it could inform marketing strategies and business decisions. She couldn't think about Agent Nick Noriega snooping around the University. Or worse, him discovering her own connection to Gus Blanity.

"Well, best of luck today, Nina. I guess I don't need to ask you about this letter. You don't have any secret time machine you failed to mention, right?" His question was sarcastic, but something about how he worded it made Nina nervous. There was no one who would police the crimes that Parker had committed, no one else knew that the Portal worked. *Or maybe*, the first doubt about the secrecy of the machine popped into her mind. Maybe she hadn't considered every variable, every potential threat to the security of her reality.

"Obviously not," Nina replied, trying to be nicer, giving a weak laugh at his question.

"Okay then. Good luck with the class," he said as he left the classroom. Nina couldn't believe it, but did he just wink at her? She couldn't be sure. And the last thing she needed was a distraction. Nina took another large pull on her iced coffee, hoping that caffeine would hit her system instantly, giving her another batch of intense focus.

A few moments after Nick left, the first student arrived in the classroom. Nina was excited, hopeful. She would help them learn about the exciting and often challenging work of marketing analytics. Her bright smile faded quickly when they took a seat in the second to last row.

She wasn't sure which was worse: having a federal agent questioning her on a whim or students who had already written her and the class off. But Nina tried to visualize all those positive notes she had posted around her kitchen. She couldn't just assume the worst. In her students, and in whatever Gus Blanity was up to with his letter.

22

Universe Alpha

Dean Marie Winchester has always been known as a woman of precision and planning. She has her routines; she has her processes. She didn't get to this position by "winging it." So, she was already perturbed to hear a knock on her office door during her scheduled work-time. As the Dean, she still taught one class each term and therefore had regular office hours. On Wednesday afternoons. Monday mornings were her quiet time to get work done and plan for the week before the meetings and the madness set in. This time was especially important to her at the beginning of the term. Sure, it was summer term, but there was always more to do. She had to protect her time during the day or else it would be dictated by others.

Assuming that it was her secretary, Renata, Dean Winchester let out a sigh that was sure to not be heard through the door and called out, "come in!" She tried to put on her most pleasant tone.

When she looked up a handsome young man stood in her doorway. Just beyond him she saw Renata's desk empty. He must have slipped by while the woman was in the lavatory or getting coffee.

"Hello, how can I help you?" Dean Winchester gave her best forced smile. Until he was in her office with the door closed, she had no intention of letting on that she knew exactly who he was and why he was there. Her eyes moved from his face down to the door handle at his palm.

Agent Nick Noriega, of the shadow agency that Winchester tolerated dealing with, closed the door behind him and sauntered over to one of the chairs facing her desk. 'What do you want now?" Winchester muttered as she crossed her arms and leaned back in her chair.

"Hello, Marie. How are you? Having a nice day? How was your weekend?" His tone was sarcastic. Implying that she had been rude, somehow remiss to not ask him those questions herself.

"Well Nick, as you know, I prefer you to make an appointment before just stopping by. I'm a busy woman-" she began. The tension between them was palpable, both barely tolerating the other.

"Apparently," Nick retorted, cutting her off.

Her quizzical expression indicated that he should elaborate on that comment. Nick pulled out the note that he had recently received from an inmate. This convicted murderer had accused her, Marie Winchester, of pushing him through a "multiverse machine" and injecting him with a dangerous psychedelic drug, knowing full well that it would lead him to his crime.

Nick laid the letter, in a protective plastic film, on her desk. Winchester glanced down at it, decidedly not leaning in to read it.

"What does that say?" She turned one of her eyebrows up. Their games of mental chess, micro-movements of who had power over whom in a given interaction were exhausting on both ends. But neither relented.

"Well, it is a pretty strong accusation about you forcing a man into another universe after injecting him with a known schedule one drug." Agent Noriega narrowed his eyes, examining her response.

Finally leaning forward, folding her hands in front of her, assuming her "Dean Posture" she responded. "Since you're the only person who has been providing me with the psilocybin to create the advanced derivative your agency needs for their work, I think the most important question you should be asking is how said schedule one drug was stolen without *your* knowledge." She paused for just a moment before leaning back again. "*If* you were to take such a preposterous accusation seriously. I'm sure a man of your rank in such an important government agency has better things to do with his time." Dean Winchester plastered a phony smile on her face.

Nick broke the tension with a laugh. "Dean Winchester, I respect your word and reputation far more than the rantings of a mad man who has been locked up for the past decade. Half of what he wrote here makes no sense and the other half would be impossible. We both know you were still working on your post-doc at Caltech in 2008."

"So, why come all the way down here to ask me about it?" Marie didn't buy his smooth tactic change whatsoever.

"To see if you agreed with my concerns over the access to the supercybin you've been creating. No one is even supposed to know about it except for us." He grabbed the letter and folded it up again in his hands.

Marie shook her head. "I mean the word about psilocybin is out. More people are advocating for its use in psychiatric treatments and in low dosages to aid in the treatment of severe mental conditions." Winchester began to rattle off these details as though she was in front of a class. She had done clinical research for her dissertation on the use of psychedelics as a new therapy for traumatized patients. It was her area of expertise; she knew just how many universities across the world were doing their own research on the topic and on that specific drug. "You said this person was incarcerated at a mental facility? Doesn't take much for someone who is already, clearly, prone to hyperbole and delusions to imagine an advanced version of the drug."

Nick nodded, agreeing with her assessment. He knew for a fact that this was fanatical writing. But he had to check it out. So far, he had been able to muscle the Dean into creating the advanced drug and providing it exclusively to the Chronos & Kairos Agency, CKA for short. He had been able to make a very credible threat to shut down the advanced research at the University for the sake of national security. And at the time they began working together, three years earlier, it was a very credible threat. Dr. Thurston and his newest protégé, Parker Lovett, were making significant advances on their version of the Portal. From what he could tell, the two of them had yet to figure out the power source equation and neither of them had even considered the physiological ramifications of such travel, hence they had never even asked the Dean for her own research on the psychedelic psilocybin.

As Nick considered Winchester's explanation, she wondered at why he was still coming to her for this drug. Yes, she was the foremost expert on the topic in the world, but surely, he had the resources with his agency to be able to reproduce as much of it as they needed. She did worry what they were using it for, why they could possibly need so much of it. She tried not to dwell on the malevolent uses like creating brainwashed assassins or altering the memories of political enemies. Instead, she pictured that her compound was used as a truth serum of sorts for interrogating terrorists, stopping future attacks. Something she could be proud of.

Nick didn't know exactly how much the guilt of her invention weighed on Marie. But, as she had shut down Thurston's research the previous year when Lovett went missing, Nick's threat of forcing the team to stop work on the device wasn't very credible anymore. But Winchester didn't seem to know that, or at least she hadn't pushed back on that account yet. He needed to make sure she continued to participate. In truth, she was the best chemist in the country, and probably the world, and the only one with the unique expertise to be able to make the drug that kept the CKA agents working.

"Well, as long as we can still continue to work together. I don't have to remind you that this is top secret for reasons of national security." Nick put on his "agent" voice.

Marie fought every instinct to roll her eyes. She had been cooperative, though begrudgingly. It was more his sense of entitlement, the way he talked down to her. Not that it was anything she hadn't been used to her whole life. Her colleagues acting superior to her. She was, after all, a woman in a man's world. And a Black woman at that. But to continue to push her like this. She wanted to remind him that as a chemist she knew how to make untraceable poisons, but she knew how that would go. A person of color threatening a federal agent. She didn't need to think too long before realizing that she should keep her mouth shut on that regard. But maybe she could give him a good rash. She smirked at the thought, something that elicited a quizzical look from Noriega.

"Yes, Agent Noriega. I am a fierce patriot and I would never want this drug to slip into the wrong hands. I'm already nervous that anyone has access to it, even you." She began to move some of the papers on her desk, unaware of what documents she was in the process of mismatching in her distracted state.

Nick Noriega assessed her as she appeared to refocus on her work. A subtle way of dismissing him. She turned, positioning herself to face her computer monitor.

"Is there anything else?" she asked as he began to speak.

"I noticed that Feminina Marks is now working here," he tried to keep his tone even.

"Yes, she starts today teaching our Statistics for Business and Marketing class. She's worked in digital advertising for years; she has the real-world knowledge these students need before they step off this campus." Dean Winchester beamed. But Nick saw through it.

After Parker Lovett was reported missing, he and Archie had stopped by and asked her questions. They asked to meet with Dr. Thurston and inspect their research findings. While Thurston had been cooperative in the missing persons investigation, he had been less than forthcoming about the research. When Nick popped by his lab, he noticed a very large space had opened up. The machine that he and Archie had been closely monitoring was gone.

The two were spooked. They had clear evidence that the machine had been used twice in the summer of 2018 and then one of their two primary assets, Parker Lovett, and the device disappeared. Given Thurston's reluctance to share their research, they had no choice but to assume that he was somehow complicit. A common logical fallacy made by law enforcement. Of course, Thurston would be less than forthcoming. He worked in a competitive field where there was only a prize for the first to make a discovery. But Nick and Archie couldn't see past their bias, past the information that they already knew.

They both met with Winchester and made it clear that they were unhappy with Thurston's lack of cooperation. They asked about where the device had been moved to? Was there a possibility that Parker had absconded with the research and the machine?

At that, Marie Winchester had let out a belly laugh. The machine was far too large to be stolen unless he had a semi-trailer and a crew to help him. Nothing on their security footage showed that.

And that was when both sides could have come clean. Winchester had reviewed the security tapes herself. Especially after Lovett was reported missing. The day-time feeds showed nothing irregular and at night the footage only recorded when the motion sensors were activated. She had seen Lovett return to the lab late in the evening of August 7, 2018 with a thick black bag draped over his shoulders. The image had been startling.

But then the video didn't pick anything up again for four and a half hours when a woman exited the building. No sign of Lovett.

Nick and Archie had seen the footage as well, they had been able to hack into the University security system. They had all seen the same thing.

Neither let on what they had seen. But both sides, CKA for their investigation and Marie for her own curiosity, had kept a close eye on Feminina Marks.

Parker Lovett was clearly seen carrying something, a *person-sized something*, into the lab. He was never seen leaving, but the woman who was seen leaving the building had the same height and build as Feminina Marks. Dean Winchester had kept her close by first suggesting that she finish her degree and then agreeing, too quickly, to allow her to teach. The woman did have experience but she didn't have an advanced degree. It was something she never would have allowed under normal circumstances. She was suspicious that Feminina was so interested in staying close to the University, she wanted to keep an eye on what she might be up to. What had she been doing in the lab that morning?

And for Nick and Archie, well Nina was a suspect in Parker's disappearance. Archie had calculated her temporal lag and it was obvious that she had been through the Portal, but whether she was a bystander, a victim, or a mastermind was still to be seen. But now, Nick was starting to realize that Winchester had her own suspicions, and if that was the case, then just how much more did she know?

There were times when he wished they could both drop the façade and show their cards. This nonverbal détente was draining. It would make his job easier and would take much less energy than this protracted game of cat and mouse. But he couldn't even tell the Dean what he needed the supercybin for. He couldn't reveal the name of the organization he worked for. It was exhausting for them both to circle the same topic.

After a pause, Nick gave a very calculated response. "Well, it sounds like she'll be a great help. And of course, that's the most important reason." Winchester opened her mouth slightly at this, at the implication that she had ulterior motives for making the hire. Because of course, she did.

Before she could retort, Nick started in with another question. "And, you've still not heard anything from Parker Lovett?"

Marie sighed and closed her eyes. "No, I've heard nothing, seen nothing, know nothing." This topic was a constant thorn in her side. Not only did she have to deal with Agent Noriega, but she was keeping an eye on Feminina, managing Dr. Norman Thurston's constant appeals for his research to start up again, and the University Board of Regents asking her to manage the optics of the missing adjunct professor.

"It's just a routine question, Marie." Nick could tell she was not happy about his bringing up this topic.

"I know, I just wish-" she stopped herself. What did she wish? That he was found? That he never disappeared? That he never came to work for the University?

"Don't beat yourself up," Nick said with a genuine note of concern. He had spoken to enough people in his life that he could tell genuine guilt from the guilt that women always put on themselves, feeling that they could have, should have done more. "Who knows, maybe he took a little trip on that machine he was building with Thurston."

Marie chortled, her laugh was broad and reaching, her voice booming. "Thanks, I needed a good laugh." Their hostilities were ended with this moment of connection.

"Seriously, one of your scientists who is working on a machine that would allow interdimensional travel goes missing without a trace, and your first thought wasn't that he absconded to another universe?" Nick was skirting a dangerous line here, but he wanted to see her reaction. Clearly Marie Winchester was not of the impression that the machine was usable.

"I'm a woman of reason and logic-" she began to respond to his outrageous suggestion.

"Exactly, this is the simplest and most obvious explanation." Nick tried to appeal to her training as a scientist.

"Not to anyone who knows the team. There is no way that Norman Thurston would allow anyone through that Portal before himself." Marie shook her head and turned to face her computer, dismissing Nick's comments.

Nick tried to point to a simple workaround. "Unless, Parker decided to do some late-night experiments." After all, Nick had seen him on the camera late at night, and he knew Marie had seen it as well.

She cut him off at this. "You think that's where he is?"

"No, I think he is hidden in some backwoods shallow grave to be honest. It's what the statistics tell me is the most likely outcome in this situation. But I have to consider every possibility since no terrified hikers have called anything in." He realized he had said too much. Nick's dark sense of humor, a bad habit he picked up on the job, was too morbid for Marie. Her face changed instantly at his words, the visual of her employee dead and dumped too grim. He pivoted quickly. "Well, I won't take up any more of your time, have a great rest of your day Dean Winchester. I'll see you again soon." And with that he was out of his chair and headed for the door.

"Agent Noriega," Dean Winchester said in her most stern authoritative voice, calling him to turn back around. "Please be sure to make an appointment next time," she gave her fake smile once more.

He walked out and Marie could finally let out a deep breath. *He must know more than he is letting on, but how much?* Was it wrong of her to give the poor girl, well woman actually, a job? She said she wanted to feel close to Parker. She had the experience. But now Winchester began to question her own suspicions and started to turn over the questions in her mind for the umpteenth time. What had Feminina been doing in the lab that early in the morning on August 8 of the previous year? It hadn't been signed, but was it Nina who had left the cryptic message instructing the Dean to put Thurston back in the classroom and restrict his research? Could she possibly have anything to do with Parker's disappearance? Nina looked like a stiff wind could blow her over, Marie couldn't picture her besting the man in any kind of fight.

Almost a year later and there were no answers. The Dean sighed, an exasperated exhale of a woman who had too many other things to worry about without this mess. She shook her head and resumed her work for the morning.

23

Universe Alpha

loud horn sounded, letting him know that he could now roll his government issued sedan through the gates. In his mind, Nick Noriega had envisioned an estate with vines crawling the perimeter fence and a grand driveway. A converted mansion, now used for the care of the mentally ill. But this wasn't a Stephen King novel. In 2019, the mentally ill who have been convicted of a crime were housed in facilities owned and operated by the Department of Corrections. Which meant high metal fences, open gravel courtyards, security checks, and full-time medical staff.

Nick parked in the visitor lot as instructed and pinned his badge to his suit jacket. The exterior of the Institute for the Criminally Insane was beige on beige. The cement walls had perhaps been stark white at one time, but yellowed after years and settled into an off-white color with water stains marring the sides. The gravel was a fine yellowish stone as well, likely a cost-saving measure as they would only need to restock on rubble every few years, instead of having a regular lawn care service.

His footsteps crunched on the gravel as he marched to the front door. Another loud buzz sounded as the door released and he entered. He expected to feel more trepidation as he approached. As an innocent man, he expected to sweat at the idea of entering a prison. While this facility was meant to provide care for the inmates first, they were still not free to leave. But with each gate he passed through, heading deeper and deeper into the labyrinth, he felt tranquil, docile. Perhaps it was the intentional design of the facility. Colors on the walls and materials of the uniforms selected for their unique properties that would promote calm and peace.

Checking in again at the front desk, he signed and timestamped his entry and stated his intent to visit with Gus Blanity. Nick read through his complete file after he first received the letter. It was light. Very light. Most criminal files that he had access to, being associated with a shadow agency did have unique advantages, came with a full incident report, court transcripts, birth certificate, report cards, and even dental exam notes. But Blanity's file started the night of his crime. It was like he hadn't existed at all before he swooped out of a dark alley and murdered Hank Jankowski back in 2008.

Of course, he knew of Nina's connection to Blanity before he ever showed her the letter. He had been curious as to her reaction. There were a lot of strange things happening all around Ms. Marks. Too many to be a coincidence, too many for her to be innocent in the eyes of the Kairos Agency. But he needed proof. For a brief moment he pictured himself ripping up a file, shredding evidence. He blinked the thought away. *Where did that come from?* He wondered this to himself. Nick Noriega was always one to follow the rules, to pursue the truth. He had never once in his life considered anything as reprehensible as destroying evidence. *But it could help Nina*, the same voice whispered in his head. Perhaps just being on "the inside" was starting to turn his mind. He would need to evaluate his own thoughts after leaving this facility. But first, he had work to do. His one source of calm and grounding in a mad multiverse, work. He was trained for this.

Following the directions of the woman at the front desk, he took the first right and completed the hallway before ascending the stairs. He expected the halls to be livelier. Patients and orderlies calmly shuffling about together. Some would need help walking, some would just want company. Too many movies tainted the image in his mind. This was a penitentiary, a cage for criminals. A nicer cage, a more understanding and cushioned cage. But it was a jail nonetheless. While the goal was rehabilitation and a level of mental health for the inmates to either stand trial or transition back into society, the primary function was to keep them inside, locked away. No one was roaming the halls except for nurses in stark white uniforms, bustling between different rooms on their rounds. Each cell appeared to have an observation window on the door and a stalwart locking mechanism. Through the small windows he could see that inside each room was a single bed and nightstand, the walls and linens all the same muted colors.

As he reached the second floor, Nick passed an orderly. Stooped low to clean up some spill on the steps, the shape confused him at first. Same all white outfit, but it was the bold and eerie white-blond hair, closer to just white, that caught his eye. The person stooping, he guessed that she was a female, had almost translucent skin. Their hair was buzzed on the sides and the top was pulled into a tight bun on the top of their head. As he reached the top step, they turned to look at him. She, definitely a she with that bone structure, blinked at him and tried to move over slightly to let him pass. As he walked by, even though they looked completely foreign and other, there was still something familiar about that face. But he could see the thin shine of a scar snaking down her left cheek. He had never seen her before. Surely, he was mistaking her for someone else.

Nick couldn't place their face and his mind kept spinning around, forcing himself to find the pattern. He was supposed to be good at this type of thing, remembering names and faces. In his line of work, it was the kind of thing that could make the difference in a case. But he told himself that this one face was just a slip, an eerie feeling of déjà vu. He and Archie had been trained to never trust that feeling, especially when they were dealing with matters of time. But he had experienced the feeling before joining CKA, so why couldn't this just be a random familiar face.

Nick shook it off as he arrived in front of Mr. Blanity's room. He set his phone to be able to record the session, he already had permission from the warden. It was time to ask Blanity some questions. Nick glanced up at the security camera mounted to the ceiling above the door, as instructed. He heard the door to the room open with a heavy clap.

Hesitantly, he entered. The front guard explained the protocol to him for exiting the room, there was a camera inside as well. But the sense of ease Nick experienced up until that moment sublimated. He was entering a cell now, with a known murderer who had no motive for his crime. A shiver went up and down his spine as he stepped into the room. There was a sterile smell of cleaning fluids covering something putrid and acidic. Nick didn't want to try to identify it.

In front of him sat a twig-thin man stooped over in a chair, facing the courtyard of the facility. Nick opened his mouth to address him when he heard the door latch behind him. He startled ever so slightly and composed himself.

"Mr. Blanity," Nick began. The man in the chair didn't move.

From his profile, Nick knew that he was in the correct room. He reviewed Blanity's mug shot a few times as he combed through the file. Nick approached the man, expecting him to acknowledge his presence in some way.

Still nothing.

Nick pulled the letter from his pocket. "Gus, I'm agent Nick Noriega. I got your letter," he tried this tack. Nick unfolded it and held it out for Gus to look at. The man still didn't look up, his gaze fixed on the scene outside the window.

"I wanted to ask you some questions about what you wrote in this letter, Gus. I think I might be able to help you." An empty but ill-defined promise. Still, no response. Nick squatted down to bring himself before Gus' eye-level. Perhaps he needed to get closer, grab his attention, to get a reaction.

But as the man's full face finally came into view, Nick saw that this was a fruitless visit. Gus Blanity was staring blankly out the window, his expression slack. His mouth agape and a small drizzle of spit slowly climbing down his front. The man appeared to be drugged out of his mind.

Well, I sure wish they would have said this was a bad time to visit before I drove all the way out here. Nick rose to his feet and shook his head.

"Mr. Blanity, if you can hear me or if you recall this visit know that I did really receive your letter, I did really visit, and that you can contact me again when you are feeling better." Nick pulled out a thin piece of paper with his name and number written on it and laid it on the perfectly made twin bed that was up against the wall behind Gus.

Nick turned and left the man to his staring. He glanced up at the security camera in the corner of the room and he heard the door unlock. He exited and made sure to close the door behind him per the instructions he had been given. He stopped the recording on his phone. Even with that short of a recording he saw that the temporal displacement reading was off the charts. *Perhaps he wasn't making up his travel back in time,* Nick thought as he puzzled over the readings.

A dark-haired nurse was making her way down the hall, her footsteps caught his attention.

"Excuse me," Nick called to her. She tilted her head anticipating his question. "Do you know how long Mr. Blanity has been sedated in this manner? I received a letter from him only last week."

Her brows furrowed as she processed his query. "We don't sedate the inmates here. We focus on behavioral therapies to help rehabilitate them." He could hear an irritation underlying her words.

Nick couldn't hide the confusion on his face as she passed on and continued her rounds. Before taking off back down the stairs, Nick peered in the room again through the window. He saw Gus Blanity looking up at him, his hand covering his mouth as he appeared to laugh at the agent on the other side of the door.

24

Summer session was always Hank's favorite. He could have always chalked it up to a lighter course load, but in general he just enjoyed the warmer weather, the bright sunshine that lasted well into the evening hours, the sense of freedom and opportunity around every corner. He was an English professor, of course he romanticized the most blissful of seasons. Even though the summer always represented a time of great pain for him, the loss of so much, he couldn't help but relish in the freedom of the warm air in June. He needn't encumber himself with a coat or jacket. An umbrella would help with the summer rains, but they usually didn't roll in until July and August. He didn't even mind the slight hay-fever that usually accompanied his extended strolls down to campus from his apartment.

This year had already been a tough one on Hank. He had been plotting and planning with Carol, trying to keep his hope alive. Savoring the early sweet sunshine on his walk to campus was indulgent, something that the person he had been a year earlier had done. But twelve months earlier he was a different man. He had rekindled his relationship with Nina, their official reconciliation was on the horizon. He didn't let his mind linger on the pain that so quickly followed. That Hank had no idea was what coming for him. For just a moment, he wanted to be that version of himself again. In love, with the weather, with the city, with his wife.

And his optimism wasn't completely unrealistic. After months of meeting, he and Carol finally had a solid plan. They had taken turns looking into Dr. Norman Thurston's routines and his schedule. Hank had an advantage; he could easily pass-through campus. He knew his class schedules, office hours, and day-time routines. Carol had been able to map some of Thurston's habits outside of work. With the new term, Hank had been worried that Thurston would be taking the summer off. But he saw his name on the classroom schedule and had been able to make note of his new class times and office hours.

Carol had been the voice of reason in each of their planning sessions. They met weekly over take out and beer, hashing out the different details of what they knew for sure, what was still a mystery, and what their next steps would be. They reviewed the small details they had from the detectives, but moreover they were focusing on how to persuade Thurston into talking openly with them. Hank was ready to just go up to the man and introduce himself. But Carol kept him to task. "Why would an English professor just walk up to the Head of the Physics Department?"

Hank didn't have a good answer as their conversations stretched from March into April into May. As Hank continued to get nothing back from Detectives Wells and Holcrum he became more and more insistent that he just go up to the man.

"I'm fairly certain he was also involved in the attack. He stopped Parker. I could go up to just say thank you." Hank had thought about this plan for a bit before presenting it to Carol.

"Hmm, could work," she bobbed her head back and forth, as though she was weighing out the chances of success. Her short-cropped hair had started to grow long, the light tendrils now reaching her shoulders, it swished against her cardigan as she continued this motion.

"What? Why wouldn't that work?" Hank knew that motion. Even if her words said it might have been a workable plan, her doubt was clear by the look on her face.

Carol picked up an open carton of lo mien and took a large bite, clearly trying to form her next words. She covered her mouth as she chewed, working the food as elegantly as she could. She finally swallowed; Hank was waiting for her explanation impatiently.

"I just don't know how that gets the conversation going with him." Carol stated plainly.

"What do you mean?" Hank was not happy that his first solid idea was dismissed so easily.

"Okay, let's play this out, I'll be Thurston. Why don't you start this conversation with me?" Carol prompted Hank to role-play with her. He immediately felt his confidence in this plan deflate. *Uh oh.*

"Uh, okay," he rubbed his hands together, uneasy about this idea, of making a fool of himself. "Hey, Dr. Thurston. I'm Hank Jankowski, I'm in the English Department."

"Oh, nice to meet you," Carol jumped in. Hank hadn't expected her to play along so easily, but began in again right away.

"Anyway, I just wanted to say thank you for what you did last year. When, uh, Parker attacked me, or us. I don't remember what happened, but I heard that you were the one who stopped him. So, thank you." Hank was earnest with his words. For all the times that he assumed that Thurston must somehow be protecting Parker, he did feel genuine gratitude. Who knows what would have happened if someone hadn't stopped that madman?

"Oh, it was nothing. I just jumped into action," Carol's response was squirrely, as though she was trying to avoid the topic.

"Well, I appreciate it-" Hank continued, trying to show Carol as Carol, not Carol as Thurston, that this was the perfect conversation starter.

"It was nothing," she cut him off, looking him square in the eyes.

Hank couldn't think of the next thing to say.

"See? He may not want to talk about this traumatic event. Especially coming out with that first. What if he is still processing the attack? What if he isn't prepared to have an open-heart conversation about it at that moment? I don't think it's the right tack out the gate."

Hank considered her words. He hadn't really thought about how the other man would react, that he might not be so open to the conversation.

"I mean, if he just walked up to you, you would be so relieved to get to ask him all of your questions. But he may not have that same reaction." Carol continued to explain as Hank processed.

"Okay, you're right." He finally conceded. "I'll think of something else."

The two returned to their list of questions that they would like to ask Thurston if and when they were able to gain his trust. And by that second week of June, they had a much better plan, tested from several angles.

So, it was safe to say that Hank was very optimistic on that first day of the summer session. He breezed through his first lecture with an energy that had been lacking for most of the year. Hank could finally see a path to finding Nina. Talk with Thurston. Gain his trust. Ask about what happened that day. See if he is hiding any information on Parker. Find Parker. Free Nina. The fact that they were both still missing kept him optimistic that they were both still alive, somewhere.

After his last lecture for the day, Hank headed over to the reception the Dean was putting on for the summer faculty. It was a new addition for the 2019 year, and Hank was not only happy for the free meal, but for the opportunity to interact with Thurston. He arrived early and scoped out the seats and then retreated to the men's room for a few moments. Hank wanted to time his entry at the dinner so he would sit down next to Thurston. But first, the physics professor needed to arrive. Based on their observations, both Hank and Carol knew that Thurston never turned down the opportunities for free food on campus. They were fairly sure he would attend.

Hank texted Carol as he waited. "At faculty reception. Thurston isn't here yet. I'll keep you posted."

He was pleasantly surprised when she wrote back right away. "Okay, let's hope this is the first of several convos so we can find out what he knows about Nina."

Hank smiled at her clear enthusiasm for this plan. Anyone else would have said that he should just leave it to the detectives, he should just move on with his life. But Carol believed him, believed that Nina was still alive out there.

He decided that he had waited long enough, he didn't want to risk both seats next to Thurston being taken.

Hank re-entered the presentation room, the maintenance staff had rearranged the rows of chairs and placed tables around the perimeter of the room, creating a large rectangle for the reception. Basic linens and table places were set, the University catering staff were bustling back and forth, filling water glasses, readying the chaffing dishes. As with anything the University did, they made it look nice, special. But Hank knew exactly what would be on the menu, it was the same one that was used for every faculty function. The dark wood paneling of the room, the podium, and microphone at the center of the room made it look like a much more special occasion than it was. But this was the distinct advantage of working for a prestigious University, the trappings of "nice" things.

Hank didn't spot Thurston yet, so he headed for the coffee table in the back corner. A little late in the day for the caffeine, but every faculty event always had fresh coffee. He loitered as he slowly poured himself a cup and meticulously added the cream and sugar to his liking. Finally, he spotted Thurston enter the room and head towards the opposite corner to take a seat. Not many other faculty members had chosen a seat yet, Hank acted quickly. He had to remind himself to look casual, relaxed.

Hank approached Thurston, who was already reaching for the bread basket nearest his place setting. "Is this seat taken?" he asked.

Hank noticed something on the man's face, perhaps a flash of recognition. "Oh, uh, no. Go ahead." Thurston stammered.

"I'm Hank Jankowski, I'm in the English Department," he started in as he sat down and reach out a hand to Thurston.

"Dr. Norman Thurston," the older man shook his hand. "And I-" he stopped for a moment, as if unsure how to finish his own thought. Hank looked at him expectantly.

"I think I was at one of your special lectures last year on H.G. Wells," Thurston finished his thought. *Was that really what he was going to say?* Hank wondered. But he knew that he had to stick to the plan, he took the opening.

"Yes, *The Time Machine*, does it stand up to contemporary science fiction? That was a fun one."

"Well, for you perhaps. But I study the quantum mechanics that could make it real. Unfortunately, my job is to put that genre out of business. Make it non-fiction." He laughed as he pressed a pat of butter into the roll in his fist.

"I'm sure there will always be more science fiction to think up," Hank continued. The two fell into agreeable commentary on the realism in modern science fiction before the University President began their remarks to the faculty.

While the other professors looked on with placid faces as they listened, or pretended to listen, Hank fumbled for his phone and tapped out a message to Carol. "Phase 1: Successful. Rapport established."

He looked up, catching something about using this term to try new exciting topics, to fine tune their research and publications to elevate the University, nothing that couldn't have been sent in an email. Hank reached for some bread as well, before Thurston ate the whole basket, when he felt his phone buzz.

"Great! I'll pick up a pizza and we can go over our next step in the plan. This is progress!" Carol's message lifted his spirit. He was looking forward to sharing the details of his conversation and how they might be able to make some headway. He felt his excitement pique. And then Nina's face flashed in his mind and he felt… guilty. *Was it bad that he was looking forward to another evening with Carol? Was he somehow betraying Nina? Had he started to lose focus on his real mission?*

"Don't worry about it, they have a big spread here. Let's connect at our regular time later this week," Hank shot back. He needed time to process these new thoughts, as well as whatever else he might be able to say to Thurston. But he also needed time away from Carol, time to sort out what this new feeling was. It was strange. He wanted to find Nina right now, had already wasted too much time without her. But he needed to delay the next conversation that might be able to help him find her. If only he could have it both ways. If he could just fast-forward to the part where Nina was back. If only such a machine like H.G. Wells described did exist.

25

Renata tapped gently on the closed door to Dean Winchester's office and popped her head in.

Marie looked over at the clock and saw that the day had flown by. Between meetings and a stream of never-ending distractions, the hours got away from her. It was as though they conspired, secretly planning to just not do their duty that day. Hours posing as minutes, taunting Marie and her never-ending task list.

It was the summer session; this was supposed to be her time to catch up on administrative items that the regular academic year didn't allow for. She shook her head and hoped that this wasn't an omen for the rest of the term.

"Sorry to bother you, but Dr. Thurston is here. He doesn't have an appointment; do you want me to ask him to come back?"

Her knee-jerk reaction would have been to say "yes." She had worked a long time to earn enough respect from her male colleagues and subordinates to get them to honor her schedule. She had a strict meeting policy. Already today she had one drop-in from her least favorite government agent. She felt the need to assert her dominance. To insist that her schedule, and her time, be respected.

But she already knew she had to tread carefully with Thurston. He had always been a bit of a trouble-maker, delighting in each chance to undermine her. But then she shut down his research when Parker went missing. Thurston was a landmine that she needed to handle very carefully. Even though she was his boss, she knew he could make her life difficult. And since he had tenure, and was good at his job, she couldn't terminate his employment. The thought crossed her mind several times, both before and after Parker Lovett disappeared.

Weighing all the considerations about her own desire for order and respect and the need to keep Thurston happy, she relented with a sigh. "Send him in."

Renata nodded and she moved aside to let Thurston duck into the office. Like a bull, Thurston charged in, his size and energy taking up the room, expanding like hot air to fill the space.

"Dr. Thurston, how can I help you?" Dean Winchester asked as she moved her current paperwork to the side.

"Well, Marie," he started in. He never addressed her as Dean Winchester or even Dr. Winchester, it was always her first-name that he used. She never invited him to be this familiar with her, he just didn't respect her. It was one of the million little ways he tried to put her down, to make her feel small. She tried to not let it get under her skin. "It's been nearly a year. My contemporaries are making great strides in quantum theory and I've been handcuffed without the ability to resume my research. I implore you to let me get back to *my work*."

Marie did her best to hold back a heavy sigh. *This again?* He really did think that the more he asked that eventually she would be worn down.

"Norman," she was very deliberate to return the same lack of respect in this subtle manner, "we've been through this so many times. Your partner on that research is missing. Has been for almost a year. The optics are not great."

"Well, how will the optics look to the board of regents when another university is first to publish findings on the same course of study. We were so close to a big breakthrough." Thurston gestured wildly, pacing back and forth in front of her desk, making a big show of his frustration.

"I think I have a better idea of what the board of regents will and will not accept, Norman." Marie corrected him. "Please, sit down."

He looked over to her, as though debating whether or not he should accept her invitation or abstain. After a long pause, he let out a huff and sat down in one of her chairs, but he kept his gaze on the desk, not on her.

Childish, Marie thought.

"Look, I know how you feel. I miss research myself. But we can't just forget that Parker is still missing. We need to do all we can to help the authorities find him." She used her best soothing voice, the one she had to use when she had to act as nurturing mother to her employees.

"It's been almost a year; I don't think they're going to find him." Thurston snapped back.

While she didn't disagree with his assessment, she also didn't like his tone. *Could he really be so callous about the man he had mentored and worked with every day for three years? Was this man that ambitious that he would insist on pushing forward without any regard for what happened to Parker?* It seemed she had read their working relationship all wrong, Marie had always thought they were more like a father-son pair instead of a professor and adjunct. At least, she got the feeling that Parker looked up to Thurston in that way.

Marie considered her next words so that she didn't let her disdain for this man's clear indifference for his missing colleague show through. "I wouldn't be so sure about that. An investigator dropped by again this morning to speak with me." Not technically a lie, although it wasn't the whole truth either.

Thurston nodded as he took in this information. "So, can I start my research up again, or no?" He didn't seem to realize that his bullish tactics weren't helping his case.

"Not right now, Thurston. I still need you to cover Parker's courses and I don't want to do anything that could interfere with the investigation. The answer is no." Marie didn't know how else to make her position more plain. These nagging tactics weren't working, but Thurston didn't seem to have any other strategies in his wheelhouse.

Instead of accepting her words, or acknowledging her position, or even just thanking her for her time, he shook his head as he stood up and huffed out of the office. And of course, he left her door ajar. Marie rolled her eyes as she crossed the room. She shut the door and sat back down to finish her paperwork for the day.

As she pushed their interaction from her mind she muttered, "prick," and shook her head. Some things just never change.

26

Universe Gamma
April 8, 2019

It was an overcast afternoon, but they didn't mind. Femi and Hank strolled hand in hand along the Leie River through the Graslei. The cute cafes that lined the walkway were calmer and a bit quieter than usual. The weather wasn't quite good enough to tempt the tourists back out of their hostels. Femi loved getting to experience the historic city of Ghent this way, like a local.

Their feet clipped along as they walked over the bricks that made up the pathway. Femi didn't know which little restaurant they would pop into for a small meal, but she didn't care. Each new place that Hank showed her in the city was delightful.

As they walked, she noticed one of the bricks under toe was loose. It buckled as she stepped on it. Femi looked down and back at the stone, the cement holding it in worn away from centuries of pedestrians. They kept on going though, not slowed down by Femi's observation. Until she noticed more and more of the bricks beneath her feet were shifting with each step. Her initial concern over the natural deterioration and the historic significance of the walkway soon turned to one of pedestrian safety. Her ankles bobbled, trying to keep herself upright. Until finally she looked up and saw Gus Blanity, standing before her with a brick in hand, ready to smash it into her skull. She had no idea how Gus could have found her here of all places.

She reached both of her arms up in defense and screamed but nothing escaped. Her throat constricted. As she felt herself crouch, ready to duck and cover she found herself awake in a dark room, the gray light of the moon casting the bedroom in shadows.

She caught her breath, trying to steady her heartrate. *It was just a dream.* But it had also actually happened.

In her months in Ghent with Hank, she had adjusted to the life of a full-time girlfriend. She read and worked on some research papers she intended to send out for publication. But she also cleaned the tiny apartment and went to the market for fresh produce and fish. She met all of Hank's colleagues at the University and dog-eared travel books with the places she wanted to see while she was there.

The routine lulled her into thinking that she had truly left her old life behind. The science, the stress, the machine, the violence. But no matter how well she seemed to be adjusting to life with Hank, it didn't quell the fear. It didn't stop these nightmares.

Hank rustled next to her, turning over in bed. He used to wake with her to soothe her back to sleep. In the first few months her nightmares resulted in her screaming out loud. Tonight's vision left her awake and panicked, but her throat had been so tight with fear no noise had escaped. It was almost as if she was more afraid now than she had been before, like her anxiety was rising with each passing day instead of waning.

And perhaps that was for good reason. She knew she had exactly thirteen days left on her traveler's visa before she needed to go back home. Her initial trip was supposed to be for one week. But then it turned out that Hank was as amazing as Nina, her alter-ego from Universe Alpha, had made him out to be. Femi let herself believe that they were meant to be together, she bought into the romance of *destiny*. Each time she delayed her flight, Hank seemed happy about it. She could just cancel the ticket and never leave. But if she tried to apply for any kind of residency and it was clear that she had overstayed the visa limits, she would likely be denied. If she stayed too long, went home, and then applied for residency, same thing. She could just stay and not think about these matters, but it was becoming more and more clear to her that a return trip might be necessary.

Once she did return, she knew what would happen. Femi had already walked through the mental steps necessary to go to the storage locker, reconstruct the Portal, and get to work on finding a way to save her dad. Her plan ever since she saw her father again in Universe Delta the previous summer had been to save him. Her own father, the one in her Universe, had died years before. She missed him. Seeing him alive and well in Universe Delta for so brief a time had been cruel. Even though she knew she *shouldn't* use the Portal for her own personal reunion, it didn't mean that she wouldn't actually do what she wanted.

Why not do what she wanted? Marie was already going on the news and promoting the quantum drive. She got to do what she wanted. Femi pushed her resentful thoughts from her mind.

She knew she should get back to sleep. She spent most nights walking this same mental path over and over. *Stay or go?* Stay and burrow further into the escapism of life with Hank? Return and live out her life's work as the co-inventor of a time machine?

Hank flopped over on his side again, his profile now visible to Femi in the barely illuminated room.

And then there was Hank himself. Her reason to stay. But also, perhaps, just maybe, a reason to go. Femi had never been one for sentimental attachments. She had never been the girly-girl who swooned over boys. She had her fair share of crushes, all unrequited, but never anything like this. She was scared of the force of her feelings for him. How quickly and completely she had fallen in love. Femi initially judged her alter-ego to be foolish with her talk of soulmates and destiny. Until she experienced it herself. In two other realities, Feminina ended up with Hank. And the way things were going, she was about to be the third. This knowledge gave her confidence in their relationship. But it also terrified her. Did she have no say over her own life? No control over who she would end up with? And in those other realities, one of them died. She couldn't bear to think that she might bring that tragedy to this reality as well.

Leaving Ghent would surely end things, break the spell. She didn't think Hank would ever go back to the U.S. How could he when his career was based on teaching literature focused on the expat experience? When his parents had risked so much to flee the United States with him when he was an infant?

Femi pictured herself initiating the conversation with him. Telling him that she was finally leaving. She imagined his possible reactions, all of them brought tears to her eyes.

She couldn't think about this anymore. Not tonight. She needed to make this decision when she was fully rested. Not when she was scared or sleepy.

She turned over and closed her eyes, wishing for sleep to find her quickly. Hank's arm wrapped around her waist, pulling her in closer. The comfort of his embrace brought a smile to her lips, the protection of his arms giving her the peace to drift away.

And before she knew it, she was wide awake again. The bedroom covered in mid-morning sunlight and the smell of eggs and bacon wafting in from the kitchen. She lay there enjoying the calm of the moment, listening to Hank move about, identifying the movement of pans and the spatula grating against the Teflon.

She rose slowly, the trepidation and worries from her mid-evening nightmare far from her mind. Sauntering into the kitchen she greeted Hank with a kiss on the cheek and set about pouring some fresh cold water for them both. She put out plates and utensils on the small bistro table in the apartment that served as a make-shift dining area.

"Should be ready in another five minutes," Hank called out, focused on getting the bacon just right. Not too soft, not burned, crisp to their liking.

"Perfect, that'll give me enough time to clear out any junk emails that came in overnight." Femi responded as she grabbed her phone from the charger and plopped herself down on one of the chairs at the table. She spotted the usual newsletters and scrolled through quickly, nothing caught her attention. She could clear out her inbox pretty quickly each day. But she did notice one email from "EZDC Storage."

Femi clicked on the message. She read it quickly and then had to reread it to make sure she wasn't seeing things.

```
"Dear Ms. Marks,
Thank you for choosing EZDC Storage for your
storage needs. We pride ourselves on making it easy
for our customers to securely store their items.
    We are sad to see you go, but please come back
at any time.
```

STORAGE UNIT: 808
STATUS: EMPTY & CLOSED
SECURITY DEPOSIT: RETURNED
CONFIRMATION NUMBER: at986201zy"

The message was so short, but communicated so much.

The storage unit that she and Marie had rented for the specific purpose of keeping the pieces of the Portal cataloged and safe was now empty. Their account was closed.

What the hell is Marie up to? Femi thought, shaking her head. Her fingers began to tap out an email to her old lab partner, the accusations flying fast and furious.

"Breakfast is served," Hank announced, his words unable to break Femi's concentration. "Everything okay?" he asked as he sat down across from her.

She knew she was being rude, but she was seeing red. *They had agreed to keep the Portal dismantled so no one could just waltz through it. This was a decision to protect their reality.* Femi's mind flashed on the image from her dream, of Gus Blanity standing before her ready to strike. This jolted Femi back into the current moment. *Maybe it hadn't been a dream after all. Maybe it was a premonition. Maybe he was already here.*

"I'm good," Femi muttered as she put the phone down. She needed to send a clear and rational message back to Marie. And perhaps she should hold off on the accusations. "Just frustrated with what Marie is up to," she avoided eye contact with Hank as she passed off this explanation.

"What did she do now?" his words garbled by the eggs in his mouth.

Feminina hadn't told Hank *everything* about their research together. He knew that they had been working on a Portal as part of their joint work on the quantum theory of the multiverse. He knew that they had developed a quantum drive and computer together. He knew that the third member of their team, Gus Blanity, had developed the supercybin. But that Blanity had turned on them and stalked Marie. And that was all he needed to know in Femi's opinion. She hadn't told him that the Portal actually worked. She hadn't explained that she and Marie had been host to a refugee of the multiverse, her own alter-ego, who had been kidnapped by another scientist from another reality. No, he didn't need to know about all that.

"Looks like she is about to make more announcements without my okay," Femi shook her head as she took her first bite of bacon. "I just need to reach out to her."

Hank nodded. He was able to ascertain that the relationship between Feminina and her old lab partner and best friend, was less than ideal. He didn't pry, which she was grateful for. There were too many layers to detail, too many years of experience and trust built and then broken to explain.

As Femi ate her breakfast, her mind tumbled over all the possible explanations for this move. But one that she kept coming back to was that somehow Gus, or Parker, or some other nefarious character had made their way into this Universe and intended to reconstruct the Portal. That Marie might be in danger, they all might.

And that was the final straw. All of Femi's logistical concerns over her visa status, her desire to save her father, her feelings for Hank were negated by this thought. That she might have failed everyone in this reality by not being a better guard of the Portal, by not being there in person to ensure that no one could use it again. She knew she would never get another wink of sleep if there was any possibility that the machine had fallen into the wrong hands. Femi would never forgive herself if Marie was hurt, or worse, because she had slinked away to Europe to forget the trauma of the previous summer.

She took a deep breath and looked up at Hank, waiting for him to meet her gaze. When his pale blue eyes met hers, she didn't hesitate. "Hank, I think I need to go back."

PART 5

"There's a special place in hell for women who don't help each other."

– Madeleine Albright

27

Universe Gamma
April 26, 2019

It was well past dark, but Femi didn't care. She would wake up the neighbors, but that was the least of her concerns as she banged her closed fist on the door to Marie's apartment.

She was exhausted and stiff from her long flight. She had managed to push all thoughts of her final goodbye with Hank from her mind ever since she departed. It was as though she was able to slip into her old self, her old ways as soon as she boarded the plane. The woman who evolved and discovered her capacity to love and feel hadn't boarded the flight that morning in Antwerp. No, Femi had left her behind, along with the tiny frame of a life she had started to build with Hank in Ghent.

The woman who spent hours on a flight, crammed in next to strangers, was the old Femi. The one who was overly logical, loyal to science only. Her leg pumped the entire flight. Partially from nerves, but also, she was seething mad. At best, Marie had gone against what they had mutually agreed upon and decided to reconstruct the Portal. At worst, someone had broken into the locker, removed everything, reassembled the Portal, forged either her or Marie's signature to close the account, and was now planning to activate the device or currently welcoming people from other Universes into their own.

Her rage hadn't subsided as she deplaned and took the metro over to Marie's place. She just had an outlet for it now. The door that was barring her way.

She had traveled back across the world when she wasn't ready to. She didn't want to leave. She didn't want to return to D.C. and all the memories and disappointments it held. But here she was, demanding that Marie open the door and let her in.

It was time for some answers.

As her fist made contact with the door again the surface shifted. Femi almost lost her balance, but she recovered quickly.

Standing before her was Sonali. Her thick curls were swept to one side, disheveled but still somehow elegant and alluring. And, as always, Sonali looked breathtakingly beautiful without a stitch of makeup on at the end of a long day. Feminina's usual insecurities were only exacerbated by the fact that she knew what a mess she must look like in comparison. And the fact that her best friend in the entire world picked her romantic relationship with Sonali over their lifetime of work together.

This was not how she envisioned this moment.

Sonali crossed her arms and smirked at Femi, waiting for the returning scientist to say something.

"I need to see her, *right now*," Femi barked. No time for manners, literally no time. If Marie had reconstructed the Portal than anyone could be waltzing through at any moment.

"Oh, hello Sonali. Sorry to bother you so late. Is Marie in?" Sonali retorted with the thickest sarcasm she could muster, mimicking the greeting she thought Femi should have given her.

"Yes, it is late. I've just flown halfway across the world to see Marie. This is an emergency. Is she here or not?" Femi didn't let Sonali's response phase her.

"You have some nerve. Literally ignoring her emails for months and then showing up and demanding to see her. Maybe she doesn't want to talk to you now either. Have you considered that?" Sonali propped her hands on her hips and pursed her lips.

Femi had already planned to push out her next verbal demand, but what Sonali said stuck in her mind. *Maybe she doesn't want to talk to you now either.* That had been part of her fear all along. That Marie didn't want to work with her anymore, that she had been replaced.

Feminina's face must have betrayed her because Sonali's expression softened ever so slightly.

"She's not in right now, but she'll be back soon. You can wait inside, but I can't guarantee she'll be pleased to see you." Sonali stood aside and gestured for Femi to come in.

The woman hesitated for a moment; her pride wounded on top of her exhaustion. Should she say that she would be fine waiting outside in the hallway or should she accept this small gesture? Her brain was too tired to weigh out the pros and cons of the situation, so she grabbed the handle of her luggage and strolled into the apartment.

It looked the same as ever. The organized bookshelves, the mess on Marie's desk. It was like the past several months hadn't happened here. Life continued on as though nothing big had changed, but Femi felt changed. How could those two things be true?

She thought back to that evening last summer, when she pounded on the door, the continuity and safety of the multiverse was at stake then as well. She had her alter-ego with her then, a visitor, an interloper. Now Femi felt like the one who didn't belong.

Thinking back on that fateful evening, she had been naïve to the depth of the risk. Feminina shrugged off her coat and sat on the couch, lost in her memory. That had been the night that her own alter-ego had shown up at her front door, a victim of kidnapping who needed to find her way home. Femi wondered for a moment how she was doing, if the other Feminina was safe in her home universe.

"Can I get you some water?" Sonali asked, the polite question must have been vinegar on her tongue.

Femi nodded silently, her pride thick in her throat, blocking her ability to respond verbally. Sonali glided into the kitchen, Femi could hear her moving about. The glass of water was set on the coffee table in front of her and Sonali walked back down the hallway.

The tense silence between the two women was nothing new. But Femi felt justified in her frustration. Sonali told Marie that she had to pick between her work and their relationship. Marie chose the relationship. And now, it seemed, that Marie was trying to pick back up on their work without Femi. The more she focused on the security issues, the chance of Gus Blanity popping back through the Portal, or another Parker, were too great. *How could Marie be so negligent?*

She didn't have to wait long to ask that question. The door to the apartment opened. Marie walked in, encumbered by a heavy messenger bag on her right shoulder and a stack of binders in her left arm, the keys to the apartment jangling in her open palm. "I'm home!" Marie called out to Sonali as though this was part of her normal routine, a comfortable pattern they settled into.

Feminina's attention snapped quickly as she watched her friend, her mentor, her partner walk in. She was just as tall and imposing a figure, her intelligence emanating from her, Marie was always a force. Her natural hair was still cut short, the gray and black curls kept tight to her head. It was late, so perhaps that is why she looked tired at first. At least, Marie looked tired before she caught sight of Feminina. With a flash of recognition her face went from calm to surprised to frustrated to annoyed.

"Hi," was all that Marie said, the word sounding like a question more than a greeting.

Sonali had come back down the small hallway and was at Marie's side, gliding her satchel off her shoulder. "Welcome home honey, you have company," she said in a sickly-sweet tone, clearly her sarcasm from earlier was still in full effect.

"I can see that," Marie responded, barely able to take her eyes off of Femi.

"Hi," Feminina spoke, her voice so low it was barely audible. All her gumption had evaporated when Marie walked in. In spite of the animosity that had built between them over the past few months of silence, now face-to-face with her best friend, Femi couldn't find the words that were free flowing through her mind just moments earlier. All her barbs and accusations scattered, unable to form.

It seemed that Marie was having the same reaction. Femi read her emails; they were long and detailed. But now her former lab partner was just looking at her, at a loss for words. That never happened to Marie. Even in awkward or tense situations she was always quick with a joke to lighten the mood.

Sonali looked between Marie and Femi. Thankfully, she was the one non-scientist in the room so she had better people skills than the two of them combined.

"I'm going to run to the corner store to grab some wine to celebrate Feminina's homecoming. I'll be back," Sonali said to Marie, who nodded silently in response. Sonali grabbed her jacket and slipped out of the apartment as Marie moved over towards her desk and leaned up against it, her arms crossed.

Feminina shifted on the couch so that she was still facing Marie.

"How could you do this?" Femi finally blurted out just as Marie spoke, "You have some nerve showing up here." The anger and attitude in both of their words were clear, even if they couldn't quite hear each other over their own voices.

After another tense moment of staring the women spoke again, this time giving each other a chance to talk.

"I needed some time to process what happened, Marie," Femi said in a trembling voice. It was the truth; it was the most bare and essential explanation for all that had happened since the previous August and it overwhelmed her because she hadn't actually voiced it before. Femi bit her lip and stared at the floor, unable to look Marie in the eye as she fought with her emotions.

Marie waited a moment before speaking. "I'm sorry." The two words that had the power to unlock the defenses that Femi had put up. It didn't absolve her, it didn't forgive anything, but it blew a hole open in Femi's tough exterior.

"How could you take the Portal out of storage? At first, I thought something happened to you, someone had done something to get the key from you. But the more I thought about, I realized it was you the whole time." Femi finally looked up from the spot on the floor she had been staring at, her eyes now focusing their heat on Marie.

Marie dropped her head into her right hand. "We have more work that needs to be done. We dedicated our lives to this, we decided we would create something that would bring our humanity to the next level. I couldn't let you stop that progress because you found some *guy* in Belgium-" Marie was staring to gesture with her hands, emphasizing her point when Feminina cut in.

"Oh, so I have to do the dirty work and dispose of the Parkers when you needed to chase after Sonali, but when I go abroad and happen to meet someone, I'm supposed to ignore that and come running back the second you snap your fingers?!" Femi's words seemed to quiet the rant that Marie was about to go on.

Marie stood silently and looked off towards the kitchen, taking a moment to compose herself. Both women were battling internally with the desire to say all the things they had pent up, the things they knew would cut to the core of the other person, and their dogged need to be calm and collected in this argument. The rational person always won out, right? But both women were losing in that regard. There was too much time and emotion invested in their long-standing friendship.

"You could have at least responded to my emails to let me know you were okay," Marie muttered.

Femi wanted to snap back that Marie shouldn't have released the news about the quantum drive, but two wrongs didn't make either of them right.

"Well, consider this an in-person response," Femi said as she flopped back into the couch cushions. "But I still don't get how you could be so careless as to put the Portal back together. Gus Blanity could be in some other Universe on some August 8 and walk right through, so long as that Portal is functional."

Marie moved closer to Femi. "I didn't set it up yet. I need your help for that."

Feminina didn't know how to respond, she hadn't expected that. *Had Marie pulled the device out of storage because she knew it would elicit this response from her?*

"I'm not going to let those men through our Portal again, Femi," Marie said, her eyes trying to communicate some kind of pain to the woman sitting before her. "But I'm also not going to let either of us throw away all the positive that this machine can bring."

Feminina shook her head. "We can't control this power, Marie. There are too many variables. There is too much that can go wrong." *Couldn't Marie see all the ways it had already gone wrong?*

"Even if it means you don't go to see your dad again this year?" Marie waited for Feminina to look up at her. "You don't have to tell me that's what you want, I'm not stupid. I was there for you when he died. I know that's what you want. You're telling me you'd skip that chance?"

Feminina didn't know what to say in response. Marie was absolutely correct. As though she had learned to actually read minds, as though she had seen into the part of Femi's brain where her plan to travel back in time and save him was buried.

In the course of a few minutes, and with a handful of very direct and brutally honest statements, the two seemed to have crossed a chasm larger than the Atlantic Ocean that had separated them for months. But this was just the beginning. If they were going to work together again, if they were going to try to do some good in the multiverse, if they were going to move past their issues, this would be the first of many tough conversations. They would have to stitch their trust back together. Carefully weave the fibers of their friendship across the jagged edges. And they would need far more than one bottle of wine to accomplish any of that.

28

"Jab! Jab! Jab!" the instructor shouted into her headset. Five-foot-nothing and full of energy, Kassandra pushed the class to punch, kick, jab, and cross every Wednesday evening. Nina had been attending for months. Her kicks were improving, her footwork more natural.

"Jump rope! Go!" The class ran back from their punching bags and grabbed their ropes as quickly as possible. Nina felt her flyaway hairs sticking to her forehead and neck, but she didn't dare fuss over it. She started to jump quickly, careful to not slam the rope into her shins.

Kassandra monitored the class, her blonde hair pulled back into a tight bun. "Good work, Mark. Nice form, Karen." She offered encouragement to the newer members of the class. She counted on some of the veterans, like Nina, to help the newbies. There were always one or two in each class. Sometimes they would come back for more punishment.

Nina pushed and pushed. And just when she thought her calves could take no more, Kassandra shouted out the next command. "Kick Drills!"

The remixed music blared through the studio speakers. The fast beat keeping time with her pounding heart, or perhaps it was her heart matching the rhythm of the music. Nina dropped her jump rope and ran back to the punching bag. Landing high kick after high kick. Left. Right. Left. Right.

In the first class, she was the one who struggled the most. Her lack of muscles certainly slowed her down as she ached all over within minutes.

But Kassandra pushed her to find that motivation. "Nina, you joined this class because you wanted to hit something, now kick like you mean it!" Kassandra bellowed at Nina while standing close by. Correcting the angle of her kicks, the torque in her abs.

And Kassandra was right. Nina found herself face-to-face with her own weakness on that fateful journey across the multiverse. Sure, the other students probably had issues with their parents or a hate for their boss. But Nina was mad at herself. For being taken, for being beat, for her complacent weakness.

"Cross Body Punches!" Kassandra ordered a new command, bringing Nina back to the present moment. With each punch Nina visualized Parker, Evil Parker. In her mind she stopped him from ever sending her through to Universe Gamma. She stopped him from attacking Hank, who she thought about every day. In her mind, she was punching Parker. Beating him away from the console, pinning him down so he could be arrested. And every so often, she pictured landing a punch on Gus Blanity. The man who was in the middle of it all. The enabler who gave Evil Parker everything he needed to carry out his plan. Who attacked her and Femi and Marie. Who killed Hank.

She let her anger out and then Kassandra blew the final whistle. "Good work today class. Let's do our cool down stretches."

Nina appreciated this part, but she always wanted just a little more time on the bag. She felt that she had years of weakness to overcome with these weekly classes. After a month or so she started to notice more definition in her abs and arms. She started to just feel stronger in her everyday tasks, as she hauled the massive bags of kitty litter up to her apartment, as she climbed the stairs each day without feeling winded.

After the class finished their calisthenics, put the bags away in the back corner of the studio, and packed up their gear, Nina headed to the locker room to rinse off. She looked forward to her protein packed dinner, following the meal plan that she subscribed to when she started her gym membership. Piece by piece, Nina rebuilt her life after having it torn apart – again. She impressed herself by her newfound independence. She wasn't pining for Parker, her Parker. There were too many complicated emotions. She hadn't been happy towards the end, and had they just broken up they would have parted ways and been just fine by now anyway.

But she didn't want to think about what Evil Parker did to him, or to her for that matter. So, she didn't dwell on it. If anything, she filled so many of her hours to keep herself from thinking of Hank again. Those few moments in the gym shower when she was rinsing off her sweat, he would sneak in. Just as he would pop into her mind when she was walking to get somewhere, or waiting for her lunch to heat up in the microwave. He was omnipresent, so she needed her routine to keep the tempting thoughts away. *She could just put the machine back together and go be with him.* But no, she didn't know enough of the science, and besides, it was early June. No quantum jitters just yet.

She finished her shower and toweled off, pouring herself back into her work clothes, now hot and clingy to her skin. In the locker room mirror she combed out her wet hair. She had let it grow a little longer than usual. And she even added bangs a few months earlier, but she let them grow out enough so that she could sweep them to the side. Nina looked at herself, scrutinizing her face for just a moment too long. Because there was something else she was trying to push from her mind. Another piece of her that broke that day last August. Hank she had already lost, that heartache was an echo of the old one. Parker she was going to lose anyways. But, not getting to say goodbye to Feminina haunted her. With her new hairstyle, Nina could almost fool herself into thinking she could pass for her much tougher alter-ego. In the mirror behind her, she pretended that Femi was about to tap her on the shoulder. The two reflections playing off of each other into eternity.

Nina turned around quickly, but not quick enough. She only saw herself looking back at her own reflection in the other mirror. She shoved her comb into her gym bag and headed out into the warm summer evening.

As she walked home, she tried to think about all the things that needed to get done. Putting her workout clothes in the wash, making dinner, starting the small little tasks around the apartment that she had been putting off. Anything to keep her mind from dwelling on the temptation. She distracted herself so well that she didn't notice the couple arguing outside the corner market, throwing curses and obscenities in some foreign tongue at each other. She didn't notice the small terrier vigorously humping the light pole to the dismay and embarrassment of his owner. She didn't even flinch when a bucket of water was tossed out in front of her, nearly drenching her dry clothes. So, of course, she didn't notice the non-descript sedan that followed her home. It blended in too well with the world, it was too easily passed over, even for someone who was paying attention. Which Nina was not.

29

The old routines came back easily, as though they had never been broken. The deep grooves of these patterns were carved into their mental pathways. The late-night work sessions that stretched into early hours of the morning resumed. The all-consuming focus with which they both threw themselves into each problem. The special language of short-hand and half-sentences that made up their disconnected conversations. Femi and Marie were back at it.

They had reassembled as much of the machine as they dared to on the weekends, leaving key pieces out so that it was not functional and no one could walk through. Not yet.

"And you're sure you won't have a spare quantum drive until November?" Feminina asked for the umpteenth time.

"Yes, the one I recreated to present is the only one that exists right now. I have to have something to present," Marie gestured with her hands to indicate that they would have been empty otherwise. "Leaving the drive in Universe Beta was good and bad. I have this one," she held up a near replica of the one they had both used the previous year. "The company that licensed the technology won't have the first batch done for months. So, this is it."

Feminina inched her energy drink, wet with condensation, further away from the device. The fragility of it exacerbated by Marie's comments.

Feminina really wanted them to be equipped with multiple copies for what they were planning. Just in case. But there was only so much time left to do all the things that needed to be done. Marie was working on the automation for the Portal to be able to move along the track effortlessly while Feminina started to run the calculations on how she might be able to step through the Portal and travel within the same universe, but to a different time. They had agreed to table the idea of a pain-free supercybin. It was a nice-to-have item, but not a requirement. And they certainly didn't trust bringing in another member of the team, not after what happened last time.

And of course, their junk food filled work sessions were back in full-swing. Sonali had made such great inroads with Marie over the past year. Cooking her authentic Indian dishes with fresh ingredients, trying healthy alternatives like cauliflower crust pizza and sweet potato fries. Anything to get Marie to see that there was more out there to eat than slimy fast food and sugar and salt-loaded snacks. Marie really enjoyed Sonali's cooking, but it didn't take away her love of take-out and tasty treats. With Femi back in town, they were both carrying on like college students. Eating as though they would never gain a pound, slamming back caffeine like it was water, working on a nocturnal schedule.

It was a Friday night, Femi and Marie were making plans for what they would do in the lab that weekend to move their process forward. Sonali returned late from her weekly family dinner. Or, it was late for anyone with a normal sleep schedule, Femi and Marie were just getting started. Sonali wished that Marie could come with her, anything to steal back some time with her girlfriend. But her parents made it clear that Marie wasn't welcome. And Sonali knew that Marie definitely would not have been happy with their latest attempts to set her up with successful men. Marie knew she shouldn't feel personally singled out by their disdain. It seemed that Sonali's parents didn't approve of much in her life, their relationship being one of many items on a long list. Still, she wished she could be there to support her. But Marie also knew that Sonali loved her parents, in spite of their blatant disapproval. She didn't want to interfere with the time she got with them.

Besides, now that she had a long task-list to tackle with Femi, Marie appreciated having at least one night a week where she didn't have to feel like she was ignoring her girlfriend. She could so easily get lost in the data, the coding, the lines and lines of symbols that would lead her to the next big jump in functionality. But when Sonali walked in that night, Marie felt the familiar pull of that guilt. She wasn't getting as much quality time with Sonali and she had grown to really cherish that. Marie had missed the thrill of being engrossed in her work, but now she missed the life that she was building with Sonali.

Marie told herself, and Sonali, that this was all temporary. They had a deadline of early August to get all this work done. This detail pacified Sonali, and at times she seemed eager to help where she could, to perhaps help the pair reach their goal that much sooner. But Marie hadn't explained, couldn't explain, that it was a fixed date that she had no control over.

"How is the work going?" Sonali chirped as she brushed past the two women at the dining room table and into the kitchen. The pair had taken over this corner of the apartment, making it unrecognizable with all the papers and folders strewn about.

"Good, getting our to do list for the week narrowed down," Marie responded without looking up. Femi usually stayed quiet when Sonali was around. She seemed to tense up, fully aware of her position as the odd-woman-out, the unwanted third wheel.

"I brought home some leftovers if you all want to have some real food tonight instead of that junk you keep ordering," Sonali offered as she held up a large Tupperware. As she cracked the lid the delicious smell of fish and curry wafted over to the scientists. Femi perked up, smelling the aroma. Marie's mouth began to water.

"Yes, please!" Marie dropped her pen and paper and stood up to join Sonali in the kitchen, offering to scoop out the dish onto plates.

"That smells amazing, Sonali. What is it?" Femi asked. Marie braced for the awkward tension that always followed their brief interactions.

"It's called Machher Jhol, but growing up I used to call it Making Jewels so my mom calls it my diamond dinner." Sonali smiled as she recounted the memory.

"That's really sweet. Thanks for sharing it with us." Marie could tell that Femi was being genuine in her response, really trying to connect with Sonali. She appreciated this, because the animosity between the two was really starting to drain her.

"Of course," Sonali nodded as she heated up the plates.

Femi stood up from the table and silently slinked away to the bathroom.

"Thank you for bringing this back," Marie smiled as she eagerly awaited the ding of the microwave.

"Well, I know how much you love it when I make this dish and my mother makes it even better than I do," Sonali gave Marie a slight squeeze around the shoulders.

"And thank you for letting us continue to take over the kitchen. At least this way I'm already home once we're done working."

Sonali was silent for a moment as she poured herself a glass of water. "I'm glad you're working from here too, I still get to at least *see* you," she said to the sink, not facing Marie, sparing her the look of disappointment that was surely written on her face.

"I know, I promised to not be a work-junkie anymore. But we really are making a lot of great progress," Marie tried to explain, still desperately hoping she could keep it all, have it all. Have the relationship she desired with Sonali without compromising her career.

"It's not the work itself that bothers me," Sonali began, still avoiding eye contact with Marie. Which, of course, made her assume that her girlfriend was about to renew her age-old complaints about Feminina. Marie let out a deep sigh, which communicated as much to Sonali.

"And it's not Femi that I have the issue with," Sonali continued, finally looking up at Marie. "It's the hours. It's these marathon work sessions all through the night, the only time that I get with you."

"We've only got a few more months, I know it's a long time, but there is a hard deadline on this work." Marie moved closer to Sonali, reaching out to her. Sonali accepted her hand and gave it a squeeze.

"I can make it a little bit longer," she said with a sly smile.

"I promise I'll make it worth your while," Marie promised, her words loaded with heat.

"I just wish," Sonali started.

"Your wish is my command, darling," Marie whispered, she was now close enough to be able to hook a lock of hair behind Sonali's ear.

Sonali let out a heavy sigh. "I just wish, you two could have found a way to work with her in Belgium. Then you would be able to work earlier in the day and I wouldn't have to share you so much."

Marie paused for a moment. Wishing for things to be different, that was exactly what she and Feminina were working on. A way to create a new outcome, a chance at a do-over. The irony wasn't lost on her. "I do too, I wish things hadn't been so strained to begin with. But she can't go back now," Marie shrugged her shoulders, knowing that this was something she couldn't change. At least not yet.

"What do you mean she can't go back?" Sonali pulled her eyebrows together, confused by Marie's statement.

"She was only supposed to be there for a long weekend for a lecture. Her visa was approved for a short stay. She ended up staying until just before the one-hundred-and-sixty-day limit that Belgium allowed. There's no way she gets approved by the U.S. to travel there, or really any other country again, for a long time."

Sonali was silent as she considered the ramifications. "Did she know this when she came back?"

"I didn't want to ask, but I'm sure she knows. I mean, think about it, how bad would it look for the Vestal Kingdom if one of our top scientists, a young ambitious female who is the best in her field, expatriated?"

"Wow, that's so sad. Because she is still with the guy over there, right?" Sonali appeared concerned, troubled over Femi's predicament.

"Hank." Marie clarified. "I think so."

"Well, I hope he can come here then, I would be sick if I couldn't be in the same country as you," Sonali added. Her capacity for empathy was one of the traits that Marie loved about her the most.

"Yeah, I don't think he'll be coming here any time soon." Marie hoped that she didn't have to spell it out for Sonali. There was no way this guy was going to move across the world for Feminina. Even if he loved her as much as she loved Sonali. He was a man, and moving here would mean voluntarily signing up for a set of laws and customs that he had no experience with. He would end up branded by the end of his first week. Marie didn't want to bring up the current laws that men were subject to. Sonali's family was still reeling from Ayush's punishment the previous summer. The stigma, the shame, it was a lot for them all to handle. Sonali started working to lobby for a change in the laws, to allow for due process, but it was an uphill battle. In their society, men were assumed guilty. If they were being punished for harassing a woman, then they must have done it. Even if they didn't commit the exact crime they were accused of, they were likely asking for it. That was a tough mindset to overcome when it was so embedded in the cultural consciousness.

Feminina slipped back into her chair at the table, not making eye contact with either woman. Marie was sure she must have overheard their conversation. Sonali must have realized this as well, she straightened up and turned to avoid looking at Femi. The microwave buzzer sounded, giving Sonali something to do.

"What do you want to drink, Femi? Diet Coke or Red Bull?" Marie asked, her arm reaching for the refrigerator.

"Uh, Diet Coke is fine. Thank you," she said. The three of them all pretending that they were just fine with this arrangement. Sonali placed a hot plate and cutlery in front of Feminina, offering her a true smile. For the first time, it seemed that she started to see Femi differently. She wasn't just the person enabling Marie's workaholism, she was just as in need of an outlet, an escape, as Sonali. Just as much a victim of the system they lived in, even though they were all mostly benefiting from it.

Marie nodded as she witnessed this moment. The night had already seen significant progress made, and none of it related to quantum theory or space-time.

30

Universe Beta
June 11, 2019

Every time he hit "play" he was transported back to that exact moment. Not physically, although he had the means to do so. No, he promised himself that he wouldn't use the machine ever again. So, he settled for the mental journey he was able to take.

As the video played, he recalled the exact feel of the buttons on the camera as he adjusted for light and focus. He remembered that his palms were sweaty, the weight and significance of the moment made him nervous. He remembered the exact feel of the legal pad in his hands, the yellow lined paper thin and smooth, the cardboard backing supple and scratchy.

Dr. Norman Thurston must have re-watched this recording a thousand times. Maybe two thousand. What he thought would have been the first of many interviews with visitors from other realities, turned out to be the lone piece of evidence that it was all real. Well, that and the holes in the floor of the lab where the device used to be securely bolted to the ground.

In his more generous moments, Thurston wondered at the magic of recorded media. How it was a time machine that had existed for decades. *How had he failed to marvel at his own capacity to go back in time so easily through photos or video?*

But lately, he had grown morose with each viewing of the video interview. *He should have asked this question instead. He should have thought to send Nina back with a way to record and transmit to him. How could he have not realized that his own protégé would use the machine for such nefarious ends? Would he have ever stopped using the machine if it hadn't all spun out of control so quickly?*

As her interview played before him, Thurston pictured another version of himself in another office in some distant reality. That version of him was watching this interview, but instead of being reminded about the lost opportunities, they were carefully cataloging the responses to go into a database of countless interviews from other multidimensional travelers. He pictured this other version of him uncovering trends in medicine and science that could help to save lives, that could expand the cultural knowledge and appreciation for the precious life that existed in this reality. He bitterly envied this imaginary, yet probably very real, version of himself who got to live out their dream.

A knock on his office door pulled him out of the fog of his thoughts as Nina's recorded answers played on. He heard her answers so many different times he had practically memorized them, down to the exact 'um's and 'ah's, the pauses in the natural cadence of her speech. Thurston stopped the video and looked up towards his closed office door.

"Come in!"

His door opened and Thurston saw one of the professors from the English department standing there. The one who ran in and tried to stop Parker the same day the interview was filmed. He had never seen this man before that day, and yet he showed up at such a consequential moment and at such an inopportune time. Thurston later found out that he was an English professor at the University *and* Nina's ex-husband. While he remained curious about this man, Thurston knew to keep his distance. For all he knew this man had no idea that Thurston had rushed in to save the visitors from other universes. He had been knocked out cold when Thurston came bumbling into the fight, his own head ringing.

"Hi, Dr. Thurston. Is this a bad time? Am I interrupting anything?" The man timidly stepped into the office while Thurston wracked his brain for the name.

"Oh no," Thurston shook his head. He could remember exactly what this man looked like as he laid passed out on the floor of the lab the previous year. He had just sat next to him at a faculty dinner a few days earlier, surely a coincidence. But his mind was totally blanking on his name. *It was Jonowski, something. Or Jaworski?* "Come on in."

"Sorry, I just thought I heard another voice," the professor continued while he ran his hands through his curly hair.

Jankowski! That was it. "Nope, just reviewing some film. How can I help you, Dr. Jankowski?"

"Oh, uh," he seemed distracted in his response. "I just happened to be proctoring an exam down the hall, I thought I would stop by and see if you wanted to grab a coffee. You can tell me more about how my favorite authors are completely wrong about the science they use in their books." He laughed a bit; Thurston sensed a bit of a nervous tension. But he was exhausted and he knew that running down the same mental spiral around all his missed opportunities to explore the multiverse wasn't helping him.

"Sure," Thurston said with a shrug and locked his computer screen. He exited and began to immediately inquire about how the essay on H.G. Wells was received by the students from the arts school compared to those in the sciences.

Hank walked in step with Dr. Thurston, his carefully constructed plan of action now shot. Carol had rehearsed several different scenarios with him over the past week. She insisted that they were still in the "building trust" phase of their attempt to get Thurston to tell them about what happened that day. But Hank swore he just heard Nina's voice coming from Thurston's office. He would know that voice anywhere. Hank re-watched all their old videos so that her laugh would stay fresh in his mind. He'd listened to all of her old voicemails, careful to hit save after each message played. So, he knew without a doubt that the other voice he just heard coming from Thurston's office was Nina's.

What could this mean? What did he really know? Hank wanted to take a time out, to call Carol and strategize with her. But he didn't have a way to stop time, and they were already halfway to the café on campus that gave faculty a heavy discount. Hank realized that he was so trapped in his own thoughts that he hadn't responded to whatever Thurston just said. Hank resumed his small talk, this time asking if Thurston had ever read any Philip K. Dick. That got him going again, giving Hank a few more moments to try and compose himself.

Crap. He was blowing it. *Get it together man*, he told himself. A chill ran down his spine as the two men walked along. He had never been more sure that getting Thurston to talk was the key to finding Nina. But he also felt like he was dangerously close to spooking him. To inhibiting the one thing that would bring her back.

31

Universe Delta
October 15, 2008

Xander was head-down in his own notes, trying to riddle out the best way to navigate across the stars when he heard the familiar and swift footfalls of Lionel Rogers. After he came clean, he had been visited by his boss often, although not at regular intervals. Xander could always hear him coming, not just by his rushed gait, but because he could hear the murmur in the halls. "Hello, Mr. Rogers." "Good day, Mr. Rogers."

Dr. Marks looked up from his desk in time to see the man breeze into his office. Always well dressed, his charcoal gray suit was custom tailored to his svelte frame. Xander was sure that the man was so focused on his business success to overcome his height. At 5'2" he was sure that Lionel Rogers likely spent a lot of his childhood on the receiving end of some not so nice comments, but look at him now. Fit, rich, and a tycoon whose name was known around the world.

Rogers closed the door behind him, all of their meetings of late had been that way. Which wasn't necessarily unusual, except that the teams in the building tended to not have closed-door meetings. They were all about sharing information, learning, and collaboration. Xander knew that there was already quite a bit of speculation about the reason for Rogers frequent secretive visits. None of the rumored theories were even close to the truth.

"So, where are we?" Rogers asked as he took a seat in front of Xander's desk.

"I was able to get the exact date, time, and location for this Unknown Universe. Thank you for getting the energy clearance."

Rogers nodded. He had pulled strings with the mayor to get a second approval to shift power reserves to their building over the weekend to be able to handle the load of the quantum energy. "With each request it becomes easier and easier for her to say yes to adopting the quantum energy that we've developed. Some local officials are concerned that it is untested en masse, but I keep telling them that we can let our city be a follower or a leader."

Xander nodded, understanding what he was saying. There was a delicate political balance at play here, the need to get the quantum energy source adopted by the city would make running these regressions, and ultimately, powering the machine back on, that much simpler. But it would require a complete restructuring of the entire energy grid for the city. Rogers was working on getting permits to upgrade the five blocks surrounding the research building. He even offered to pay out of pocket.

Marks knew that this wasn't out of the goodness of his heart though. While Rogers' initial reaction was one of a compassionate father, one who understood the raw panic and terror that Xander was going through, the scientist knew that he wouldn't have been so generous if not for the potential business impact. Primarily, the negative public image of an experiment gone awry. Xander was quick to point out that the experiment had been a success. Everything that followed was the disaster. And while Rogers was committed to bringing Nina back, Xander knew that being able to use and license all of the components of their test: the power, the quantum computer, the Portal, would all equal massive dollar-signs. It was a win-win for Rogers to do all that he could to help.

"If we can guarantee that we can switch the quantum power back on again for August 8, it would make me feel more secure in our plan," Xander added, reminding Rogers of the very real deadline they were under.

"I'm doing everything I can, Xander. We'll get her back." Rogers spoke earnestly. His business-like manner stripped away for a moment, he was speaking to him not as a boss, but as a fellow-parent. But as quickly as the sentiment appeared, it vanished. Rogers was never one to sit still, to let a moment be, he had too much to do, too much to manage. Always flitting from one priority to the next. "How is Ramona settling in?"

"She's doing great, very efficient. Keeps to herself a bit, but she's new. I'm sure she'll start to make some friends around here." Xander offered his honest appraisal. Rogers had been acting on multiple fronts in order to find a way for Nina to come back home. When Xander explained that he would need a quantum drive to save any coordinates on, his boss started calling around. He needed the best computer science engineer with extensive research experience in quantum computing. At their first follow-up meeting, Rogers said that everyone he asked kept referring him to one scientist: Nina Marks. Xander smiled proudly, although both men were frustrated by the lack of progress. But a week or so later, a new name finally popped up on Rogers' radar: Ramona Hernandez.

"Good, I'm glad she was able to start so quickly." Rogers nodded approvingly. They had both been a little hesitant to hire someone so quickly without a full background check, but even with months to complete the task, the clock was ticking.

"And very convenient she was already living here in D.C." Xander added. "She got to work right away; I'm thinking she'll beat our estimated date for a prototype by at least a week."

"That's excellent news!" Rogers smiled for the first time since Xander broke the news to him. Then he leaned forward, "So if she can get this done ahead of schedule, could we boot up the machine earlier?"

Xander told himself that this was a question based on a concern for Nina's well-being, a desire to help her return that much sooner. "Potentially. We have to time our movements with the quantum jitters and we know those will start coming on August 8. Before that it is a total guess."

Rogers rubbed the shiny bright skin on his bald head, a habit Xander had observed many times now. "Right, right. I keep forgetting about that part." Rogers explained away his question.

It's the one element I can't forget, Xander thought. The utter agony of having to wait a full year to try to get his daughter back. And if they failed, having to wait again. "Yep, just the one day," Xander looked down at his hands, folded on top of his desk.

"But with time travel we can keep retrying as many times as we need that day," Rogers stated with a questioning tone.

Xander nodded. "Exactly." His boss' understanding of quantum theory was very rudimentary, but he had the right idea.

"And if we get it right the first time, then we just have all day to be able to run more experiments," Rogers added in. He smiled and stood up, leaning forward to give Xander a pat on the shoulder. "It will all work out. We're all working hard to get Nina back."

And just as quickly as he had swept into the office, he was gone, back down the hallway off to handle some other issue.

Xander sat at his desk in silence trying not to let his own frustrations get the best of him. *Focus on getting Nina back. Focus on getting Nina back.* But it was hard to do that when he was certain that as soon as he brought her home that he would be fired and that his invention would be kept in use, leaving their entire universe exposed and at risk.

One thing at a time, Xander reminded himself. *One thing at a time.* Or maybe, just maybe, he could do two things, in two places, at one time.

PART 6

"One must work with time and not against it."

– Ursula K. Le Guin

32

Universe Alpha
June 20, 2019

He mopped his brow with his exposed forearm. His long-sleeves were rolled-up because he was here to get hard work done. The soreness in his back, the numbness at the tips of his fingers from maneuvering the small gears and bolts, and the musk of his own sweat were all signs that he was doing something real.

It didn't really matter to Norman Thurston that his boss had strictly instructed him to leave the project alone. He would have rebuilt it anyway, although he had spent hours calling himself a coward for waiting until she was gone to a conference in New York.

At first, it felt wrong to continue the project with Parker missing. But it had been almost a year. Science couldn't stop because one man disappeared. Thurston missed his protégé, but he knew that there were other physicists waiting in the wings to earn a post at the University and to continue this field of study. So many dreamed of finding the way to broach the multiverse. Winchester didn't understand that. She remained too sentimental about Parker's disappearance. Or perhaps it was her own image that she was concerned about.

Thurston rolled his eyes as he considered her motivations. He spent his hours that week between classes working on moving the dismantled pieces of the device from storage back into the warehouse section of the lab. With the project "officially" closed down, he was easily able to hide his progress in plain sight. No one was coming around to check on what was happening in that area of the lab. He laid the track and bolted it to the ground, the holes already drilled from the previous year. He unpacked the boxes with the quantum computer components. All the processing power he could ever want, but in pieces they were just inanimate parts incapable of anything. All he had left to do was find the actual Portal frame.

After Thurston mopped the sweat off his forehead again where it continued to pool and spill across his face, he wiped his hands on his trousers. The grease from the wires was making it more difficult for him to finish putting the quantum computer together. But he was nearly done. He promised himself he would just work on it a little each day, but found himself getting lost in the rebuild. At first, Thurston reasoned that by doing this bit by bit he could hide what he was doing a little easier. But he didn't have any classes on Thursdays during the summer term so he had more time to continue getting it back together. And besides, Winchester would be back on Monday. He could finish the quantum computer and at least get back to some of the regressions he had been hoping to run before she arrived.

Just as he twisted the last wires back into place and secured a cap, he realized that the construction was done.

Astounded that he was able to finish in days what had originally taken him and Parker months to design and create, Thurston rounded the console and sat down in front of the computer. He pressed the power button and held his breathe. Would he be disappointed? Would he have to dismantle and then redo everything because of one missing chip or screw?

But, to his surprise, the monitors flickered to life. Thurston could hear the fans within the console begin to spin as the system loaded. He knew it would take a few moments before he could log in. Even with so much power, the computer still had to come to life. Thurston wanted to sit and wait for the exact second when he could log in, but he was too excited to sit still. He started to take the boxes that he had emptied and stack them together. He needed to work in an orderly environment and he didn't want any clutter to ruin the moment when he could type his first command into the computer in almost a year.

After he collapsed the boxes into one another, he headed for the large metal shelving on the far side of the lab. He could keep the boxes here and when he was inevitably forced to take it apart again, he could easily find them.

It was just as he tipped the boxes up onto the top shelf that something shiny caught his eye. Against the far wall, tucked between the shelving and the concrete was something big and metallic. Thurston hardly ever used any of the items on the shelves and certainly hadn't been to this side of the warehouse in over a year. He didn't have any reason to.

So, perhaps it shouldn't have surprised him that the one item he needed to complete the machine was right there all along. *Could it be a coincidence? A happenstance? That the moment he finished the track and the console, that the one missing piece would present itself to him?*

Thurston pulled at the frame and felt the weight of it tip into his arms. He knew that it would potentially damage the doorway, but he had no choice but to drag it out a bit further and shimmy it onto the floor.

Finally, on its side, Thurston saw the Portal before him. Even though he designed it with Parker and he knew the dimensions, the true scale of it didn't hit him until he saw it with his own eyes once again. It was sturdy, and therefore heavy. Thurston was already sweaty, what was another bit of hard labor to maneuver the doorframe back onto the track?

Thurston lunged down and braced the short side of the doorframe, readying himself to push it along its length. He noticed that the side closest to him already had scratches running up and down in a cross-hatching pattern. Whoever dismantled the device had slid it over here on its side as well. Thurston shook his head, frustrated that Winchester would allow someone to so carelessly handle such expensive equipment. (Even though he was about to do the same thing himself.)

With a huff, Thurston pushed and the frame inched closer to the track. It all came back together so easily. It was as though the machine wanted him to rebuild it, it wanted to be back on. Thurston accepted all these fortunate events as a sign that he was on the right path, that the machine was going to do his will. It never occurred to him that he was taking the exact actions that the machine, that the forces of the multiverse, wanted him to take. He maneuvered the edges onto the track and heard the frame click into place.

With the device constructed and the quantum computer booting, Thurston only had to wait now. Such a funny thing to have to do, to *wait* for a time machine to become functional. He glanced down at his watch.

7:08 pm.

Goodness, where had the time gone?!

As if on cue, his stomach grumbled. All of the day classes had been dismissed, all of the night seminars were in session.

Thurston glanced over at the screen and saw that the rebooting process was still in the early stages. He grabbed his blazer and hand-combed his hair.

He was already down the hall, thinking about his favorite order from the sandwich shop just off campus, when the glow of the Portal started to illuminate the lab, but he couldn't see it.

He was already out of the Sciences building as the roar of the machine filled the space, and a foot stepped firmly onto the slick concrete floor.

33

Marie nodded her head along to the music. Her wireless headphones were snug in her ears and fully charged for a long day of work. Her playlist was set with her favorite artists to keep her energized. It finally felt like life was back the way it should be. Not the way it had been, because it had been fractured before. She had been too much of a workaholic. She had taken Sonali for granted and it showed. She had relied too much on her best friend. But ever since Feminina returned, it seemed that all was right in the universe. She had a great relationship with the woman she loved, she had her best friend back, and they had spent months working on rebuilding their invention. After Sonali's comments, it hadn't been the tireless nights that they had committed in years prior. Instead, they worked reasonable hours and worked around the schedule that made the most sense for each of their relationships.

Except for this one day.

Sonali had been understanding about why they needed to be in the lab at exactly midnight. Marie assumed that Femi had communicated a similar reason to Hank. While both Marie and her best friend were in healthy, loving relationships, neither of them could tell the *whole* truth about what they were working on. It was still too dangerous. And, even between Marie and Feminina, they thought they were a little crazy. They had agreed to a story: they needed to be in the lab that early because they would need to pull a lot of power off the grid and this way it couldn't disrupt the daily usage for lights, air conditioning, and the like. The power was free, but the grid was still fallible. When Sonali had a few follow-up questions, Marie had jargoned her with scientific terms until she said, "oh okay, makes sense," and dropped it.

Marie didn't like that she lied to Sonali, she didn't want any dishonesty in their relationship. But she couldn't tell her that she and Femi were working on a Portal to another universe. Especially because Sonali's first question would have been about if it worked, at which point Marie would have had to explain all that had happened the previous year. And so on and so on. No, it was best to keep this one secret, *for now*, she assured herself.

She pushed these thoughts from her mind and refocused on the task at hand. The quantum computer was booted. *Check.* The Portal was advanced to the correct location on the track. *Check.* Outgoing and incoming vial of supercybin for Feminina to inject and carry with her. *Check.* The coordinates for Universe Gamma when Femi's dad was still alive were input for the exact day and time that the pair had agreed on. *Check.*

Feminina was about to head back in time to see her dad again. The pair knew they could travel to any other universe that they wanted. But this was their first experiment to travel back in time in the same reality. There were paradoxes that could prevent Femi from ever stepping foot through the Portal. They both knew that she might walk through and never cross back again. But Feminina said it was worth the risk to her. Worth the potential pain to save her dad from ever getting sick. And they would both learn a lot along the way. It had been a year since Femi had seen her dad in Universe Delta. With each passing day, Femi had become more and more convinced that this was the right move. Who was Marie to argue with those kinds of emotions? Ration and reason would never apply.

Marie was concerned that Femi might get stuck in the past, but her stubborn lab partner was set on this idea. She wanted to see if she could get her dad help before the cancer took hold. During that time, she would help them develop the quantum drive and map a trail so she could get back home. With any luck, Feminina would be back in the lab again about a minute or two after she left.

Marie reviewed her list one more time. But everything was all set. Now she just needed her lab partner to arrive. Marie looked at the time on the computer monitor. It was 11:59 pm. Marie rolled her eyes. This whole set-up was complete to help Feminina see her dad again and she was about to be late enough to miss the first quantum jitter of the day. Marie shook her head as the track on her playlist changed over. *Figures, that girl is going to be late to her own funeral.*

Marie stood back from the console and placed her hands on her hips. *Nothing to do now but wait.* She eyed the countdown timer running on the top left monitor. The first quantum jitter would open in under two minutes. Once that one passed, she would be able to see the countdown for the next one. Marie knew that even if Femi came running into the lab right that second there was no way she was going to make that first jitter.

Might as well pop open the first energy drink of the day, she shrugged and turned towards the lab table where she had a backpack full of snacks. Her head bobbed to the beat of the song that pumped into her ears. As she reached the table, she noticed a weird change in the room, the lighting seemed both darker and brighter. And the music in her ears was muffled, drowned out by some loud ambient noise that had just started in.

"What the-?" she asked aloud as she turned around and saw a figure stepping through the pearlescent quantum foam of the Portal.

It's funny, in life the small choices or coincidences that end up having major consequences. The train that you miss that crashed. The elevator that you just made it onto that happened to be the exact location where you bumped into your soulmate. Of all the random events that happen in all the universes, it really does seem that every once in a while, a person finds themselves in the right place at the right time.

Or for Feminina, she wasn't in the right place at the exact right time.

She and Marie planned to meet at around 11:30 pm on August 7, 2019. They had mapped the path back in time to 2009, back before her dad was diagnosed with cancer. They knew how to operate the machine, the console, and the quantum drive. And if something had to be fixed or they had to troubleshoot an issue, they had all day to be able to course-correct. But they seriously doubted that it would be necessary.

Feminina had slept most of the afternoon so that she would be well rested for her trip across The Plain. Her alarm clock went off promptly at 10:55 pm giving her just enough time to shower, dress, and grab a snack to go. She took the time to blow dry her long brown-black hair, but she wasn't overly concerned about her looks for this trip. No press conference would be waiting to greet her when she departed or when she returned.

As she headed down the stairs, she heard a boom in the distance. By the time she reached the door to exit onto the street she could hear the tapping of raindrops on the cement outside.

She planned to walk to the University. She didn't even want her hair wet from a shower. She most certainly didn't want to be soaked through in rain by the time she got to the lab. Not only would it be uncomfortable to wear wet jeans, but she would completely fry her phone. She also didn't know how much moisture would interfere with the Portal. When traveling the multiverse little things like this mattered. Damp hair, not a big deal, but she wasn't going to risk that. Hence, she took the time to dry it. Soaked through clothing, could cause a problem. She might end up in the wrong place, or the wrong time, or the added moisture could exacerbate the headache.

Femi marched back upstairs and grabbed her umbrella. She headed out into the rain; her perfectly planned schedule was now much delayed. She sidestepped puddles carefully, trying to avoid her shoes and socks getting soaked through.

After her careful tiptoeing and walking so that she was strategically likely to stay drier, she did not arrive at the lab until a little after midnight. *Well, I definitely missed the first jitter,* Feminina thought as she tried to open the door to the building while keeping the umbrella held over her head.

Once inside, she shook off the umbrella and rushed down the corridor.

"I'm so sorry Marie," she began to call out as she turned into the lab. At first glance she didn't see her lab partner anywhere.

"Marie!" Feminina called out. The light was on in the lab, so she knew for sure that Marie had to be there. She looked around again, but the wide-open room didn't leave many places that Marie could be without Femi noticing. Marie's handbag was slung over the desk chair at the console. *So, she has to be here somewhere,* Femi thought.

She tried back in the hallway, looking to see if Marie had perhaps ducked into her old office or the lavatory.

But Femi didn't see any trace of Marie.

She walked back into the lab slowly, her guard now up. As she stepped up to the console, she heard something crack under her shoe. A small puddle of orange liquid was on the floor. The remnants of one vial of supercybin, the glass and the liquid, were ruined under her heel.

Something was wrong. Femi could feel it. And every second that the Portal lay on its tracks, set-up and functional, left more opportunity for someone unwelcome to walk through.

Femi pulled up the logs on the console quickly. Her mind jumping to the worst conclusions.

And sure enough. She saw the exact moment when Marie's signature, the decay wave that uniquely identified her, switched from Universe Gamma (their home) to a different one. And it appeared she hadn't left alone. A mustard yellow line appeared next to Marie's.

Feminina began to feel bile rising up in her throat.

It was happening again. After a year of worry and then months of planning for every contingency, there was an unknown variable, some factor they didn't predict, that had interfered with their plans.

Femi needed to figure this out, and fast. But without her lab partner, who could possibly help her? And in time for her to catch the next jitter, which was only a few moments away?

34

**Universe Beta
June 17, 2019**

He had put it off long enough, but it was finally time.

His week had taken a negative turn quickly. He wasn't sure what was worse. Calling to make the damn appointment, waiting for the date and time to come, or the events that precipitated all of it.

Hank trudged along from the metro stop, begrudgingly taking each step. But he knew that this was his penance. This was the thing he had to do in order to get Carol to help him, to believe him.

After his distracted discussion with Dr. Thurston, Hank rushed home to call Carol and tell her everything about what he heard coming from the professor's office. Carol seemed interested in this information, but relayed her doubts. "How could you be sure it was Nina's voice if his door was closed? Maybe it was the radio or a podcast or something."

Her rational explanation made sense. She was using logic to find the most simple solution. But Hank knew that it was Nina's voice that he heard, just like he knew the sky was blue and that gravity just worked. "No, I would know her voice anywhere," Hank pressed on, remembering Nina's favorite line from an old movie. *I still look for your face in crowds.* She had loved to re-watch it over and over again, which struck him as funny since it had to do with baseball and Nina never actually liked the sport. But it had been a line she loved to repeat aloud at that exact moment in the film, and it was one of the first things she said to him after they reunited. The memory, the crisp sensory experience of her face, her hair, her voice, almost knocked the wind out of Hank.

"Okay, but, what could this mean? We already think that Thurston knows more than we do, so we've just confirmed our theory. We still don't know what it is that he knows just yet." Carol was absolutely right. Hank replayed his memory of this phone conversation as he rounded the corner and found himself in front of a gray office building, a half dozen names on the door with an alphabet soup of degrees and designations. He confirmed that the one he was looking for was there.

The foyer of the building was utilitarian and blank, just a hallway of elevators and one door at the far end leading to Harris Winslow, Chiropractor. Hank called for an elevator, his mental replay getting to the part where he really messed up.

"Well, clearly we need to move up our timeline, we need to find out what he knows and bring it to the detectives." His words had been more frenzied, it was like he was shouting into a phone tree, trying to get through to Carol.

"Maybe they already know what he knows," Carol quipped, ready to bring Hank back down. And then he snapped. He couldn't take her level-headed pragmatism anymore. He couldn't stand being told to wait and be patient. He had enough of it.

"Whose side are you on anyway, Carol?!" he bellowed through his phone. Her stammering didn't stop his verbal attack. "It's like you just want to drag out this whole process. Why? So, you can take Nina's job at work? So, you can feel important because you know as soon as she is back, you'll go back to being her less successful friend? What is it?"

Hank regretted the words as soon as they crossed his lips. If he could undo it, unsay them, he would. But you can't put vapor back in a bottle, you can't undo something, you can't go back in time. *If only he could.*

He heard Carol's breath hitch and then the line disconnected. Hank was mad at the world, the failure of the detectives to find Nina or Parker, his own inability to keep her safe, Thurston for having more information and not sharing. He was angry at the position he was in. And Carol happened to be on the wrong end when his gasket blew.

He tried to call her back, but she didn't answer. He texted apologies and never received a reply. For the first time since she had run over to his apartment to assert that Nina was alive, that she couldn't be dead, Hank felt utterly alone and hopeless. *Had he just alienated the only other person who was rooting for Nina to return?*

———

As hours passed with no response from Carol, Hank knew what he had to do. This outburst wasn't what should have prompted him, it should have been her intervention months earlier, it should have been his own newfound habit of nursing his woes with whiskey each night.

The elevator dropped him off on the third floor. Hank turned right and saw the name that he was looking for. Dr. Andrea Syvilak.

Guess it's time to get my head shrunk, he thought as he braced himself for what would happen once he walked through the door. As though just entering would put him in an emotionally vulnerable position. And perhaps it did. He already knew that what he said to Carol was wrong. He was aware that he wasn't coping well. But he didn't know how this psychiatrist could help him. Unless she knew exactly where Nina was.

Hank sheepishly went through the routine of checking in with reception, filling out forms, and waiting to hear his name called. And then it was time, the slender female doctor called him in. The room was exactly what he expected, but it was also not what he had pictured. Muted tones, degrees on the wall, soft pillows on a pair of chairs facing each other. But no couch, no incense burning or healing crystals. *Thank goodness for that*, Hank thought as he plopped down in one of the plush chairs.

"What brings you here today, Hank?" she started in, her voice crisp and professional. Clearly the opening line she began each new patient relationship with. She sat back with her notepad in hand and her legs crossed. The completely forgettable visage of a professional female, all neutrals and muffled features.

"I think I've lost my mind," was all that Hank could think to respond with.

The doctor let out a small laugh. "We all do from time to time. Where do you think you left it?"

Her small joke broke some of the tension that Hank was feeling. "Well, it's a long story," he thought as he ran his mind back to that horrible day, their last day with Anna.

"We've got time," the doctor prompted him, pointing to the clock on the wall.

And with that small opening, Hank just let it all fall out. How Anna died, how it ruined him and Nina in such different ways, how they stopped being "them," how he pushed her away and she didn't push back, how they lost each other, divorced, and reconciled. And then he got to those fateful few days. Nina agreeing to move back in, saying that her relationship with Parker had been over for a while, that she wanted to come back home to him. Her abrupt silence. Her erratic behavior that final day. The body in the basement. Her plea for help. The attack. The darkness. And the lack of progress in finding her.

The doctor listened intently, making a few notes as he went along. But the clock on the wall wasn't listening at all, it just kept moving along, each arm advancing in its metered and programmed fashion. Methodically marking the passage of time. Of another hour that separated Hank from Nina.

As he finished his tale, the doctor gave him a moment to add anything. "Thank you for sharing that with me, Hank. It sounds like you have been through a lot."

Hank raised his eye brows and nodded in agreement. "I just don't know how much more I can take."

The doctor closed her notebook and placed it on the side table by her chair. "Well Hank, I think we'll have a lot to cover next week as we start to figure out how we can help you manage this all. It is a lot for one person to carry. But I want us to have a clear goal. Have a clear point where you will feel like you are better, that you are able to handle all of this."

Hank conceded that was a good idea.

"So, what do you think the remedy will be? What will make you happy again? Make you feel like you aren't losing your mind," she used air quotes around his words as she repeated them back to him.

His initial thought was that he could be happy again once Parker was apprehended and Nina was back safe. But Carol's warning from February haunted him. Nina would be changed from this experience. He was changed from this. They would have to work so hard to find each other again. Hank wanted his life back. The life he and Nina built years earlier, the family they made with Anna. It might have sounded like a facetious answer, but it was the honest truth.

"I want my girls back," he murmured as their faces lingered in his mind, their giggles playing in his ears.

The doctor nodded as she made one final note and closed her journal.

35

Universe Gamma
August 8, 2019
12:10 am

The surest way to get going was to actually get going. Feminina's first thought was to travel back in time as planned. Her father, Xander Marks, was one of the smartest men she ever knew. With his help they could prevent this from ever happening. Together they could figure out where Marie was and get her back.

Only, it would take them time to develop what they needed, and there was no guarantee she would even arrive back in time in her own reality unharmed. Then Marie would really be out of luck. And *if* she saved her dad, *if* they created the machine and necessary elements on their own, she didn't even know if they could pinpoint where Marie had been taken. While going back in time could undo everything, if she didn't know who was behind this, it could all repeat again anyways.

She hated to admit it, but she would have to scrap her plans to go back in time until Marie was back. She understood the paradoxes at play and that she could reverse what had just happened by saving her dad, by fundamentally changing the trajectory of events. But Femi would be driving herself crazy for years worried about what would happen to Marie. And in the meantime, until she caught back up to this exact moment in time, their Portal could be open to more unwelcome guests.

No, she needed to go to after Marie. Some allies would be nice, but not necessary. *Although, I won't be able to do this alone.* Femi felt exposed without Marie. Operating a time machine was not easy to do alone, she would need help and she wasn't exactly known for her warm personality and charm. If she went looking for help, she would need to find it in a universe that had a quantum drive, supercybin, and an operational Portal.

Feminina tried to eliminate the other known multiverses on her list before she keyed in a search for the quantum drive signature.

Universe Delta might work, but her dad had been so emphatically against their sharing information. He was so upset about how the machine had been misused, he would ask her what they had been thinking when they decided to use it again. And then she would have to tell him his fate. A compelling reason, to be sure. And while she was willing to risk some ethical quagmires, she wasn't ready to see her dad look at her as though he was disappointed. She knew she couldn't handle that part.

Universe Beta had an operational machine, at least as of the previous year. But the people who knew how to operate it were dead. At least the Parker from that Universe was gone, pushed out into the void by her own hands a year earlier. And the other professor, Thurston, well he was in bad shape when Femi and Marie had left that reality. She couldn't count on him to be alive and willing to help her.

That left Universe Alpha. Home to her alter-ego, a functioning Portal, and presumably, a version of professor Thurston who was alive and well.

Three for three, works for me. Feminina pulled up the records that were saved on the quantum drive for Universe Alpha. If Femi couldn't convince Thurston, the third on her list, to help then perhaps Nina could, she was likable in a damsel-in-distress kind of way. Feminina had heard of women playing into that archetype in the 19th century. She assumed it was a cliché that was alive and well in Nina's barbaric and antiquated society. Even though she was only going there to save Marie, Femi's scientific curiosity was piqued. She had to admit that it would be interesting to experience another reality. All she had seen on Universes Beta and Delta were the labs where the Portal had been housed. She hadn't really ventured out into those worlds; she hadn't been able to experience all that was the same and all that was different.

And this time would be no different. She needed to help Marie first and foremost.

While she pulled up the logs, she started to question some of her reasoning. While Alpha had things that she needed, her mind flashed back to that caffeine and sugar fueled evening from one year ago. Nina had stumbled into their reality late in the day, putting Femi and Marie on a very tight deadline to solve for and power up the Portal to get her back.

While she didn't want to make Marie wait any longer than she needed to, what if they couldn't get everything together in one day? What if they needed a little more time?

Well, first I need to see if Alpha's Portal is even available. Feminina reminded herself of this as she pulled up the frequencies she needed on the main screen in front of her.

Nina, alive and well.

Thurston, alive and well.

Marie, the Marie from that Universe, alive and well.

Store of supercybin, present but not as heavy of a frequency as the one showing on Femi's home screen for Universe Gamma.

Quantum Drive, present but not particularly close to the Portal based on the proximity readings she could see. By the estimation provided it was in the same city at least, even though it wasn't in the same room.

Portal located at the University coordinates, operational.

Feminina clicked on the squiggly line that represented the Portal. She was relieved that it was functional, but also somewhat disappointed in Nina for not deconstructing it. *She's leaving herself exposed*, Femi thought as she shook her head. *Or trying to get back to Hank.*

Just thinking of him made Feminina wince. She was getting by with the video calls and letters to her Hank. But she missed him so much that it physically hurt. Every day that they were apart she felt that she was losing him, that they were drifting further, like two items floating on the vast open ocean.

Feminina shut down that line of thinking, just as she had done numerous times over the past months as she prepared to leave for a time jump. *No time for silly infatuations.* She knew that she was lying to herself, that what she felt for Hank was so much more, but if she admitted that to herself then she would have to question every decision since she booked her return flight to the United States. And now was certainly not the time to get emotional.

She refocused on the frequency in front of her. There had indeed been a large gap in the availability of the Portal. It had gone offline a year earlier on August 8, 2018. *That must have been Nina dismantling it.* And then the frequency resumed again on June 20, 2019.

Sentimental fool, Feminina thought as she shook her head.

But, Feminina did see the benefit to arriving on that day. That would give her six weeks to work with Nina and come up with a plan to find and rescue Marie. A much longer timeframe than they had to work with the previous year. *This could work.* Feminina plotted the course and watched as the Portal slid into place on the track. *Thank goodness we got that part updated.*

The next quantum jitter was about to open up in just a few moments. Feminina injected herself with a vile of supercybin and waited for the Portal to open. She clenched and unclenched her fists. Her neck rolled from one side to the next, a few crackling pops sounded. She swung her arms back and forth, loosening them as though she was about to enter a boxing ring.

When the sheen of quantum foam filled in the edges of the Portal and the roar of the machine began to fill the room, Feminina steadied herself with a deep breath.

I sure hope this works, she thought as she stepped through the film and across The Plain.

PART 7

"The most common way people give up their power is by thinking they don't have any."

– Alice Waler

36

Growing up, her dad had always told Nina how lucky she was. She had the longest birthday of the year. Her special day was longer than everyone else's. Or, at least most years it was.

Born on June 20, 1988, Nina was always a fan of the summer solstice. It never bothered her that school was already out for summer when her day rolled around. No special class cupcakes or parties for her. But she got to spend the whole day doing what she wanted. Reading or playing or tagging along behind her father on his errands, which she found endlessly fascinating.

Each year, Nina would spring out of bed with renewed hope and energy for the upcoming year. She would wake to bright sunlight streaming in, the sun already "up" and proclaiming that it was her day. She would exhaust herself until late in the evening when the sun finally relented, retreating across the sky.

Even in the year that she lost Hank, she still had her dad. Once he was gone too, she still did her best to make the most of the extra daylight on her birthday. To make it a cheerful day. She wasn't really successful with that until she met Parker.

And this year, she had no one. Carol and Sonali had planned a brunch for the three of them that upcoming Sunday. Nina was excited to see them again and tell them all about her first weeks at the University.

But today, on her *actual* birthday, she was alone. She had been trying to think of something she could do that would make the day feel more meaningful. Yes, she was thirty-one now, but she still delighted in the childishness of birthdays. She didn't want to just go home and sit on her couch with her cat. Although, she knew her night would eventually end up that way.

Nina found her feet following the familiar path to the Einstein Memorial. It had become her secret sanctuary. She knew it was mostly for the tourists and the school kids. Well, it was really for good ole Albert, but he wasn't here to enjoy it. She wondered if his spirit could somehow sense that someone who had traveled across the folds of spacetime was visiting his place of remembrance. Would his oversized statue become animate and beckon her to share what she had seen, what he had missed experiencing because he didn't live long enough to discover it for himself?

In spite of the good weather and the late sunset on a Thursday night, the monument was fairly quiet. Only a few idle groups loitering quietly nearby. With the after-work rush, all the pedestrians around her were eager to move along. Get home and rest. Get to dinner and eat. Get out of work clothes and go have some fun. Everyone was going somewhere purposefully, except Nina.

She loitered in front of the massive bronze statue, humming the happy birthday song to herself. As she finished the tune she stepped up to the exact spot where she could hear her own voice. Nina closed her eyes and savored the silence, as though she was about to make a wish for herself. In her mind, Nina envisioned her alter-ego celebrating in Universe Gamma. Would she be toiling away in her lab or out to drinks with Marie? Nina pictured Feminina having a blast, living their best life. If Nina couldn't have a fun-filled day, then at least one of them should.

With her wish in mind, Nina opened her mouth.

"Happy Birthday, Nina," she spoke out loud. And sure enough the sound reverberated back to her.

"Happy Birthday, Nina," she heard. "Now open your eyes."

Confused, Nina did open her eyes. But not because she had heard her own voice command it. Rather she was utterly confused. She hadn't spoken those words, yet they were echoed back to her. There was only one possible explanation for this.

Nina spun around, looking for the answer. And sure enough, standing before her was the *other* birthday girl. Feminina.

37

Universe Alpha

"Surprise!"

Nina heard her own voice say the word, but the lips of the woman across from her had moved to form the sound. The coy smile on her own face was enough to make Nina want to jump up and down. Feminina looked exactly the same. Pin-straight hair with long bangs. She had the same facial features and silhouette that Nina saw in the mirror every morning.

Nina could hear the air expel from Femi's lungs as she wrapped her arms around the woman. She acted on instinct. She was so glad to see her alter-ego. Nina had been so terribly lonely for most of the last year, she hadn't realized that what she wanted was a chance to see Feminina again until she was standing in front of her.

"How are you here right now?" Nina wondered aloud as she finally released Feminina who had disengaged from the hug several seconds earlier.

"Well, I thought you understood the mechanics of it all last year, but I'm happy to explain," Feminina retorted with an air of sarcasm.

"No, no. It's not the multi-dimensional travel that I'm confused about. I just can't believe that you're really here!" Nina smiled as she took in the moment. "Although, the only Portal in this reality has been dismantled. Unless you arrived before I took it apart and then laid in waiting for a year-" Nina's mind started to run through the temporal scenarios.

"Oh, the Portal in the University lab is *definitely* operational," Feminina cocked her head and gestured to her own body for emphasis.

Nina began to wordlessly direct the two of them to take a seat on the edge of the large granite steps of the memorial. She shook her head in disbelief. "That's not possible, I took it apart last year, right when I got back."

Feminina furrowed her brow as she considered this. "You dismantled it? Piece by piece? And packed the parts away in boxes and put those in storage?"

Nina felt like she was being scolded. "No," she shook her head. "I took the Portal off the track. I left an anonymous note for Dean Winchester in Beta and in Alpha saying that the research needed to be shut down and that Thurston should go back to teaching."

Feminina silently assessed what Nina relayed, her blinking eyes the only sign of movement on her face.

"And you expected that to work?" Femi finally retorted.

"Yes!" Nina answered before elaborating. "Thurston in Beta was going to dismantle it anyways, but on the off chance that Evil Parker came back, I wanted there to be some kind of note expressing how important it was to Marie. And I work at the University now and this Universe's Thurston is teaching intro physics and the machine is completely gone."

"Well, I hate to break it to you, but I just walked through the Portal in the University lab." Feminina's sharp reply dripped with annoyance.

"What?!" Nina couldn't believe it. *Who put it back together? And why now?*

"Yep," Feminina nodded her head.

"That can't be. What if the Portal in Beta is open too? Anyone could walk through the Portal here any moment. We have to go back and take it apart!" Nina stood up and started to march off in the direction of the University.

"Not so fast," Feminina tugged at her arm to pull her back. "It's a good thing it was open, I need your help."

Nina listened patiently as her alter-ego relayed the series of events that unfolded in Universe Gamma. Feminina and Marie dismantling their Portal only to set it back up so Femi could try to go back in time to save their dad. Marie missing, potentially taken, that morning. Only it was six weeks in the future. Only it had happened two hours earlier for Femi.

Feminina finally finished by recounting what she saw after she stepped through the Portal. The University lab that looked near-identical to her own.

"I figured I would walk through and see you standing there, but no one was around. I strolled right out of the lab with no issue. And then I was outside and on campus and I had no idea where to even start looking for you. So, I started walking. I used to go to the Albert Einstein Center all the time when I was a kid, so I started walking that way. And then I saw you standing here by this statue."

Nina couldn't believe it. Any of it. And then something clicked. It must have been Thurston who reconstructed the Portal. *Why today?* The thought popped across her mind just as quickly as the answer. *Dean Winchester is out of town. What a slick bastard.*

"Yeah, I've been coming here a lot lately," Nina nodded. It was the one thing she could respond to, so much of the other information Femi had just provided her needed to process in her mind.

"I guess we have some of the same habits," Feminina smiled, this gesture seemed to be an apology for her earlier snarky remarks.

"I guess so," Nina agreed. After a deep breath she jumped into action. "Okay, I have a million questions for you and I'm sure there is a lot we need to catch up on. Let's head back to my place and we can order in a birthday dinner."

The air didn't seem any different here. The city streets looked similar enough. But there was something distinctly different about this reality, this version of her life. Feminina couldn't quite place it. Sometimes in life she thought that one city looked like another looked like another. Downtown New York looked like Chicago and could be easily mistaken for London or some other world city. But having been to several U.S. cities in her childhood, and visiting a couple of European cities with Hank, she realized that they were each distinct in an indescribable way. It wasn't just the architecture or language on the printed signs. It was something more ephemeral.

That same feeling of otherness struck Femi as she walked in step with her alter-ego.

Her momentary frustration at Nina's naïve attempt to take apart her Portal had washed away. It wasn't truly her responsibility, or not one that she had asked for. And Femi and Marie hadn't exactly given her line-by-line instructions on how to take it apart before they had been separated. She was curious about how Nina had managed to get a job at the University. It seemed that her overly sentimental and emotionally minded alter-ego wasn't all doe-eyes and romantic notions. She had to be pretty smart, and noble, to try to guard her entire reality against interlopers from other universes.

Feminina was about to open her mouth to ask Nina what they would get for dinner when a loud whistle called out.

"I could entertain a pair of twins all night long," a gruff voice called out to them. And she knew this person was referencing them because to the outside person, that is exactly what they looked like. Identical twins. Feminina spun and saw that a construction crew was exiting a worksite for the day. They had their hard hats under their arms and grease on their brows.

Nina must not have noticed that Femi had stopped for another half-second. But a half-second was all it took. Femi turned and marched towards the man who had cat-called them, jumped the barricade, and kept walking straight for him.

She could hear him joke with his buddies, "well, one is better than none."

In a swift motion, Femi kicked his legs out from under him and grabbed the nail gun on the work bench to her right. She pressed it squarely against his shoulder. His colleagues, stunned, looked on in silence.

"What did you say?" Feminina hissed. Nina ran up from behind, screaming for her to stop.

The man mumbled something. His skin was tanned from dirt and sun exposure. His eyes darted back and forth, as if expecting someone to come and help him.

Feminina ordered him to repeat his words.

"I'm sorry, I'm sorry. Okay?" She could hear the fear in his voice and it pleased her.

"I don't think I came all the way over here just because you said 'I'm sorry' as I passed by with my friend." Feminina hadn't ever had to respond in this manner, she had only ever heard about the revolutionaries who came before her. The brave women of her world who had championed women's superiority and paved the way for her and others.

The man below her squirmed. Femi shifted the nail gun ever so slightly and fired a nail into the dirt just above his shoulder. He let out a yelp and a stream of wetness appeared on his pants.

"Femi!" Nina pleaded with her. It was just then that Feminina realized that Nina had been calling after her almost the whole time. Something about hearing her own voice pulled her out of this violent trance.

She stood up and brushed past the other men on the crew, all dumbstruck by what had just happened. Too scared to stop her, lest them find themselves on the ground with urine-soaked work pants too.

Feminina popped back over the barricade and continued down the street as though nothing had happened. Nina rushed to catch up to her. "You can't do that here!" Nina lectured her alter-ego as they continue to walk, her tone furious.

"And why not?" Feminina snapped.

"You can't assault people because they say something mean or rude to you," Nina tried to explain.

"Because?" Feminina prodded like a toddler with too many questions.

"Because?! Just because someone is an asshole, doesn't mean you can physically hurt them!" Nina was shouting as they walked.

Feminina stopped as Nina caught up to her. The two of them stood face-to-face. "First of all, I didn't hurt his person, only his pride. Second, don't tell me that you can't hurt people because we're all equal and supposed to play nicely. He does not see us as his equal, or he never would have said such a thing. That man has no respect for us and likely no respect for any woman. He may not have physically harmed us, but I would bet he has acted against a woman at some point in his life. Call it karmic retribution."

Nina opened her mouth to try to counter her alter-ego's arguments.

"No, I've lived this, remember?" Feminina pressed on. "Men will treat women this way until they *learn* that we are the superior gender. You have to show them your power or else they will continue to act this way." Feminina started walking again, not waiting for Nina's response.

"Oh, and does cutting out their eyes help them *learn* in your reality?" Nina hissed as they walked in-step again.

"Yes, it does." Feminina said plainly. "Now what are we going to eat for dinner. I'm starving and this headache really isn't helping."

38

Universe Alpha

Laden down with pizza, breadsticks, wings, drinks, and several pints of ice cream, the Femininas climbed the stairs up to the apartment. Nina fumbled with her keys as she tried to keep the wings and ice cream from tumbling onto the ground.

Once inside, Feminina easily navigated to the kitchen and set the hot boxes of pizza on the counter. Nina reached over and placed her items down on the breakfast bar before turning her attention back to the door. She set the deadbolt and chain and grabbed a metal bar and placed it just under the knob to lock it in place.

"Well, now I feel secure," Femi said in a sarcastic tone as she observed Nina's ritual.

"I've been a little," Nina paused, considering her next words, not wanting to appear weak to this formidable version of herself. "On edge." She picked the right words.

Feminina nodded her head. "Yeah, me too." The visitor crossed her arms, clearly uncomfortable with this admission. Nina was relieved to know that she wasn't the only one. She assumed that Femi's unease stemmed from the same root as her own: Evil Parker, Gus, the existential terror of knowing the fate of the multiverse was your responsibility. Feminina crossed back out of the kitchen and moved towards the living room area. Nina took her cue and entered the small galley kitchen to set out the plates and utensils, playing the role of dutiful host to herself.

First, she brought out a pair of water bottles and set them on the coffee table. Bonnie had already jumped up on the armrest of the couch, clearly confused and assessing if this new person in her territory was okay to go near. Feminina didn't seem to notice the cat glaring at her, instead her attention shifted to the books with sticky notes popping out of them left piled in the center of the table. Her hands hovered just above them, as though she was considering a touch.

"Doing some light reading?" Feminina asked flatly.

"Uh yeah, just to-," Nina stammered, stumbled to find words. She was already heading back into the kitchen. She was never good at lying and had no poker face. But this was the literal definition of not being able to lie to herself.

Feminina called out. "You're trying to find a way back?" The books were all about quantum theory, the more accessible ones written by a few big-name celebrity scientists.

Nina quipped back as she placed the ice cream in her freezer. "Why would I do that? I'm working a dead-end adjunct professor job with a bunch of kids who hate having to listen to me just so I can watch over the Portal to make sure no one else uses it." Her dismissive tone was clearly an act.

Feminina moved silently off the couch and was standing back at the entrance to the cramped kitchen, leaning on the edge of the refrigerator. "No one, but you!" Feminina retorted and crossed her arms.

Nina glanced down quickly, a reflex. A way to manage the feeling of being caught. "You don't understand, Femi," Nina's voice was on the edge of breaking.

"Don't understand what?" Femi fired back. If anything, she understood exactly what Nina had lost, and she certainly knew more about the mechanics of how the device worked.

"He's my soulmate," Nina looked her in the eyes as she said this. She knew her alter ego probably thought it was silly and ridiculous, but Nina was a romantic. "You don't know him," she started and then she caught an echo of her last reaction on Feminina's face.

Guilt. Caught in a lie of omission.

"Wait, you met Hank?" Nina's expression changed in the span of time that it took light to travel across the cramped apartment.

"I didn't know if I should tell you. I hadn't planned on finding him. But when we got back last year, Marie and I had a bit of a falling out. I wanted to use the machine to try and save dad. She wanted it off, but still wanted to use the data to publish research. I thought I wasn't going to ever be able to try to save dad. So, I thought, if I couldn't have one of the men I loved, then I wanted the other." She paused, as if waiting for Nina to react. "I flew to Belgium and met him. I don't know what I expected, I guess I thought I could prove your soulmate theory wrong. But you were right," Feminina smiled and then looked down at her feet, as though ashamed. Nina was still processing, unsure how to respond.

"Ugh!" Femi clapped her hand against her forehead. "I feel like I'm telling my best friend that I'm dating their ex-boyfriend. Which is weird since my actual best friend doesn't date men."

Nina laughed at her joke. "I'm-" she began. And then she felt it, truly. "I'm happy that at least one of us gets to be with him." After all the heartbreak, knowing that she had lost Hank in her reality, that he had lost her in Universe Beta, it was nice to know they could be together somewhere in the multiverse.

Feminina offered a weak smile in return, she didn't want to mention that they would likely never be reunited. Nina resumed her busy movements. Paper plates were set on the counter as the women dug into their birthday feast.

"So, we'll celebrate and have a good birthday, but then we should probably get to work figuring out how we can find Marie." Feminina started in with several slices of pepperoni pizza and a few hot wings.

"Okay, that sounds good," Nina replied as she loaded up her plate with extra breadsticks. "Oh, I have your quantum drive by the way," she added before leaving the kitchen to set her plate on the coffee table.

"Sweet! That is definitely going to be very useful," Femi said with a mouth full of cheese and sauce. "We could probably try to plug it in from your computer here and see what we can do with it. I'm not sure how it would interact with a regular computer."

Nina laughed out loud a bit. "Yeah, it will fry the laptop."

Feminina gave her a quizzical look, opting to let her face ask the next obvious question as she chewed her food.

"I tried already. Lost two laptops in a month." Nina admitted sheepishly.

Feminina finally swallowed her large bite and took a swing of water. "Note taken. So, we'll have to find a way to use the quantum computer that your Thurston set up when he turned the machine back on today."

Nina nodded in agreement. That was going to be tricky, the Dr. Thurston in her reality was not necessarily a friendly person. In fact, he was kind of a jerk. Nothing like the fatherly figure she encountered in Universe Beta.

"That will be the first item on our list of problems to solve," Nina replied. Feminina nodded as she continued to dig into her food, her fingers saturated in sauce as she pulled away at the chicken wing in her hand.

"Oh! Napkins!" Nina remembered and sprung up from the couch. Her mind was starting to think of the next items they would need to add to the list as well. Figuring out who took Marie and where. *Would this person come after them as well?* But she had to remind herself that they needed to handle this one thing at a time. Nina carefully opened the cabinet next to her, trying to avoid getting pizza grease on the door. She grabbed one napkin first to clean her own fingers and then reached for a stack to bring out to Feminina.

That was when she spotted the bright red bag, still unopened. Sure, they had more than enough food to last them all weekend, but Nina remembered her visit to Universe Gamma and her innocent little question about the location of her favorite snack in a convenient store. She grabbed the bag and headed back out to join Feminina.

"More food?" Feminina asked, incredulous. "I mean, I can eat, but we still have dessert," she reminded her alter-ego.

"Trust me," Nina said as she popped open the bag. "It'll change your life." She smiled, knowing this might violate some law of multiverse travel. But surely enjoying a foreign snack, and one so delicious, was one of the perks of such an invention. Nina couldn't imagine life without Doritos and all their many flavors. She tipped the open bag, inviting Feminina to grab one.

After wiping the chicken wing sauce from her fingers, Femi tentatively reached in and grabbed one crisp triangle. She popped it into her mouth.

Nina watched as her eyes grew wide. "Happy birthday," she chirped as Feminina enjoyed the chip.

"Oh my gosh! What is this?!" her alter-ego asked as she grabbed the bag and placed a handful of chips on her plate.

39

She knew it was the right thing to be there for him, but she still had a feeling that she should stay away. His temper was too erratic, his last comments too cruel. But somewhere in the back of her mind the words of her grandmother reminded her that she needed to do for others what she would want for herself. If Carol lost the love of her life, she wouldn't want to spend their birthday alone. And Hank had assured her that he finally started going to see the psychiatrist that she recommended.

Still doubting if this wasn't a disaster in the making, Carol knocked on the apartment door. In the past year this had become a familiar place to her. She knew the exact spot on the couch where she would sag a little too much, a very comfortable position but horrible for her back. She knew that she had to jiggle the handle on the freezer sometimes when grabbing ice for a glass of cola. She knew that the upstairs neighbors enjoyed salsa music on Thursday evenings and it reverberated through the floor boards and down into Hank's apartment. She could already hear the beat from out in the hallway.

In the time between that initial knock and when Hank opened the door, Carol considered walking away, but she heard the lock sliding and then she was face-to-face with him. He didn't look bleary-eyed from crying or alcohol. If anything, he appeared to be much more put together than she had seen him in a while. His hair clean and pulled back behind his ears, his clothes weren't wrinkled.

"Thanks for coming over," he breathed, apparently relieved to see her.

Carol nodded and followed him inside. They hadn't spoken since his tirade the other week. Once she set down her purse and sat on the couch, he offered her a drink. Not the usual water or cola, but some of Nina's favorite wine.

"We should celebrate because we know she is still out there and we will find her." Hank said to himself, or perhaps to Carol, as he brought the glasses out. Carol accepted one and placed it on the coffee table while Hank took a sip.

"Yes, we'll find her," Carol finally spoke. She didn't know what she would say. She thought of telling him off, but that anger only lasted for a moment. Now she was just disappointed. Not with Hank, but with herself. For thinking that he might apologize. For wasting her time helping someone who was so unhinged they couldn't even say thank you for all of the help she provided. And, worst of all, for the daydreams she started to have of her and Hank. *Together.*

He must have noticed her reluctance, her silence. "Carol," he started, waiting for her to meet his eye line. "I feel like such an asshole."

To her surprise, as well as Hank's, Carol did something uncharacteristic. She didn't make apologies for him. Instead, she agreed. "You should."

Hank sat down, accepting her words. "I've been so focused on finding her, I just feel like I can't sit still. Each second that passes, I feel like I'm a failure all over again."

Carol thought of responding, reminding him that he needed to work through these emotions with a professional. He needed help. But he must have read her mind.

"I'm meeting with that doctor you recommended. There's a lot to go over, so I'll be there again every week for a while. But I want to be a better version of me. For myself. For Nina. For my friends." He added the last as he stared into Carol's eyes. She felt a jolt run through her. That was probably going to be as close as she would get to an actual apology, and she was willing to accept it. Because Hank was looking directly at her. His words had stung, but she had to admit to herself that she had imagined what life would be like if Nina was never found. If she and Hank kept working together and then finally their conversations changed from the investigation to just everyday life, and then... Who knew? But neither of them could admit this out loud, could say it, or speak it. And she didn't even know if a thought like that would have even crossed his mind. He was so focused on Nina; she was the only one for him. Even if he did ever look at her that way, she would always be the second choice. But that didn't stop her heart from pounding, her cheeks from blanching.

Finally, Hank broke his gaze and stood. "I hope we can still work together to help find her. Two heads are better than one."

Carol nodded. "Of course, I'll help," she gave him a half-smile.

Hank nodded, standing awkwardly. He seemed unsure of what to do or say next. Carol, as always, was ready to help him along.

"Well, what do we need to unpack tonight? Any progress with Thurston?" She finally picked up her glass and took a sip of the crisp white wine. It was a little sweet for her taste, but this was Nina's day, so she didn't mind.

"Yes, actually. Lots to tell you there. But first, let's eat. I made Nina's favorite dish and I figured I owed you a real meal after all that takeout."

Carol hoped her face wasn't betraying her. That the look on her face didn't reveal what she was feeling inside. *Remember that Nina is your best friend!* "Sounds great," she cooed and followed him over to the dining area of the apartment.

40

Universe Alpha
July 5, 2019

Nick was never one to sit and watch the clock. He had a job that required odd hours, so he rarely found himself without work to do. He didn't count down to five o'clock so that he could make a dash for the door. But today, he had already put in thirteen hours. Every time he glanced down at the clock on his computer, time seemed to just jump ahead. He might have suspected some kind of temporal anomaly, but they had alarms for that. No, it was just a normal busy workday. Nick was exhausted by 8:45 pm when he finally went to log out of his console. He already started to imagine the soft feel of his sheets, the hum of his window AC unit blowing on him, when he received a message. Just a second or two later and he would have already started the shut-down process. Just another moment or so and he would have already been out the door, ordering takeout that he could scarf down before crashing into bed.

But, he couldn't unsee the message. "New information on Parker Lovett case, pop over. – Mona"

Their internal chat system was efficient, but Nick wanted to curse it. He had been going blind staring at the same footage over and over again, looking for some kind of clue. And now he had to investigate this new file, the allegations made by Gus Blanity. Both had to do with the University in some way, all circumstantial links but nothing solid. So instead of focusing on Lovett, Nick had been distracted, trying to chase down information on this Blanity guy. The promise of a lead on the whereabouts of Parker

Lovett was a welcome surprise. Maybe he could finally resolve this one and put it in the archives.

Nick finished shutting down his computer and headed further back into the office, away from the exit. He would see what Mona had for him and then he was definitely leaving. He made this promise to himself, hoping he wouldn't have to break it.

As he sauntered over to Mona's workstation, Nick rubbed his eyes. She was visible in the far corner where she sat with the other analysts, most of whom had already left for the day as well. The white glow of the computer monitors gave her skin an eerie pallor, making her usually tan complexion look like a cool mocha.

"You spend too much time staring at that screen, Mona," Nick called out as he approached.

She looked up and raised an eyebrow at him. "And you don't?" They always had an easy back-and-forth as they spoke with each other, exchanging quips and barbs between their work conversations.

"What have you got for me? You are making me late for a very exciting evening," Nick asked as he plopped down on a rolling chair at the console next to hers, scooting closer.

"Oh yeah, what does she look like?" Mona retorted as she moved some windows on her double-screen set up to display exactly what she had found.

"Dark blue, freshly laundered with not one, but two, memory foam pillows." Nick said with a mock excitement as he yawned.

"Sounds fun," Mona closed off that thread before diving into the elements on her screens. "So, we know that Parker Lovett has been missing since August 7, 2018. Or at least that was the last time anyone reported seeing him, and we can verify that with the security camera feeds from the University." Mona pointed to the items on her left monitor, the ones closest to Nick.

"What are those frequencies?" Nick asked, ignoring what she had just said and looking over at the right side of her set-up.

"You know, I put together this information and have a way that I plan to present it, and you just cut to the chase every time." Mona turned her head and waited for Nick to meet her eyes. Even though she had a significantly lower pay-grade within the joint-agency, both Archie and

Nick knew that they would be up a creek without a paddle if not for Mona. They respected her and she was able to snap back at them because of it.

"Time is of the essence here," he quipped back, his pun falling flat. "Okay," Nick nodded. "Sorry."

"Thank you," Mona continued as she minimized the screen with the fuzzy screenshot of Parker entering the University with a large item. "So, we all started looking for him on footage the night of August 7 and then early morning of August 8."

Nick nodded; this was all a very familiar recap for him. "But all we found that morning was a female exiting the building-"

"Who we currently believe to be Nina Marks, but without much concrete evidence. Yes." Mona picked back up, not pausing to let Nick linger on that theory. "But I started to wonder about the energy incident from two weeks earlier."

"We poured over that footage when the alert first came in. You spent two full weeks studying every camera angle on the Sciences building." Nick reminded Mona.

"Yes, we looked at the footage, but none of the other metrics that were recorded. We saw the energy surge, but we didn't see anyone leave the building for a bit and when someone did emerge it was Parker. Which wasn't unusual since he left around quitting time." As Mona explained this, she minimized the next window and moved the charts Nick had initially pointed to over from her right to left computer monitor.

Nick sat up at attention. "Why didn't we look at this before?" His tone had a bite of accusation.

"Oh, I don't know, we had another major energy surge and a missing person to track down. There are dozens of cameras and after looking at a thousand hours of footage the earlier surge didn't seem consequential. And then you know, we got busy. Do you want me to continue?" She was on the defensive. To be fair, they had both missed this potential information. It was highly uncharacteristic of Mona to miss any details, but Nick knew that Archie had her running down information on his mysterious person-of-interest in the triple homicide from four years earlier.

Nick acquiesced and Mona pressed on. "So, a couple of weeks ago I pulled the data back up and looked at the frequencies that were recorded prior to and after the energy surge. We get them for everything, so it was tough to pull them out, but I was able to isolate Parker's signature." She pointed to one of the squiggling lines on the screen.

Nick nodded, looking at where Mona was pointing.

"Do you see that?" she asked.

"Oh, I'm allowed to ask questions now?" Nick retorted. He squinted to see a bit clearer. He noticed that the line appeared slightly darker, bolder, during the reported energy surge.

Mona elucidated on what was on the screen. "I looked closer at that first energy burst we observed last summer and spotted a thicker dot at this point," indicating on the screen. At first, I thought the power surge just amplified the frequencies we could see near the machine at the University. Then I realized it was actually a different frequency, but only imperceptibly."

Nick looked at the line before and after the spike. It did look slightly different, but if there was any pattern at all it wasn't discernable to him.

"Translate please."

"There was a second Parker Lovett in our Universe."

Nick nearly jumped out of his chair. This was literally what his job was supposed to prevent. "Why didn't we get an alert on this sooner?!"

"It's a quantum computer. It's fast but we're talking about all signatures across the multiverse. It takes a while. Besides, no one had run that specific query, we were so focused on pulling the video clips." Mona waited for Nick to ask another question.

"So, if there was another Parker in our universe, there should be two signatures, not just one." Nick stated as his mind worked through the implications of this discovery.

Mona nodded. "You're right, there should be. But we don't have any." Mona paused before continuing. "My theory is that our Parker, the one from this Universe went missing on July 25, not August 7."

Nick started to think about all that he had learned so far about Parker Lovett. He had a great working relationship with his mentor, but they had argued shortly before he went missing. His girlfriend said he had been acting different, kinder right before he went missing, she had surmised it was guilt for all the extra time at work. "Holy shit," Nick whispered as it all clicked into place. "We had a person from another Universe here for at least two weeks, but now they are missing too."

Mona looked over at him with a look of worry in her eyes. "We haven't had this before, at least not that I can find. I could set the quantum computer to search for this new frequency now or possible other anomalies, but with Jump Day approaching everyone is pulling as much as they can from the system. Even the most powerful computer in the world has limitations."

Nick looked at the frequencies again. "Okay, so we assume that neither version of Parker is in this reality. All we have to do is find our Parker and bring him back to restore continuity."

Mona began to move her mouse again, "One step ahead of you. I isolated a frequency here. I believe this is where our visitor came from and where they went back to."

"So, we know where Parker is?" Nick sounded relieved.

"Not exactly, but we have a lead for the first time in almost a year," Mona corrected him.

"Well, it's a start." Nick sighed, concerned about what else they could be missing. "Good work on this, Mona," he added, knowing that he never would have thought to look at the data from this angle.

"Mmmmhhmmm." Mona crossed her arms and nodded. Nick continued to stare at the screen, struck dumb by this evidence. "Looks like you'll need to add your name to the schedule for next month. You're going on a little trip."

As Mona said the words, dread and excitement poured into Nick's system. He was finally going to cross the threshold and travel across the multiverse.

41

Universe Delta
July 29, 2009

The day was drawing closer. While the rest of the team was pleased with their progress, Xander wasn't so sure. He had this gnawing feeling that something was missing. Rogers had cleared the use of the quantum energy again for the entire day of the August 8. Jiro, Katsumi, and Hajime were all prepared to monitor and record every detail. Ramona had built two functional quantum drives, one of which they had already used to save the coordinates for the Unknown Universe. Thankfully, Ramona didn't ask too many questions. She seemed content to get the work done and took pride in it, but she wasn't prying.

Still, even with every element in place, Xander felt like there was something he wasn't thinking of. Some fatal flaw that would derail the entire rescue mission.

Hajime continued to assure him that the plan would be successful. "Only another week or so until Nina is back." The optimism of his team buoyed him as the hours stacked up.

Xander tried to stay focused, visualize a positive outcome. He was working in the lab with Ramona as they ran diagnostics on the Portal device. She had only been told that it was an experimental travel set-up. Which was technically true, he just left out the part about reaching other realities.

"Looks like the machine is functioning properly, sir," Ramona called out from behind the console as Xander stared out at the city. The lights of the buildings and memorials twinkled before him. Xander turned from the wall of windows, acknowledging her words.

"Good," he nodded as he slowly approached the console. He felt a deep tightening in his lungs and reached for a tissue in his pocket. His movements were rushed, jerky, as he tried to forestall the coughs. He covered his mouth just in time as the painful heaving began.

On top of everything else, he couldn't afford to get sick.

"That doesn't sound good, have you been to a doctor?" Ramona asked, concern in her voice.

Xander knew that she was right, but he didn't have the time to worry about his own health right now. "I'll make an appointment for next week, after our trial," he wheezed out as his chest relaxed. Her worry was endearing. Surely if Nina was here, she would have already just booked the appointment and sent him on his way. It wasn't lost on him that Ramona was near her age. He had thought many times that they would make great friends, when they finally got to meet.

Ramona looked on, observing him carefully. "You know, you have a team to help you out. You can't do it all on your own. Let me take over some of what needs to get done so you can make an appointment."

As Xander pocketed his tissue, Ramona's words sank in. *A team.*

That was just it. That was what was missing from the plan. He had a full team in his reality helping him out. Not just the core team that knew about the project, but Rogers and an entire staff that kept the building operational, the power on. But once he stepped into this Unknown Universe, he wouldn't have that. And while Nina was there, he couldn't count on her being able to help them get back. *What if she was injured or incapacitated?* As the gears in his mind began to turn, he remembered the three travelers who had visited the prior year. Two of his daughter's alter-egos and their companion, Marie.

"Yes, of course," Xander breathed.

At this Ramona perked up, "Yes? Okay, I'll get my laptop so we can look up a good pulmonologist and start a list of what you need me to assist with." She shuffled off before he could correct her, before he could clarify that his words were unrelated to her offer. It was the first time he had seen her so eager to please.

After she left the lab, Xander began to move quickly. He sat down at the console and checked the coordinates once more. The prior year they had sent all three visitors back to Universe Beta. This reality had a functioning machine, supercybin, a quantum computer, and scientists who could all help him. Not that he didn't have all of this right here, he had a team and all the resources he needed at his fingertips. But *out there*, in the unknown, he would have to work the full problem of finding Nina and keeping the multiverse safe without any help based on their current plan. He was just following after Nina. But, with a little help, perhaps he could get Nina back and keep Rogers from monetizing the Portal. Maybe, just maybe, he could save everyone.

His new plan started to form and for the first time in almost a year as he let himself think, "This could work."

42

June slipped right into July without Nina noticing. Feminina seemed content to work all hours of the day and night trying to figure out a plan for her to find and rescue Marie. Even after only a couple of weeks, Nina was getting used to having Femi around.

Femi crashed on the couch after her late evening work sessions. Bonnie originally seemed dubious of this stranger, but within two nights she was curled up next to her. When Nina left for work, Femi would wake-up to shower and sleep a bit more soundly on the bed before getting up to tack down the right plan again.

The tiny table that sat adjacent to the cramped kitchen became the command center for the entire operation. How to get into the Sciences building without costing Nina her job? What if the machine was taken back down again? How to access enough supercybin to get Femi to wherever Marie was and then take her back home to Universe Gamma? Their list of questions and contingencies had only grown since Femi arrived. The list of solutions was still thin.

Nina arrived home from work to find Femi splayed out on the couch. She was staring at a cable news program as she shoveled bright orange triangles of cheesy goodness into her mouth.

"You know if you eat enough of those, you are going to turn orange," Nina said as she closed the door behind her and dropped her bag to the ground. She needed to review the assignments her class had turned in, but her usual evening routine had been preempted by Femi's arrival.

"Wouldn't be the worst thing ever," Femi replied as she licked her fingers. Bonnie sniffed at the plastic bag, tipping her paw in tentatively.

Nina plopped down next to Femi and stuck her hand in for a snack. "What, how are these almost gone?" She asked without thinking, because obviously she knew how.

"Sorry," Femi offered with a coy smile. "I just can't believe these don't exist in my Universe. It's so unfair!"

"You have universal healthcare and free electricity," Nina quipped back.

"I guess that makes us even," Femi joked with her. Nina snacked on a few chips as Femi resumed watching the news. When her brain couldn't focus on the myriad problems involved in bringing Marie home, Femi was trying to absorb as much as she could about life in Universe Alpha. Nina often found herself having to explain the most mundane elements of their society, things she took for granted.

"Ugh!" Feminina shouted as the commercial break ended and the news program resumed. "Your President is objectifying women on TV! Have you seen this?!" She pointed to the man with whisp thin blonde hair and an excess of self-tanner.

"Yeah, it's actually not the worst thing he's said," Nina said as she licked the cheese dust from her fingers and stood up from the couch. She remembered how upset she had been when that man had been elected in spite of his recorded statements against women, minorities, his own party. But it had become something else she'd grown inured to over time. And with the weight of the multiverse resting on her shoulders, she didn't have the energy to worry about politics anymore.

Nina was nearly to the kitchenette when she heard a knock at her door. She spun quickly and locked eyes with Feminina. They had identical looks of shock on their face, eyes wide and lips drawn into a tight thin line. Nina scrunched her eyebrows, as if to ask Femi if she was expecting anyone. Femi gave an emphatic shake of her head.

In their weeks together they hadn't actually created a plan of action for this specific situation. But the benefit of being the same person is that they did think a lot alike. Without any verbal or non-verbal cues, Nina crossed to the front door as Femi tip-toed into the bedroom. Nina looked back to see that the door to the bedroom had been closed before she dared to look through the viewfinder.

It was that Agent Noriega again. Nina rolled her eyes. *This guy was like a dog with a bone.* And while he wasn't completely off about suspecting Nina of having something to do with Parker's disappearance, she knew she couldn't explain that he had actually been killed by his evil alter-ego. So, she put up with the continued questioning. But perhaps it was time to start acting like an innocent person and get indignant with his repeated intrusions.

Nina huffed and placed her hand on her hip as she opened the door. "Agent Noriega," she identified him without any cheer.

"Hello Ms. Marks, how are you doing?" His chipper tone and wide smile looked phony to Nina.

"Well, I just got home from work and now I have a federal agent at my door, how do you think I'm doing?" Nina smirked and then let her cheeks fall quickly.

"Ah, sorry to bother you, but I thought it was better to try you here than at work. You didn't seem to like that last time." His hands were folded behind his back, as though he was waiting for Nina to respond. She didn't give him anything. "May I come in?" he finally asked.

"Do you have any updates on Parker's disappearance?" Nina diverted again.

"Potentially, I have a few questions to ask you, if you don't mind." Nick was better at this than Nina had expected.

She stood aside as he strolled into the apartment. Nina closed the door and tried to anticipate what more he could possibly ask her. She crossed her arms and waited for him to fire away with his questions.

Nick looked around the apartment, scanning it. For what, Nina had no idea. But she started to feel nervous that some evidence of Femi might be left out. Thankfully, her alter-ego had organized her papers and notes on the kitchen table into neat manilla folders earlier that day so her plans and schematics weren't sprawled out for Agent Noriega's wandering eyes to catch.

Finally, Nick turned to face Nina with a school-boy smile on his face. *Was he waiting for her to offer some water?* She was not about to give in. "So, what do you want to know?" Nina was annoyed at this point, what was his game?

Nick reached into his jacket pocket and pulled out his miniature steno notepad and pen. "You haven't heard anything from Parker in the past week or so? Have you?" He clicked his pen as he finished the question.

"No," Nina shook her head. "Why, has he been found? Has he contacted you?" She would be genuinely shocked to hear from her Parker. But that hopeful thought was quickly chased away by the possibility that Evil Parker, or another version of Parker, had come to this reality as well.

"No, ma'am." He didn't look up as he responded to Nina. "So, he hasn't stopped by, knocked on the door, let himself in?" Agent Noriega's eyebrow popped up with this question.

"No, nothing like that. But you must think he is in the area then if you think he potentially contacted me?" Nina felt her pulse start to race. She and Femi had discussed the possibility of more people coming through the Portal while it was still up and operational at the University. But Nina's optimistic mind had first thought of other potential visitors who would come in peace.

"I'm just trying to make sense of the new information we've received," Nick tried to pacify her, but the raw panic was building.

"What new information?" She blasted her inquires at him fast and furious. Nick Noriega may have stopped by to question her, but she had flipped the table without planning to.

"I can't tell you that, Ms. Marks," Nick offered as he finally looked back up at her from his notes. His exasperation seemed to disappear as he took in the look on her face.

"When we spoke last summer, you mentioned that Parker had been acting a little strange right before his disappearance. Can you tell me more about that?"

Nina uncrossed her arms. At these final tender memories, she felt her defenses fall a bit. These were her last good memories with Parker, but she always had to remind herself that it was Evil Parker, not the man she had known and loved. "His behavior wasn't strange. He just started to be a bit more affectionate, caring. I thought he was maybe feeling guilty for all his extra work hours. Trying to make more of an effort in our relationship."

Agent Noriega nodded, taking in her words. "But those kinds of acts, weren't normal from Parker. He wasn't usually the affectionate type."

"No, he was a scientist through and through. Romance wasn't logical, so he didn't see the point. But I thought he was trying to rekindle something." Nina's words were laced with a final sadness, one that she did feel for Parker. But she also felt a deep regret. That she didn't realize something was amiss sooner, that she had so easily been duped by his doppelgänger. Remembering herself and the role she needed to play in that moment, she made a move to cover her face. "I just don't know why he would walk away; something must have happened to him."

"I promise, I'm still on the case and I'm working every possible lead to try to find Dr. Lovett." He seemed to think that this was the reassurance she needed.

"Okay, well, please keep me informed," she repeated the words she had given to him so often.

"Yes, ma'am," he said and started towards the door again. Nina found it odd that he had only asked a couple of questions before retreating, but perhaps her own dogged queries had scared him off. Or assured him of her innocence.

The snarky comments that Nina had thought of saying when he first arrived evaporated. Her stern warnings of harassment or demanding an advance phone call were nowhere near her tongue. "Have a good evening, Ms. Marks. If you do hear from Parker, please contact me immediately." He nodded at her and then slipped back through the door, letting himself out.

Nina stood still, in shock from the large potential just unveiled to her in the past few moments. She could hear Nick Noriega pounce down the stairs through the paper-thin walls of the apartment building. As his steps diminished, out of hearing range, she heard the door to the bedroom behind her click and open.

Nina sensed Femi walking up behind her. She knew that she should turn and talk through this information with her alter-ego, but fear was freezing her blood, her joints, her body. Visions of every nightmare from the past eleven months began to flash in her mind. If Evil Parker was back, she would never be safe.

"Nina?" she heard her own voice whisper as a gentle hand pressed down on her shoulder.

"Mm," was all she could muster in response.

"I won't let him touch you," Feminina cooed.

How did she know? How could she possibly sense the depths of Nina's fears? And then it dawned on Nina that Femi had been prey to the same nightmares as well. Or, maybe not the same exact ones, but some version thereof. Nina had relived the fear of being kidnapped, finding her own dead body suffocated beneath plastic, being pushed out into the multiverse without any help. She had been kicked and hit and used as a punching bag by someone she loved. Or at least, someone who looked exactly like the man she loved. It was a lot to process and her nightmares let her know that she wasn't anywhere close to working through the trauma. But for the first time, Nina stopped to consider the impact on her alter-ego. Feminina had been attacked by Gus as the three of them tried to leave Universe Gamma. She was with Nina in Universe Beta when the pair of malignant Parkers tried to fight back. And, she now knew, that it had been Femi who had pushed them both out into the void. She knew that the chances of their survival were slim to none. Femi had that guilt on her conscience as well.

Nina reached up and squeezed the hand that lay on her shoulder. It was comforting to know that she wasn't alone with this burden anymore. It was nice to think that she might be able to provide some strength for someone else who knew what she was grappling with.

"He didn't say that Parker was back, he just asked if he had reached out." Nina was ready to address the information streaming through her brain.

"But if this detective thinks that Parker might have reached out to you, then he must have some evidence of Parker out and about. Facial recognition on a security camera, transactions on his online accounts, something." Feminina rationalized.

"Yeah, or maybe he got some weird tip." Nina shrugged, trying to think of the least menacing explanation. "This guy is probably thinking he is looking for a body instead of a missing person by now." Nina tried to pull from a lifetime of poorly written crime dramas to inform her assumptions.

"Okay, that may be the case. But *we* know that there is a Portal standing open just a few blocks from here. Parker, any of them, could have walked through after I did." There was an air of impatience in her tone, as though Feminina couldn't believe she would have to explain that to Nina.

"Well, *I* know that, but then why hasn't that version of Parker popped up yet?" Nina shook her head, there was something that just wasn't fitting.

Feminina was exasperated. "Look, we'll just have to be on alert."

Nina nodded in agreement. Then she rushed to the door and flipped the deadbolt, locked the chain, and added the security bar to the knob. She had relaxed on her routine ever since Feminina arrived. But no more.

"Alright," Nina said with a nod. "Let's get to work," she gestured at the stack of orderly folders on the kitchen table. Nina knew that they had a lot to go through by August 8, she understood the timeline they were under. But Nick's visit had reminded her of just how dire the consequences could be if they failed. *Looks like those papers will go ungraded another night,* Nina thought as she glanced down at her messenger bag.

Feminina popped open a can of cola and passed one to Nina who had grabbed the Doritos from the couch. Once seated, Feminina divvied out the folders based on their areas of expertise. Feminina focused on the ones labeled "QuantComp", "Supercybin", and "Drive." Nina looked at her pile: "Campus Security", "Winchester", and one aptly designated "The Thurston Problem." Nina let out a brief sigh and returned to Dr. Norman Thurston, the unknown variable in the house of cards the two Femininae needed to construct. Although, she was tempted to start a new one with Agent Nick Noriega's name on it as well.

Nick slid into the driver-side of the car and pulled his phone out. It had been vibrating ever since the radiation alarm was triggered, not soon after he stepped into Nina Marks' apartment.

"So, how did it go?" Archie asked with feigned interest. He was still convinced that she was no good, but he didn't want to insult Nick with his little middle school crush on the prime suspect in their investigation. At least, Archie considered her a prime suspect

"Well, there is more quantum radiation coming out of that apartment than there ever should be." Nick passed his unlocked phone to Archie while he rushed to put on his seat belt.

Archie's eyes bulged at the readings, not that Nick saw his reaction.

"So, we know she has definitely been involved with the jump we monitored last week from the University."

"Maybe, maybe not," Nick equivocated.

"Um, hello? How else do you think she has this level of radiation in her place?" Archie waved the phone at Nick, who was now looking over at his partner.

"Maybe Parker Lovett finally returned from his trip across the multiverse," Nick offered as a solution.

"You think he was there?" Archie was stunned that Nick hadn't returned with the rogue scientist in custody.

"When I asked if she had heard from him, her reaction seemed genuinely surprised. And then she kept asking me questions about whether he had been seen in town, was he in contact with me? She seemed genuinely shocked at the idea."

Archie wanted to point out that Nick was clearly biased in this case, but he let his partner continue. "So, either to her, Parker really is missing and the idea that he is back is a shock because he has been gone for so long, which in my mind rules out the potential that she killed him."

"Or?" Archie prompted.

"Or she should be teaching in the drama department, not business statistics." Nick muttered. It was the first time Archie heard him express any doubt about Nina Marks' story out loud.

"What else?" Archie asked. He wasn't trying to distract his partner from a potential heartbreak or disillusionment. Archie wanted answers and he knew that with a fresh mind Nick would recall more.

"There was definitely someone else there and my guess is that whoever that person was is the one spiking these readings." Nick said as he turned the key in the ignition and checked his blind spots.

"What makes you think that?" Archie inquired.

"You live alone, right?" Nick asked.

"Yeah, but?" Archie didn't get the connection.

"Ever shut your bedroom door when it's just you at home?" Nick inquired.

"No," Archie shook his head. "That's kind of-"

"Weird," Nick finished the sentence for him. "Really weird." He pulled out of the parking space and drove back to headquarters so that they could both revisit the mounting pile of oddities that seemed to reveal themselves every time they interacted with Nina Marks.

PART ∞

"A gender line… helps to keep women not on a pedestal, but in a cage."

– Ruth Bader Ginsburg

43

Universe Alpha
August 2, 2019

Feminina allowed herself a midday break from planning and panicking to do a little anthropological research. She was still worried sick about Marie, she thought about how upset she would be if she couldn't save her. Then she would think of what she would say to Sonali. *No, this plan would work.* But when her doubts were louder than her optimism, she decided to silence them by exiting the apartment and going on an observation stroll.

Nina hadn't exactly suggested that Femi not be seen in public. They both understood the potential issues that could occur if they were seen in two different places at the same time, but honestly, not many people were really looking. Besides, Feminina needed to move around. She missed her daily strolls with Hank in Ghent. She had been so devoted to the project when she arrived home, that she hadn't resumed the habit. Femi needed to stretch her legs. She brought along Nina's journal so she could add her own thoughts to it.

Yes, of course she went snooping through Nina's apartment. She had uncovered all of the items of interest within the first few days of being there. Again, something she didn't tell Nina about. Femi was just curious and Nina didn't have any spooky skeletons in her closet. Nina did, however, have a shoebox full of her multiverse souvenirs. Femi read through the entries in the journal she found. She relived Nina's experience of the previous summer through her own words.

In the name of science, and posterity, and reminding herself that this was real, Femi decided to add her own words, a second chapter, a part two.

After her first outings Feminina balked at the sexualized advertisements, the litter, the obvious segregation of neighborhoods. She realized that this Universe was so unlike hers in so many ways. But also, just as imperfect. For so long Femi had lived believing that her country was the best, her way of life was the only way of life. As a woman, she didn't want to live anywhere else in the world. Why would she? Until she met Hank. And saw what life was like elsewhere. More carefree, less rigid, less fair to women, but somehow more equal. As she strolled and made her way to a small café off campus, Femi thought about whether it was the reality that was flawed or just the country. Or maybe it was all people who were flawed, who felt the need to act as though their gender, or race, or opinion, was the only one that mattered. As though other experiences weren't valid.

She added these thoughts in the blank pages before her, the only difference in the structure of her penmanship and Nina's a slight lean to her "f"s and "t"s. Lost in these musings, letting the ice in her coffee continue to melt and water down her drink, Feminina was in her own little reality. So, she was caught completely off-guard when a voice broke through her concentration.

"Nina?" the male voice sounded both concerned and annoyed. Not used to responding to that name, Femi finally realized they were talking to her. Turning, she saw a man. Tall, dark, and handsome was a phrase she had picked up from this reality, and it certainly fit. But the whites of his eyes covered his irises, adding a bit of mystery to his otherwise attractive face.

She blinked once or twice, trying to determine how to respond. Femi decided to do her best impression of Nina.

"Oh hello! So sorry, I was off in my own little world," she bubbled. "Care to join me?" That slipped out a little too quickly. She wanted to channel Nina's general positive attitude, not get herself in a bind since she had no clue who this person was.

"Uh sure," the man responded, clearly confused by her response. *Maybe I need to tone down my Nina-ness*, Femi thought to herself.

"So, how are you doing?" Femi asked as she took a sip of her drink. She casually closed the journal and slipped it into her messenger bag that was hanging behind her chair. The man across from her changed his expression, as though he had just figured something out. He took a sip from his coffee as well, assessing Femi with his milky white eyes.

"I'm great, Nina." He started in. Something in his tone worried Femi. *Was this some ex-boyfriend or something? Was Femi messing things up for Nina?* "How are you doing? Don't you have a class right now?"

Femi, usually so sharp and quick on her feet, used to being the smartest person in any conversation, suddenly found herself a little dumb. She had no context for how to respond. She started to get an uneasy feeling, an eerie otherness.

"Oh well, sometimes I can play hooky, you know." Femi shrugged off the comment and stood, acting as though she had planned to leave just then.

"What's the rush?" the man asked, his white eyes following her movements. It was in that moment that Femi recalled the ancient myths she learned in school, of oracles and seers. And she felt very seen, very exposed. As though this stranger who somehow knew Nina was looking into her person. Into the dark memories of condemning the Parkers to the void. Into the moment of terror when she realized Marie was missing. Into all that she had done and might do.

"Just realized I forgot to feed my cat," she made up an excuse as she slung her bag over her shoulder. Trying to regain her composure she looked over at this stranger to offer a good-bye. He just stared straight back, unblinking.

"Say, you're not from around here, are you?" he asked. What an odd thing to ask Nina, if he really knew her. But how could he know? How could anyone know? Femi's mind was spinning as she dashed back to Nina's apartment. For the first time in Universe Alpha, she was scared. She couldn't flip the locks fast enough. Her heart was pounding in her chest.

Maybe he was a figment, a phantom. Some sign from the multiverse that she had been tampering too much with space-time, some manifestation of quantum energy spun into human matter to warn her. Or perhaps one too many shots of supercybin had permanently damaged her brain.

She waited anxiously until Nina got home, unable to focus, unable to sit still, until she could tell her alter-ego everything she had just experienced.

44

Universe Alpha
August 7, 2019

Time is a funny thing. It's a social construct really. As humans we all needed a way to count the days, to make plans to meet, to connect. Time allows us to do that. But without the word "minute," or "hour," or "year," or even "decade" what are these things that pass us by? Each revolution of the Earth on its axis, each elliptical journey around the Sun: it's just progress. It's just waiting.

And that is what he had been doing for eleven years, down to the day.

Gus Blanity sat on the edge of the cot that had served as his bed since he had been tried and sentenced back in early 2009. The justice system in this Universe was significantly slower and more lenient than he had experienced in his own home reality. He just had to sit in this room. No hot irons. No surgical procedures. No public humiliation. He might have been content to stay in this little box forever, but his anger and resentment were like grains of sand. They slowly wore away at his patience, his ability to hold his thoughts in. These grains were really bits of disdain, of anger at what had been taken from him, and they eroded his ability to cope, to keep calm.

And then one day, all of them had started to blur into each other after years of staring at the same blank walls, someone showed up and changed his outlook.

At first, he flinched at the sight of them. He recognized them immediately, but they looked so different. They looked harder, meaner, scrappier.

He didn't believe what they were saying. He had spent years in this reality trying to explain what happened to him. How he had ended up here, how he had been wronged. But his mental state was called into question, and once that happened, it seemed near impossible to get anyone to believe him. But then this person showed up and started telling him things that he already knew, promising him revenge, escape. He started to question his own sanity. But he felt their touch on his back, he heard their footsteps in the hall, he could smell the stale remnants of lunch on their breath when they got a little too close.

This was real.

But he kept a small kernel of doubt in his mind. Would they come through? He would know shortly. If this was all an elaborate and very realistic hallucination then he would still be sitting on that tiny bunk when the sun came up. But if they were real, if they had promised things that were in fact possible, then-

He heard the lock to his cell rattle. He couldn't see anyone through the porthole in the door, but then again, he never saw them before they entered on their daily rounds. Too short.

The door swung open and he saw their silhouette in the hallway. The fluorescents were all out inside the building, but the floodlights outside were still on and the illumination seeped through into his room.

"It's time," he heard them whisper.

Unsure if this was real or not, Gus hesitated. He had clawed back his sanity over the years. He had accepted that he would never leave this facility and, in that realization, he had found a kind of calm. He was beyond exhilarated at the idea of leaving, of going home. But if he got his hopes up and this turned out to be a figment of his imagination, he might lose it.

It couldn't have been more than a second or two. They were impatient and he would hear it from them if they were kept waiting. He stood up and shuffled to the edge of his room, his prison cell. And then, his foot crossed the threshold. One foot in the hallway, one foot in the cell. It was like standing across a state-line, he was in two places at once. In his past and in his future.

Gus moved his second foot across and looked directly at them, he gave a silent nod. The plan was real. Everything they had told him about this evening was going to happen.

They turned down the hallway, their steps so light and silent that they seemed to move like a ghost. Gus followed. He hazarded a glance behind him to make sure no one else was looking.

If he had known back when he arrived in this reality that all he had to do was wait for eleven years before he was able to go back, maybe he would have weathered his sentence a bit better. But it didn't matter now.

He was out, and he had a score to settle.

45

It was time to go. Time to move. There was no blaring alarm alerting him to the urgency of the moment. No, if there had been a timer at all it had been internal. Ticking away the seconds with each beat of his heart, with each breath he took. His body wasn't counting down though. If anything, it was marking the time like a prisoner. Adding days to the wall with thin hash marks. 365 days since he last saw his daughter. 365 days since she was safe in her home reality.

The Portal remained up for the year, she could have come back at any point. But she hadn't. That meant that she wasn't going to come back on her own. He needed to brave the unknowns of the multiverse and head out after her. And after a year of planning and waiting, now it was time.

Xander Marks gathered himself and stood up from his desk. He left a sealed note on top of his ink blotter. *Just in case.* His hair had grayed considerably in the last year. Each brown piece now steel, each gray strand now a stark white. The stress of the situation had aged him. He wondered what time travel would do to him as well.

He stalked the hallway, perhaps for the last time. He felt the weight of these moments weighing on him. Or maybe it was something else starting to strain his breathing. But he couldn't be sure. He was so nervous, but this was the only way. He had to try.

Ramona waited patiently for him in the lab after she finished the system checks. Even though he had asked her to go home and get some rest after their official workday had concluded on August 7, she had stayed. Her thick black hair was now swept up in a messy bun, her dark eyes were rimmed with exhaustion. Even though her skin was considerably darker than Nina's, he recognized that look. That exhilarated expression Nina wore with the pride of working late. That youthful willingness to sacrifice sleep and health for science. It was an echo of how his daughter looked one year earlier.

Only, this time was very different. Rogers was in the conference room across the hall, a live stream set up with the team in Tokyo. Once Ramona gave Xander the thumbs up he said, "alright, I guess it's time to go." He offered a sheepish shrug as he clapped his hands together.

"Good luck, Dr. Marks," she said with a smile as she pushed back from the console and stood. Xander had told a little lie, a fib really, to both Ramona and Lionel Rogers, the only two other people who would be in the building at the time of the first jitter. While the team in Tokyo knew better, from first-hand experience, Xander told his new assistant and his boss that they couldn't be in the same room with him when the machine was in use. He tossed around enough jargon about quantum irregularities and basically implied that if they were all in the same room that the machine might suck them into a wormhole. So, they would be in the conference room, with the door closed and Xander would be in the lab, with his door closed. Two separate systems he explained.

But really, he just needed the time to go and switch out the coordinates and execute *his* plan, his alone.

Xander stood at the console. He sat there for weeks on end at first, determined to find her. Then, once he had given up hope, he had avoided that room as much as he could. But thankfully, his resolve had rebounded.

Standing there in the first moments of the day, he pressed the single button that he needed. He had mentally reviewed this plan over and over in his mind. He knew that a one-way ticket to the Unknown Universe without any help was a suicide mission. But he knew the exact location of just one other reality than his own. The one that he and his daughter had seen their guests off to a year ago. Universe Beta they had called it.

He found the record in the system quickly after the idea had occurred to him a week or so earlier. But he knew that he couldn't arrive at the same exact time that they had sent the travelers to. No, they had returned to fight off a megalomaniac who was wreaking havoc across the multiverse. Xander knew he would have to arrive a day or even a week later. He wanted to aim for one day though, too much could happen in a week. *Or just a few moments*, he thought to himself, remembering how quickly Nina had been taken.

But when he tried to plug in just a twenty-four-hour advance the Universe location disappeared. So, he tried one hundred and sixty-eight hours. The same result. It was almost as if the Portal to that Universe had closed within hours of the travelers arriving.

It finally occurred to him that their first order of business once they had the situation under control would have been to dismantle the Portal. But surely, they would have given it a chance again. Initially he hoped that it wouldn't be too long. Then he remembered that he was only planning to use this location as a change station. Then he could find some help, a team who had already traveled the multiverse as well. That was his plan.

And after reciting it over and over again for days, it was now time to take action on it. That single action, pressing the one button he needed had pulled up the exact coordinates for Universe Beta one year after the travelers went back, ten years ahead of his own time: August 8, 2019. The Portal moved accordingly on the track.

The first quantum jitter of the day was about to open the Portal. The sheen of the quantum foam between the edges of the frame gave off a faint glow in the lab. The supercybin injection stung for the shortest second. Xander took a deep breath and closed his eyes. He pictured Nina's face in his mind for just a moment before he stepped through the Portal and into the multiverse.

46

What makes a day on a calendar so special? It's just a specific twenty-four-hour chunk of time. We give meanings to different days to mark celebrations, remembrances, holidays. We count the years that pass by how many times that specific date has come and gone. But it could really be any day. Christmas doesn't *have* to fall on December 25, you can celebrate it a week later and the sentiment is still the same. Memorial Day, Labor Day, Arbor Day. All these days that we ascribe special meaning to, they were created by us, we humans control them.

But Dr. Norman Thurston knew better. He knew there was a cosmic significance behind this day. August 8. This day that passed every calendar year without any fanfare or notice. How could people not sense it? Couldn't they feel that the air around them charged, buzzing with possibility?

Thurston had been anticipating this day all year. Had been hoping for something to happen, but also dreading the possibility of what it could bring. So much could go wrong, so much could go right. But much like a child anxiously awaiting Santa Claus on December 24, Thurston stayed up to watch the clock strike midnight. As the day passed from August 7 to August 8, nothing happened. Or at least not anything that he could tell from the armchair of his home office. So, he convinced himself to go to bed. There would be something waiting for him, either fascination or failure, in the morning.

When he awoke, he showered, and ate, and headed in to the city. Nothing barred him from completing any of those tasks. He had no emergency meeting requests from the Dean. No breaking news stories of cosmic wonders spilling out of his lab. Nothing. It was as though it was just another day. But how could that be? There were jitters, ripples, in space-time that would allow people to walk across worlds. But everyone he passed seemed completely absorbed in the minutia of their own lives.

And then in his own classroom, his office, his lab, nothing was out of place. Nothing was moved or different. Of course, he knew that with the machine disassembled nothing could have happened. But still, he wondered what temporal abnormalities might have conjured up a reconstructed Portal overnight. But there was no one else around to take such matters into their own hands. Parker was gone. The Dean was happy with his decision to stop their research and refocus on teaching. Especially after the incident the previous summer with massive energy surges, a SWAT team descending on campus, and the whereabouts of Parker and Nina unaccounted for.

No, if anyone was going to do anything on that day, it would have to be him. And he had sworn to never allow the machine to be used again. So, he trooped on through his lectures, through lunch, through his poorly attended afternoon office hours.

As the early afternoon slipped away, Thurston stood at the edge of the lab, looking out on the vast open space where his life's work once stood and imagined it still functional. The gleam of the steel. The whirring of the fans inside the quantum computer. The blinkering of lights on the monitors. He glanced over at the boxes on the metal shelves, each component sitting idly, ready to work.

Thurston convinced himself to go over and just look at them, to pay homage to them on this very special day. And once each box was down, he found his fingers deftly assembling the components. His hands operating on autopilot, like a person transfixed in front of a jigsaw puzzle, he couldn't not fit the pieces together.

Just to make sure all the odds and ends are still here, he told himself in the few conscious moments when he caught himself in the act. It was as though he was watching himself do this, that some greater force was driving him to complete this forbidden task.

Time slipped by without notice as the track, the console, the computer, the screens, all came back together. He hadn't been as thorough in disassembling each piece, instead leaving several modules connected, which made the process that much easier. As though he had been planning for the day when he would do just this.

As the final bolt was screwed into the ground to secure the track, the quantum computer finished its reboot. All that was left to do was add the frame.

The fog of work that had masked Thurston's actions from his own consciousness seemed to lift. Was it enough to just see the device back together again, to celebrate this anniversary with the invention he had poured years of his life into? Surely, just seeing it 99% assembled was enough. He had already been reckless, careless. Putting this much together was a huge risk. One he had promised himself he would never take.

"What have I done?" He whispered aloud to no one at all. This was a dangerous errand; he should take it apart immediately. All the delayed alarm bells started to ring out in his mind. This was foolish, irresponsible, potentially fatal. He told his feet to move, to get to work taking it apart again. But the sentimental part of his mind wouldn't allow it. He missed tinkering with his creation. He missed the excitement and the possibility of it all. He missed the person that he had been when their research filled every moment of his day with the promise of discovery. But he had seen the reality of what the machine could do, and it had broken his heart. Looking at it now, with fresh eyes, he felt transported back to the man he had been a year earlier, one who thrived on the potential of what lay before him.

And then, the next thought popped into his mind. That he should complete the machine, just once. What could it hurt to see it all together for just a moment? *Just one minute. I'll set a timer*, he told himself. All his rationalizations and excuses manifest as he heaved the large frame up onto the track. He didn't care that he had sweat through his button down or that his glasses were slick on the bridge of his nose. He didn't seem to even notice how hungry he was or the lightheaded feeling that often accompanied his empty stomach. He had a singular focus, a mission to complete.

Once the frame clicked into place on the track, Thurston stood back. He let out a gasp. Both in awe and horror. He looked down at his watch.

9:08 pm. He would only give himself until 9:09, 9:10 at the latest. In his heart, he felt a deep disappointment. Because he half expected something to happen when the frame was set. *I guess I should be relieved*, he reminded himself. It was difficult to be noble in that moment.

He glanced back down at his watch. Already the minute had passed, the seconds just flew by. "Alright, enough is enough," and he hung his head, his feet starting to move forward, ready to carry him through the motions of undoing it all again.

But then, the room filled with light, stopping Thurston in his tracks. The roar of thunder that filled the warehouse would surely give him away, he desperately hoped it would fall silent.

And then, a polished brown leather loafer appeared on the floor as someone stepped through the veil of space-time, across the Plain, and into his lab.

47

Universe Beta

"**D**r. Xander Marks," the gentleman before him extended a hand in greeting. His expression was polite, although Thurston had to admit that he noted a slight sadness to this man's eyes. Was he disappointed? *Surely, if I had walked through a time machine and saw someone on the other side who wasn't my own alter-ego, I might feel the same way.* Thurston didn't begrudge the man any potential shock on his part. He was shocked himself.

"Dr. Norman Thurston," he offered his hand as well. He couldn't help but release a nervous smile. "Did you say Marks?" The name finally filtered through his brain.

"Yes," this stranger's eyes lit up slightly.

"Any relation to Feminina Marks?" Thurston asked. In his studies of the multiverse, he first thought that coincidences were statistical inevitabilities, but after experiencing how the Portal worked, he believed less and less in them.

"Yes, she is my daughter. Is she a scientist on your team here?" Thurston observed as this stranger looked around the lab, perhaps hoping for a glimpse of Nina. The soft wrinkles on his forehead erased as his ears perked up, pulling the skin a bit tighter.

"No, no. She was dating my lead scientist up until last year," Thurston began. As he spoke a bit of memory popped up in his mind. A conversation with Parker years back, one of the first holiday seasons he and Nina had spent together. The week of Thanksgiving, Thurston had inquired about Parker's holiday plans. He said that he and Nina were headed to a tropical beach to escape the chilly D.C. weather. When Thurston had asked why they weren't spending time with family, he explained that Nina's parents were both gone too.

Don't tell him, Thurston thought immediately. He was sure that so many rules and implied laws of ethics in multiverse travel had already been broken, but he couldn't tell this man, wherever and whenever he was from, that he had already died in this reality.

"Ah, okay," the same look of disappointment crossed Dr. Marks' face. "Well, do you happen to know where she is?"

Thurston realized this would be hard for him to hear as well, but he didn't have nearly as many qualms about the potential ripple effect through the different realities by telling him. "No, no one does actually," which was a bit of a lie. Thurston knew where *a* Feminina Marks was, safe and sound back in Universe Alpha. "She's been listed as a missing person for a year now."

Xander Marks took half a step back as though he had just been punched in the gut. "Not here too," he breathed as he pressed his hand to his chest.

"What? What's wrong?" Thurston asked as he guided the man over to one of the rolling chairs by the console.

Dr. Marks took a few deep breaths. Thurston scurried back into the classroom section of the lab and grabbed some water from his desk. He offered it to Dr. Marks when he returned, only seconds after leaving his side. He bent forward to see if the man before him had turned blue from lack of oxygen.

"Nina has been kidnapped," Xander Marks stated.

"Yes, yes. She was kidnapped by Parker, brought here from Universe Alpha against her will, but she went home. I checked the logs and wiped them." Thurston nodded his head, hoping his answer would calm this man's worry about his daughter, or his daughter's alter-ego. *A parent's love must know no bounds,* Thurston assumed.

"No, *my* Nina was kidnapped." This visitor's voice was ragged, the words were tough for him to get out. "My Nina was taken a year ago," Marks looked up at Thurston, his eyes now pleading.

Thurston stood up, his spine straight, the tiny hairs on the back of his neck prickling with electricity.

"What?" The professor who often found that he spoke too much, droned on too long, was at a loss for words. He stood there, dumbfounded, as Dr. Marks relayed the events that had unfolded 365 days earlier. Or at least, in his universe those events had taken place a year earlier. To Thurston it happened eleven years prior.

He now recognized that Marks was his counterpart, his cosmic colleague, also dedicated to developing a Portal to travel the multiverse. He also learned that this had been the man who had helped Nina, her alter-ego, and Dean Winchester's alter-ego get back to him in time to stop Parker. It seemed that their fates were intertwined.

Thurston listened in horror as Marks detailed the moments that passed immediately after their visitors left. A too brief celebration cut short by his daughter's disappearance, Marks' skin lost its tan luster as he recounted those first panicked moments.

Was Nina destined to be kidnapped in each universe where she existed? Was she doomed to be a victim of the Portal no matter where she was?

"So, why did you come here?" Thurston finally asked after Marks finished his story.

Marks looked up and explained the pressure he was under. Only a select few knew what happened. He needed to continue to produce new results for his think tank, but he could barely concentrate knowing that Nina was missing. A harsh cough wracked Marks' body. His fist was quick to his mouth to cover it up. Thurston stood back, letting the man catch his breath and take a sip of water before continuing.

"I need your help. I have the coordinates for this Unknown Universe, but I can't go in there alone. I figured that if so much had started in Universe Beta, I would be able to find help here. I was able to find the exact moment that the two Ninas and Marie went back to this Universe, this lab. I didn't want to jump right into the thick of the fight they were in. So, I looked ahead, but there was a huge gap. No access to this Universe until-"

"Now," Thurston whispered, cutting off the other man's words. He gazed over at his invention, the device he had created with Parker, now fully assembled for the first time in a year. It was truly a Portal, a doorway, an entry and exit point.

After a few steadying breathes, the wheels in Thurston's mind began to turn. He had to help and more importantly, he had the means to help. *It looks like I'll be getting my adventure after all,* he thought wistfully.

"Come on then, we have no time to waste. It's already late in the day and we need to plot our course." Thurston looked down at the man, still catching his breath in the desk chair.

Xander Marks looked up at Thurston and a rueful smile crossed his face.

48

**Universe Alpha
August 7, 2019
11:30 pm**

The sound of their footsteps, in sync, reminded Nina of marching soldiers. As their heels struck the sidewalk at the exact same time, the *clip-clip* of their shoes seemed to echo into the night. For a late Wednesday evening, the streets were eerily quiet. In the bustling Washington, D.C. that Nina was used to, the city quieted but never fully settled. She assumed that Feminina, at her side, was used to the silence. Nina had seen how the Washington, D.C. of Feminina's reality, Universe Gamma, had been a shell of the one she knew.

The two women were on their way to the University. Nina had checked earlier that evening before she left work, the Portal was still up. Together, they had worked on a plan for the past month on how they would enter the building, access the Portal, and head off into the multiverse to find Marie. And then they made a back-up plan. And then they made another back-up plan.

Nina's apartment had served as their command center and now they were about to take action. But first, they needed refreshments. Nina thought this was silly, they could eat before they left her apartment. But Feminina reminded her that they had to plan for things to go wrong. If they missed the first few jitters while the quantum computer was recalibrating or as they were measuring the exact location of the frame on the track, they would need some kind of sugar energy to keep them going.

Nina didn't push the topic further. It also seemed to be good luck. It had been almost exactly a year earlier that Nina had barged into Feminina's life and asked for help getting home. Femi and Marie made a point to stop for snacks first. Nina was not going to question their methods since it worked. And Nina thought that Femi might feel a little nostalgic for this tiny and silly ritual. Feminina never admitted it out loud, but Nina could see the worry in her eyes. While their plan had them intercepting Marie the instant she was kidnapped, almost six weeks of time had passed for Feminina. She left her Universe on the morning of August 8 and traveled back in time and across the multiverse to find Nina and get her help. She had to worry about what was happening to Marie, who took her, where she was for six weeks. Nina's stomach churned slightly as she thought about that kind of persistent anxiety.

The pattern of their shoes stopped abruptly as the two reached the door to the corner market. An electronic bell chimed as they passed from the muggy evening air into the crisp air-conditioned respite. The bright fluorescent bulbs cast every item in the store into sharp detail. Nina and Femi split up. Nina headed to the back wall of refrigerators and grabbed the energy drinks she knew they both liked. Femi, of course, headed for the aisle of salty chips.

As the two met up at the counter, Nina laid the cold cans down carefully. Feminina plopped a large red bag down.

"You know, if you keep eating those your fingers are going to be dyed nacho cheese orange for life," Nina muttered.

"Worth it," Feminina replied with a mischievous smile. Nina knew better than to give Femi a hard time about her new Doritos addiction. If everything went to plan, Femi and Marie would be back safe in their home Universe within the hour and Femi would never get the chance to eat one of those delicious triangles again.

The overnight clerk in the store eyed the two women warily. His dark eyes flashed between the two of them and then up. Nina was starting to get used to the looks when she was out in public with Feminina. To anyone else they looked like identical twins with slightly different haircuts, although Nina had been growing hers out long before Femi arrived. Nina assumed that these suspicious glances were the same that she had noticed over the past month and a half. People saw twins and were either curiously fascinated or deeply suspicious. Not of them, but of their own eye sight.

Until, Nina caught a reflection in the plexiglass partition. She turned and saw that the local evening news was on the television above their heads. As the images before her processed in her mind, she didn't catch the words Feminina was saying. She didn't even hear what the newswoman was reporting. She only read the headline that was scrolling across the screen.

"BREAKING NEWS: INMATE ESCAPED FROM CORRECTIONAL FACILITY. CONSIDER ARMED AND DANGEROUS."

It wasn't even the mug shut of Gus Blanity that had her jarred. She recognized him immediately. Nina had been bracing for this moment for over a year. She had worried that he would try to escape and avenge himself. Before she knew where he had come from, before she understood how they were connected, she had been able to tell herself that he was just deranged. That he only attacked her and Hank because he was crazy and they had been in the wrong place at the wrong time. But after everything Nina experienced the previous year, she understood. Gus had come after *her* that night eleven years earlier, and killed Hank instead. And now he was out, on the loose. It was like a nightmare come to life. She had dreamed it so many times, maybe that was why she wasn't so shocked to see his face on the screen. She had been mentally preparing for this.

But it was the face next to his on the screen that tripped her up. A headshot that looked like it would be used for a security photo showed a woman with pale white skin, piercing eyes, and blindingly white hair.

Feminina must have been growing impatient, because her words were getting louder, starting to register in Nina's brain.

"Um hello, Earth to Nina. Can you please pay the man so we can go?" Femi's direct request went unanswered. And Nina felt her move, sensed her shift on her feet to turn and see what Nina was looking at.

For the final seconds of the news segment the two of them stared up at the screen in disbelief. The face staring back at them was one that they knew all too well. Her cheek bones, her mouth, her chin. In spite of the androgynous look of the person in the photo, the features were very distinctly *feminine*. The scar on her one cheek didn't throw them, nor did the hair, nor the lack of visible eye brows.

It was *them*. It was *us*. It was *her*.

49

Nick tried to not tap his foot as he waited for the coffee to drip. He was already keyed up, but it was the middle of the night, he could use all the caffeine his body could handle. The office was buzzing with energy. All agents and support staff for both divisions were on call. It was going to be a long work day for them all, but it was their only reliable shot to move their cases forward.

For the first year, Nick wouldn't be sitting idly waiting for Archie to return from his jumps. This year, Nick would be heading out on his own. His first time across The Plain. The more he had looked into Parker Lovett's disappearance, the more he began to suspect that he had been placed in another Universe. Dr. Norman Thurston, Parker's boss, had both the means and potential motive to get rid of Parker. If Thurston wanted the glory of discovery and if he sensed any chance that Parker would leave the lab and take their research to another team, it could have been enough to drive Thurston to act. *But how could someone force another person through the Portal?* The timing had to be perfect. And then there was the growing evidence that Nina Marks was up to something, though he still didn't know what.

Nick didn't know exactly what evidence he would be looking for, but he had a strong sense that he needed to travel to the Universe that Mona found as she scrubbed through the data logs from the University from the past year. Find Parker. Solve the case. While the records from August 8, 2018, the previous year, were gone, there had been some activity that they were able to record in the past six weeks. He had a hunch, he had a location, and he would see what he could find.

He glanced up at the clock on the wall, a jolt of nerves shot through him as he realized how soon he would be taking off. Archie had given him some pointers. Some tips on how to manage the headache, how to address people so he wouldn't necessarily get caught in a bad situation. Archie was slated to take off and return at least three to four times that day, depending on what his evidence turned up. Nick worried about the volume of jumps Archie did each year. The toll on his body was becoming more obvious, less avoidable. But it was a tough job to tell what changes in the past would impact the present.

As though he had conjured him up just by thinking of him, Archie approached Nick.

"You ready?" Archie asked as he leaned back against the breakroom counter.

"I guess we'll find out in about fifteen minutes," Nick responded with a shrug. He was trying to play it off like he could handle this, like he wasn't scared of what was on the other side of The Portal.

"It'll be weird to come back and not see you waiting for me," Archie noted.

Nick reached for the carafe and poured himself a mug of fresh coffee. "Well, at least on one of your jumps I won't be there. Should be back in more than enough time to help you out with your new clues later today."

"Uh, tomorrow," Archie corrected.

"Right, tomorrow," Nick agreed. He took a tentative sip from his coffee mug as he moved away from the counter, leaving room for others on the team to duck in and grab their liquid energy. Archie moved with him, the two standing in the middle of the breakroom. Nick had his own set of worries, but he felt the need to warn Archie to take care. To watch out for himself. Nick wanted to say that he had a bad feeling, but he was trying to convince himself that it was just nerves. "Hey, Archie," Nick began, still searching for the right words to say to his friend, his partner.

Archie locked his calcified eyes with Nick's rich brown ones. "Yeah?"

But before Nick could say anything, his phone buzzed in his front pocket. Reflexively, he grabbed it with his open hand and unlocked the screen. Archie did the same, his phone must have gone off as well.

Nick re-read the alert on his screen, unsure if he was seeing it correctly. PERSON OF INTEREST ALERT: GUS BLANITY ESCAPED. AT LARGE.

Archie didn't even excuse himself before he ran from the break room and badged into the Chronos side of the hallway. Nick didn't have any time to be offended, he was busy trying to do the same, having to pause for a moment to set down his coffee and pocket his phone so he could press his thumbprint to the scanner. If he had a moment to think, Nick might have wondered at what news Archie received at the same exact time. It didn't seem that Blanity had any connection to the cases that his partner was working. Unless Mona just decided to ping them both.

Once inside the Kairos office, he saw the other agents lined up, all eagerly discussing their jumps. Nick headed straight for the back corner where Mona's face was illuminated by the monitor she was staring at intently.

"What's going on?" Nick asked as soon as he was within earshot.

"Exactly what I just put into the system. Gus Blanity escaped from custody. I've been able to pull the security cameras for the Institute. It looks like he might have had help," Mona rattled off these details without breaking her focus from the screen. Nick moved around to her side of the console so he could view what she had found.

Nick didn't need any further explanation. He recognized the cropped hair and scar on the camera right away. The orderly he had seen when he visited Blanity two months earlier was locked in the frame. Mona paused the video feed just as the pair headed down the side stairwell, before they passed out of view. No doubt about it, this was the same person he had seen on his visit.

And as if all the pieces were finally falling into place, Nick heard Archie's voice in his mind. *Pale face. White Hair.* As Mona advanced the video, he saw the orderly flip the hood of their black sweatshirt up, covering the scar. This was Archie's mark.

There were no coincidences.

Nick dashed out of the Kairos control room. Ignoring the nervous excitement of the other agents gathered towards the front, the rising murmur of side conversations. Nick was about to try his badge to enter the Chronos side of the office when their door flung open as well.

Archie nearly ran into Nick.

"One of your suspects escaped!"

"Your murderer helped my suspect escape!"

Their words cut over each other.

Each took a deep breath. Nick nodded at Archie, as though they had communicated telekinetically. But they both knew the same thing. Archie's murderer would be looking for a way out of this Universe. Gus Blanity would have the same motive. There was one Portal set up in their joint-agency office which they both knew was protected, secure from this duo. That left only one other option, the Portal at the University lab.

The two men marched resolutely down the hallway and out to Nick's car. They were on their way just as the clock struck midnight.

Perhaps they could resolve both mysteries in *this* Universe after all.

50

**Universe Beta
August 8, 2019
11:37 pm**

Even though they were sitting only a few feet from a time machine, it seemed that time was running out. As the clock counted the hours: 9:00 pm, 10:00 pm, 11:00 pm, Dr. Xander Marks tried not to panic. He had already traveled so far, and waited for so long, but he refused to think that he might lose his chance to find Nina.

This Dr. Norman Thurston seemed to be incredibly smart. He wished he had known him in his own reality. *Or perhaps he would have been an adversary trying to beat me to discovery,* Xander thought. He smiled at this idea, that he had perhaps met his academic match.

As Thurston worked, he asked Xander questions about his power source. While Marks would have found this distracting, to have one problem in front of him while inquiring about a different line of scientific inquiry, it seemed to fuel Thurston. As though this man's brain needed multiple inputs in order to effectively process what was in front of him.

If he had been able to, Xander would have crossed into Universe Beta as early on August 8 as he could have. But it only came online that evening.

Had this been a purely academic trip, he may have tried to explore a bit more. His only other trip through the Portal had been a year earlier (or a decade earlier) in his own Universe, traveling from Washington, D.C. to Tokyo and back. But this was a whole new reality. The lab here appeared to be functional, though far less clean and organized than what he was used to. Perhaps that was the difference between life in a University with limited resources and the well-funded think tank that Xander had become accustomed to.

Unfortunately, there was only one console, so Xander had to stand by as he watched Thurston pull up path after path on his own quantum drive. He told Xander all about how he had hidden it after the incident the previous year. The women who had traveled to see him had brought their own drive with them. That one had been taken by the Nina from Universe Alpha, the first Nina to be kidnapped, when she returned and sealed off the Portal to her reality. But the drive that Thurston and Parker had developed was kept locked away in a safe in his office. Xander nodded, following the logic. It was refreshing to converse with someone already so fluent in the paradoxes of the multiverse and thinking in more than two dimensions.

Xander felt his pulse begin to race as Thurston's fingers rested and his eyebrows furrowed.

"No, this can't be right," the scientist muttered. Xander felt his shoulders deflate.

"What is it?" Marks dared to ask.

"Oh, uh. It's not related to the Unknown Universe, that regression is still running," he pointed to the screen in the upper right-hand corner of the array.

Xander nodded, relieved.

"It's just – uh, it looks like the Portal to Universe Alpha has been opened again," Thurston moved his cursor to see how long ago it had happened. He felt betrayed in his blind trust of Nina to protect her side of the multiverse. But then he realized that she wasn't the only one there with the means and know-how to rebuild the machine.

Thurston pointed to a thickness in the yellow lines in Universe Alpha. "Two Ninas in one Universe," Thurston whispered.

"My Nina?" Xander popped up from the chair he was sitting in.

"Oh no, this is the one you saw last year, from Universe Gamma." Thurston responded absentmindedly, trying to riddle out what in the world was going on. "Hmmm," his voice carried as his mind pondered the ramifications. Xander looked on as Thurston advanced the monitor. "Yes, it looks like she arrived a little over a month ago, and then,-" Thurston's words stopped just as abruptly as the yellow lines on his screen.

"They're gone?" Xander asked, confirming what he could see on the screen.

"It appears so," Thurston looked over at the scientist beside him, both of them uncomfortably close as they leaned into the monitors. He scanned this man's face for signs of concern, worry, dread, as more of his daughters turned up missing in the multiverse. He sighed, knowing that Xander would want to confirm the timestamps, there was no hiding information from a grieving man. Especially not one who valued reason and logic, those were the two items that would comfort him the most.

"Yes, it appears that first thing this morning one of them left, and then later closer to midday the next one went out as well." Thurston gestured to the differing lines as he zoomed in for a closer look of the exact spacetime stamp of their departures.

"Could they be heading off on some fun adventure?" Xander asked, a sad hope on the edge of his voice.

"Perhaps," Thurston nodded; it was still a logical explanation. Although, given how Xander's daughter had been kidnapped, it didn't seem to be the case.

Xander opened his mouth to ask another question, but he was interrupted before he could begin. The alarm on the top monitor started to ring. Thurston wheeled himself closer to that side of the console, nearly running over Xander's feet in the process.

"Oh, sorry," he added. "Looks like we have a lock on the time and location for your Universe Unknown." Thurston clicked on the alarm and with a few simple keystrokes he had the calculations for the exact position to adjust the Portal.

The two men set to work quickly, grabbing a measuring tape to guide them to the exact dimensions they needed. As they began to carefully walk the Portal down the track, they realized that they were heading far to the right. Neither of them questioned the distance until the Portal was locked back into the track. They checked the math, and then checked it again.

"Well, I guess we'll be off to see what the future looks like, Dr. Marks," Thurston said as he wiped his brow. The Portal slid smoothly along the track, but it was still heavy and the added pressure of getting it just right was enough to make him sweat.

"Looks like it, Dr. Thurston." Xander nodded as his accomplice headed back to the console to save the coordinates and back them up to the quantum drive. He approached the man at the console, trying to ease the very palpable tension in the room. They were both nervous, Xander had so much riding on this trip going right. And Thurston had never made a trip across the Plain before.

"You know, when we get back, I could come and show you how we created our automatic gliding component for our Portal," Xander began to offer.

"Automatic gliding component?" Thurston looked up at him abruptly.

"Yes, the coordinates go straight from our console and the Portal moves along the track to the precise location." Xander nodded, impressed that he and Nina had considered this and built it in, even before they had the ability to travel to other universes.

Thurston glanced over at his machine and shook his head. "Why didn't I think of that?"

"Well, you did come up with the quantum drive, so we'll call it even," Xander smiled and crossed his arms.

Thurston grabbed four vials of supercybin from the locked box under the console. It had been in storage with the rest of the machine so he had pulled it out too. Or at least, that was what he told himself. *Turns out it was good to bring this along as well.*

"Two for the road, two for the way back," Thurston stated as he set the orange cylinders on the console and began to reach for the key again.

"Wait! We'll need an extra vial for Nina too, to bring her back home." Xander pointed to the vials on the desk.

"Right, right. Here, let's bring five and then a few as back-up. Just in case. Don't want to get caught in a reality we can't escape all because we didn't pack enough of this stuff." Thurston grabbed eight vials in total and put six of them in a padded envelope. Nice and cushioned for the trip, he pocketed the envelope and passed one of the remaining vials to Marks.

"Orange?" Xander asked as he eyed the vial, rolling it between his fingers.

"Yes, is yours a different color?" Thurston inquired, genuinely curious as to the differences.

"We added a painkiller and it turned from this shade of orange to a clear liquid," Xander stated, his lips tight. He must have just figured out that his head was several minutes away from a jarring headache.

"Ah," Thurston breathed out his disappointment. Yet another thing he hadn't thought of. But he had no time to dither and chide himself for not being more forward thinking. The alarm for the next quantum jitter chimed.

0:60

"Time to go then," Xander stated, eager to be on their way to find his daughter. He had been so relieved to meet another physicist of his caliber to help with the calculation that he hadn't stopped to think about the next step. Nina had been kidnapped. And to ward off whoever had been strong enough to pull her away, he was bringing his aging body as well as an equally out of shape and graying scientist.

Thurston felt his anxiety spike. This was it. He was going to finally set out into the multiverse. It hadn't been how he had envisioned it. He told himself time and time again that he wouldn't take this action, no matter how tempting. But there was a young woman, a damsel, in distress. He had to act because he had the means and the knowledge to do so.

0:30

Thurston's hand trembled as he held the vial up to the crook in his elbow.

"Here, I'll do yours if you do mine," Xander offered. The men exchanged vials and injected each other.

They both stood before the Portal, mesmerized by the pearlescent sheen that formed between the borders.

"You do the honors, Dr. Thurston," Xander offered.

Thurston nodded and stepped into the unknown void of space and time for the first time.

51

Nina could feel the cola cans *thunking* against her back as she and Femi half ran/half walked to the University. They had paid the convenient store clerk hastily and Nina had stuffed their goodies into her backpack as quickly as she could. The campus lights were in sight now, a glowing beacon in the city. Even though the streets were well lit at night, the University took it to a whole new level with flood lights keeping each corner of campus illuminated, and supposedly, safe.

As they approached, Femi flipped the hood up on her jacket. This had been Nina's idea to conceal their faces from the multiple security cameras. It turned out to be an eerie premonition given what they had both just seen on the news. Nina popped her hood up as well. She was already sweaty and hot in the humid evening with long sleeves and the exertion to get to the lab quickly. She was eager to get inside, take the pack off her back, and remove the jacket.

Femi swiped Nina's access badge at the door and opened it for Nina who followed. *No getting around that one*, Nina remarked as they planned out the morning. But she would report her card missing later in the day on August 8. Or at least that was the plan. But now it felt like the plan was disintegrating, dissolving beneath their feet.

Femi and Nina ran down the hallway and into the lab, already bracing for the worst. But it was empty.

"Thank goodness," Nina exhaled as she flipped on the light. Femi was already charging through the plastic tarps to the Portal. Nina set the backpack down and took out their snacks. The chips were probably all crunched from the run over and those cans would need to sit for a little bit before opening them or else they would explode everywhere.

Nina followed Femi through the tarps and watched as she began to power up the quantum computer. Nina passed her the quantum drive wordlessly. They had gone over this plan so many times they both had each step memorized. And Nina didn't have to ask Femi if she was nervous or worried about what they had seen just a few moments earlier. Aside from being able to see the tell-tale signs of anxicty on Femi's face: the creased brow, the silent determination, Nina just knew. Because she was nervous too.

This plan had to work. Marie was missing and Femi needed to find her. Nina had to help. *And now the man who attacked them a year earlier was on the loose in the same city with–*. Nina couldn't finish the thought. She couldn't accept that any version of herself in any universe would help that man.

Femi was quick at work, her fingers moving at incredible speed. Nina moved towards the Portal, stooping to unlock the clamps. It was one item she could do now to make it that much easier for them. First, Femi had to locate Marie in Universe Gamma. Neither of them had been able to use the drive in their planning. This step could take minutes or it could take hours. If Marie were here, it would have taken seconds. Of course, the one aspect of their plan that required a computer science expert couldn't be executed by her since she was the one who was missing.

"How's it looking?" Nina asked as she unlatched the second clamp.

Femi looked over at her with one of her signature glares. Chastened, Nina held up her hands as if to apologize.

Nina stole a glance at the clock on the wall. She saw the second hand make its final move to announce that it was officially August 8. She hadn't specifically expected that something would happen at the stroke of midnight, but she felt her anxiety kick up a notch. Nina was now hyperaware of everything around her, the inanimate pieces of furniture and lab gear sitting in the dark corners of the lab, the hum of the computer. Nothing out of place.

Until a loud piercing metallic sound disturbed the silence. Nina snapped her head towards the direction of the noise. It had come from the hallway. Someone or something was just outside.

52

**Universe Alpha
August 8, 2019
12:06 am**

Even with his excellent driving skills, Nick couldn't make the red lights turn over any faster. Archie had fidgeted in the passenger seat the entire drive over. It was annoying, but Nick couldn't be mad at him about it.

Nick finally saw the lights of the campus ahead. He parked in the faculty lot, the one closest to the University Sciences building. During the day he might have had trouble finding a space, he might have even been fined or asked by campus security to leave. But at this hour, no one was there to object.

The two dashed out of the car, Nick remembered to click the button on his key and lock it after he was already a few feet away. Archie was running beside him, although Nick could see him limp a bit out of the corner of his eye.

No time to think on it, though. They were at the door to the building already. Nick hadn't planned on how to get into the building without an ID badge. With all the resources he had access to as part of a shadow government agency, he didn't have a magic pass card that worked on all doors. Advanced mobile apps to track temporal lag? Yes. The ability to access records that should have otherwise been behind firewalls? Of course. But no universal badge.

Archie acted as Nick started to think through ways to get into the building. Every time Nick had been there before it had been during the day when he could slip in behind someone or ask a student to hold the door for him. He always managed to get in just fine. But no one was here to do that now. As Nick prepared to explain this to Archie, he saw Archie's hand close around the handle to the door. And it opened.

"Looks like someone didn't check that this was latched behind them," Archie said as he walked in.

"Or maybe they wanted it to be left open," Nick muttered as he followed Archie into the dark entranceway.

The stairwell to the left was illuminated by the eerie glow of the flood lights from the parking lot, a wall of windows following the flights up and up. Nick usually turned and went up those steps when he visited the Dean. But today he would be going straight, just like he would when visiting Dr. Thurston. He knew the layout of the building by heart. Mona had pulled enough security footage, and the blueprints, that Nick was able to act on instinct of where to go next. Archie followed Nick, both gently jogging past the closed classroom doors.

About halfway down the corridor a loud crash thundered off the walls. Nick and Archie both picked up their pace, screeching to a stop at the lab and taking a hard-left turn to enter.

Confusion was the first thing to hit Nick as he looked at the classroom section of the lab. It was empty, save for a lone backpack sitting on one of the long slate tables. Perhaps forgotten by a student.

But then the lights and the motion beyond the plastic tarps caught his attention. He locked eyes with Archie. The two of them nodded slowly, in perfect rhythm. Hesitantly, they each stepped forward, inching towards the partition. As the adrenaline pumped through his system, Nick saw each small detail in focus. Every minute sound stood out clearly, from the squeak of his shoes on the linoleum to the grunts coming from the other side of the flaps.

As Archie and Nick breached the partition, they wordlessly knew to each take one half of the view before them. Archie on the left and Nick on the right.

Nick took it all in at once. A Portal, not dissimilar to the one back at the Kairos-Chronos headquarters, was fully assembled next to a console.

Nick wasn't surprised, but he was still angry at the fact that he had been assured by Dean Winchester that the device had been dismantled. He knew that it must have been put back together after the recorded energy surge six weeks earlier, but he still felt his ire flare. He would have to deal with that lie later, and for good reason.

Before him were four people. The first had their back turned to him, working away at the console of the machine. With their black hoodie pulled up over their neck, he couldn't see who it was. But the other three he had a clear view of. First was Nina, laid on her side, fumbling as though she was trying to stand back up from being pushed down. But then he also spotted Nina standing, trapped in the arms of Gus Blanity.

Seeing him now, Blanity appeared to be very much animated with no trace of a sedative in his system. His forearms were straining as the woman fought back, but the knife he held to her throat kept her from making too much trouble.

As Nick tried to riddle out how he was seeing Nina in two places at once, the figure at the console whipped around to face him and Archie. They had certainly not taken any pains to make their entrance a secret.

As the figure stood from the swivel chair, they lowered the hood on their sweater. Petite frame, jagged scar, and that blinding white hair. It was the murderer that Archie had been after. It was also the orderly that Nick had seen at the asylum, he was sure of it.

But somewhere in his mind, it also registered that, even though it seemed impossible, this was also somehow… Nina?

53

Universe Alpha

His rotting breath was almost too much to take. Hot and stale and wretched. Like one of those smelling salts that could knock people out or revive them, but in this case Gus Blanity's gross breath was about to make Feminina faint. But she couldn't do that. For multiple reasons.

The first of which being the sharp knife point that he had on her neck. If she passed out, she would crush into the blade and that would create a big bloody mess that she wouldn't recover from. The second reason being that Nina was hurt, she needed to help her. The third reason that she needed to stop these creeps from taking off into the multiverse.

Feminina hadn't forgotten her mission to find and rescue Marie, but she was now very concerned that this duo could do more damage and bar her path. *No coincidences, right?*

She had run through the potential moves she could use to get out of Blanity's grip and get to the console to do some damage to the freak who helped him escape. But each move could cause him to tighten his grip or pull that knife in just the wrong way. She didn't dare act.

The person that Blanity had come in with had quickly knocked Nina to the ground, then stepped over her to the console. Nina seemed to be getting up. *Poor girl has had one too many concussions,* Femi thought to herself, remembering the details of what happened to her alter-ego the previous year.

How could such evil exist in the world, in the multiverse? Why were they both in this position, *again*, but this time on the losing end?

And how could this person help Gus do it? Feminina wasn't a fool. She knew who it was. This woman looked like her, like them. But her arms were puckered and scaly with burns, visible under the rolled-up sleeves of her hoodie. The left side of her face was divided by a dark scar, on either side the skin was singed. That half of her face was tight, her lip curled up in a snarl.

She was us. She was another Nina, but she wore her scars on the outside. Feminina was too stunned to think that one of her alter-egos, that some other version of herself, would be capable of aiding Gus Blanity.

And just when it looked like all hope was lost, that no one would come to their aid, the cavalry arrived. Well, sort of.

54

Universe Alpha

Nina felt irritated more than anything else. She had been knocked down and hit her head, again. It just pissed her off. *Like, come on bad guys, can you target my kneecaps just once and give my brain a break?* It didn't seem like she had been knocked out for more than a few seconds, but in that time so much had happened. The creepy stranger who looked like Nina, only not, was at the console, entering coordinates for who-knows-where. Feminina was struggling to break free from Gus' hold, but Nina caught the glint of the knife in his hand. She knew Femi couldn't attack the way she had seen her take down that construction worker. It was going to be up to Nina to somehow subdue these two bad guys.

Light on the toes, fists up to protect your neck. The words of her kickboxing coach barked into her mind, urging her to get up and to fight.

As she did so, she noticed that there were two more people in the lab now. Nick and his partner, Archie. *Great, just what I need*, Nina thought to herself.

One problem at a time. She was on her feet as the frail looking version of herself stood from the console. Nina caught sight of the scar, it looked nasty.

"To the left," she called out. Her voice was familiar, but harsher. Gus shuffled with Feminina in his grip, he kicked the Portal on the track. It floated easily down the line. *Good thing I unlocked those for him.*

The woman with the bleached hair moved to cross behind Blanity and settle the frame.

"Freeze!" Nina spun around to see Archie pointing a handgun at the woman in the black hoodie.

"Cool it, remember gunpowder and quantum energy don't mix well," Nick called out to him. *What does Nick even know about physics?* Nina lost her concentration for a moment.

The bleach blonde smirked and continued on her way, feeling certain that she wouldn't be harmed. There was something about her colorless appearance, she was like a ghost. But even though she was as white as unfiltered light she seemed infinitely troubled. She was dark and menacing. Nina couldn't come to think of her as another version of herself. No this was a femme fatale, a stranger who just happened to share her facial features. Well, most of them. Nina didn't have the scar, and she still had eye brows.

No, this was not someone she could call Nina-4 or some other number. She was a totally different species of Nina. The Dark Femme, that is what Nina decided to call her as she watched this new alter-ego finish positioning the frame and lock the clamps.

"I said don't move," Archie repeated. Nina noticed that his voice sounded much deeper than any of the other times she had spoken to him, perhaps a more authoritative tone. Nick seemed to be taking the opposite approach, inching his feet closer to Blanity, trying to move while the attention was on his partner.

Nina tried to refocus, to look for a chance to spring on the Dark Femme, to kick her in the gut and have her doubled over. This isn't exactly what she had trained for. In her nightmares she was always fighting off Parker or Gus. Never another one of her alter-egos.

The Dark Femme crossed closer to her, moving back to the console. Nina's eyes flashed on the monitor. The timer was active. Only another 50 seconds until the next jitter. Everything was in place. *She must be going for the supercybin.*

Nina lunged, aiming to meet the Dark Femme at the cabinet and block her way. Before she could stop herself, she caught sight of the metal. Pulled from the loose recesses of her hoodie, the Dark Femme had produced another knife.

"No!" Nina heard three of the voices in the lab call out, she couldn't discern just who had said it because she was flat on the floor, underneath Archie's broad frame. He must have pounced, trying and successfully knocking Nina out of the path of the knife.

She couldn't focus on the Dark Femme taking out the vials and injecting herself and Feminina before filling a third syringe for Gus. She couldn't see the foam beginning to appear in the frame of the Portal. She couldn't hear Nick grunt as he pulled Archie off of her, the roar of the machine was just too loud.

Once she was free of the weight, she turned onto her stomach and looked up in time to see Gus guide himself and Feminina through the Portal. Nick crouched over Archie, checking that he was okay. The Dark Femme looked down at her and smirked before she crossed through herself.

And just as quickly as it had all happened, the energy was sucked out of the room. The Portal stood still, empty, as though three people hadn't just disappeared into it.

"No!" Nina cried out.

"Nina!" she heard Nick call for her but she was too focused on what had just happened before her own eyes.

"Go," she heard a ragged voice whisper behind her. Nina turned to see Nick on the floor, Archie slumped against him, a knife sticking out from his stomach. It all clicked into place for her now. The burgundy stain on Archie's shirt was far too dark, too fast. Nick's face said it all, Archie needed help right away.

"No way man, we got all day to chase after them, we need to get you patched up," Nick tried to reassure his partner.

Nina wanted to object, but she knew Nick was right. *Wait, how did he even know what just happened? Shouldn't he be freaking out?* She spun to face the vacant Portal one more time, perhaps hoping that Feminina would be waltzing back through, unharmed.

She didn't.

"Nina! I need your help," Nick called out to her. She turned back as he whipped off his jacket, holding it tight against Archie's stomach.

Her feet were already moving back from the machine, inching towards Nick. Nina would have to help him carry Archie out, there was no way he could do it alone. Her impulse was to chase after Femi, but just as her alter-ego had needed her help, Nina knew she wouldn't be able to chase her alone. She would probably also have some explaining to do.

No, she needed help, and a plan, and some back-up. Then she would be able to follow. But to get all of that done today? In less than twenty-four-hours?

Nina narrowed her gaze and pointed at the machine, offering it a final threat: "This is so not over!"

Epilogue

Universe Beta
August 8, 2019
10:30 pm

Hank folded the empty pizza box and crushed it into his tiny kitchen trash bin. It had been a somber day for him. He took off from work so he could visit Anna's grave. And then he stopped by the police station to see if Detectives Wells or Holcrum could give him any updates on Nina's case. He knew it would be a fruitless request, but he had to ask anyways.

Carol had suggested that he still go into work, to see if Thurston was doing anything on this day. But Hank just couldn't face that building, that place where he had lost the love of his life – again. Even his therapist had suggested that he not face that room again until he was ready. She didn't think he was ready yet.

Because it was based on medical advice, Carol had dropped the subject. But they still met up for dinner and a rehashing of their latest theories. They enjoyed pizza and beer while they picked apart Hank's interaction with the detectives that day. "Did they seem like they were giving you the brush off because they were too busy, or because they didn't want to give anything away? If they are working a lead, they may not be able to say anything." Carol was becoming an expert in dissecting each of these small conversations. The clues were cold, the potential for new information was drying up. They were like castaways at sea, slowly divvying out the last of the rations. Cutting them smaller and smaller, savoring each little morsel with more determination as the end drew near.

With a heavy heart, Hank realized that once he did flat out ask Thurston for his version of what happened, that might be it. If the other man didn't recall anything, if he flat out lied, or shut him down, then… what? This was his last hope for tracking Nina down himself. Perhaps that was the real reason that he and Carol were going along with this longer plan of gaining his confidence, because once they crossed his name off their list, there was no one else left.

As this thought settled on him, he heard a knock at his door. Carol had left twenty minutes earlier; he wasn't expecting anyone else. *Eh, maybe she forgot something*, he thought as he moved out of the kitchen. He wanted it to be Carol returning, imagining her coming back to comfort him.

But then, he realized it could be the detectives stopping by with news. His steps quickened, closing the space between the front door quickly.

After he unlocked and swung the door open, he saw a young woman looking up at him with crystalline blue eyes. Her face was framed with a thick tangle of dark brown curls, they stuck out at all angles. He had never seen her before in his life, but there was still something incredibly familiar about her. Something about the line of her jaw, the slope of her nose. Even the shape of her mouth as she let out a soft gasp. She appeared to be just as shocked to see him as he was confused to see her.

"Can I help you?" The words popped out of his mouth by default. His brain was working on overdrive to try and place her. *How could she look so familiar? What was she doing here?* And then a giggle popped up in his mind. A day at the park with his girls. One pushing the other on a swing. One flying higher and higher, her laugh soaring with each push. *No, it couldn't be.* Even if she was alive, she would have only been 9 years old, not a grown woman. In spite of the logic that told him otherwise, his brain couldn't stop his mouth. Not before he hazarded a guess at her name.

"Anna?" he breathed. A name he kept locked in his heart, tucked away, so that the pain could never slip out.

She must have been working through her own mental calculus as well, finally brought into the current moment. Her voice was clear and her tone was urgent. She nodded and started in with her demand: "Dad! We have to go now! Mom is in danger."

Acknowledgements

In a world of infinite entertainment options, thank you so much for reading this book. And most likely, you've also read *The Infinite-Infinite*, so thank you times two.

This series has been a fun way for me to explore the different aspects of the self and the ways in which we rebuild and adapt ourselves over time. How we envision a new life for ourselves and then make it happen.

Getting this book done and out to you has been fun and challenging. Within the past two years since *The Infinite-Infinite* came out we all experienced a global pandemic, but I also had another life-changing experience. I became a mom, and with it a new array of worries and joys have appeared. Thank you for your patience as I worked on this next piece of the story.

I hope that you will indulge me and take a moment to read through the long list of thank yous that will follow. This book and the world that you just visited would not have been possible without the following people:

Thank you to my amazing husband for his continued support and devotion to my creative pursuits. Thank you for always being my first reader and putting up with the weird things that I say as I consider plot points. Thank you for being the de facto President of my fan club and cheering me on. None if this would be possible without you my dear.

Thank you to my mother who instilled a love of reading in me from a young age.

Thank you to my amazing editorial team. Debbie and Jeff, this book would be riddled with plot holes and errant commas without you. Your work and time dedication to this story have shaped it into a readable book instead of just a pile of my crazy ideas.

Next, I want to thank those who have been supporting my work. The cliché of the penniless writer persists for a reason, royalties are slim for even the best of us. Those who have taken the time and continued to financially support me through my Buy Me A Coffee membership have helped to keep me going. Thank you so much to Jason, Teresa, and Sheila for your support!

I must end with the most important note of thanks, and that is to you! Thank you for supporting my work. Whether you purchased this book or checked it out from the library, I am extremely grateful that you spent your time with Nina, Hank, Marie, and Parker (and their alter-egos). I will always cherish the time that you have given to this story and I hope to continue to entertain, inspire, and thrill you all for years to come.

About the Author

M.K. Williams is the author of multiple novels, self-publishing guides, and short stories. You can follow her for more in-depth information on these books at 1mkwilliams.com. To receive updates on upcoming books, please take a moment to subscribe.

If you enjoyed this story, please consider leaving a review for *The Alpha-Nina*. Each review helps other readers discover this book. Thank you for your support.